Praise for the Book

"A thoroughly entertaining series debut, with enjoyable yet realistic characters and enough plot twists—and dead ends—to appeal from beginning to end."

—*Booklist*, starred review, on *Booked 4 Murder*

"Filled with clues that make you go 'Huh?' and a list of potential subjects that range from the charming to the witty to the intense. Readers root for Phee as she goes up against a killer who may not stop until Phee is taken out well before her time. Enjoy this laugh-out-loud funny mystery that will make you scream for the authors to get busy on the next one."

—*Suspense Magazine* on *Molded 4 Murder*

"Engaging characters and a stirring mystery kept me captivated from the first page to the last."

—Dollycas, Amazon Vine Voice, on *Divide and Concord*

"Well-crafted sleuth, enjoyable supporting characters. This is a series not to be missed."

—*Cozy Cat Reviews* on *Death, Dismay and Rosé*

"A sparkling addition to the Wine Trail Mystery series. A toast to protagonist Norrie and Two Witches Winery, where the characters shine and the mystery flows. This novel is a perfect blend of suspense and fun!"

—Carlene O'Neil, author of the Cypress Cove Mysteries,
on *Chardonnayed to Rest*

Books by J. C. Eaton

The Wine Trail Mysteries

A Riesling to Die
Chardonnayed to Rest
Pinot Red or Dead?
Sauvigone for Good
Divide and Concord
Death, Dismay and Rosé
From Port to Rigor Morte
Mischief, Murder and Merlot
Caught in the Traminette

The Sophie Kimball Mysteries

Booked 4 Murder
Ditched 4 Murder
Staged 4 Murder
Botched 4 Murder
Molded 4 Murder
Dressed Up 4 Murder
Broadcast 4 Murder
Saddled Up 4 Murder
Grilled 4 Murder
Strike Out 4 Murder
Revved Up 4 Murder
Pinned 4 Murder
Puzzled 4 Murder

The Marcie Rayner Mysteries

Murder in the Crooked Eye Brewery
Murder at the Mystery Castle
Murder at Classy Kitchens

The Charcuterie Shop Mysteries

Laid Out to Rest
Sliced, Diced and Dead
Death on a Serving Board

Puzzled
4
Murder

J. C. Eaton

BEYOND THE PAGE
PUBLISHING

Puzzled 4 Murder
J. C. Eaton
Copyright © 2025 J. C. Eaton
Cover design and illustration by Dar Albert, Wicked Smart Designs

Beyond the Page Books
are published by
Beyond the Page Publishing
www.beyondthepagepub.com

ISBN: 978-1-966322-01-6

To Vivian Hennessey, who donates the Sun City West puzzle each year, in memory of her husband, Jim

ACKNOWLEDGMENTS

Without the support of Sun City West librarian Tracy Skousen, this puzzling romp would not have been possible! Loved the puzzle room tour!

And Sun City West Puzzle Solvers, your expertise and patience astounded us! Thanks for letting us peek over your shoulders last summer.

Double thanks to Regina Kotokowski, whose enthusiasm for puzzle solving put this idea into our heads, and whose incredible editing skills as a beta reader were invaluable. You are amazing!

Susan Schwartz in Coorparoo, Australia, we can't begin to thank you enough. You have been with us as an editor and beta reader for over a decade! Your eagle eye and attention to detail made our novels shine! Super hugs!

Larry Finkelstein and Gale Leach, we would be writing on stone tablets if it wasn't for you! Thank you for keeping our computer and website running! Now we can go back to rubbing sticks to make a fire!

Dawn Dowdle, our agent at Blue Ridge Literary, who passed away far too soon, remains with us in her wisdom and her guidance. Her voice is always in our ears! We miss her every day.

Kudos to Dar Albert from Wicked Smart Designs, who creates the most eye-catching covers imaginable. We don't know how you do it, but don't stop! You amaze us!

Finally, to our editor, Bill Harris, and the talented staff at Beyond the Page Publishing, we are indeed appreciative of all you do.

Finally, we thank you, our readers, for picking up our cozies and welcoming our wacky characters into your lives!

CHAPTER 1

Bagels 'n More
Surprise, Arizona

"They just got black garlic schmear, Phee," my mother said as I took a seat between her and my aunt Ina. Before I could respond, she continued, "I was getting tired of the garden salad schmear but I didn't like the chive and garlic one they had."

My aunt bit into a pretzel bagel laden with salt and wiped her chin with a napkin. "Garlic gives me heartburn. Not like your uncle Louis. That man was born with an iron stomach."

An iron stomach and selective hearing.

My aunt went on. "Did I mention I got an invitation in the mail for one of those life-extending seminars? A free lunch at the prestigious Cooper's Hawk Restaurant in Surprise. I can bring friends. Let me check the date and I'll let all of you know. It's a ways off."

"Count me out, Aunt Ina," I said. "Those things are notorious scams meant to lure you into spending money on something you don't need or will never use."

"It's at the Cooper's Hawk! All we have to do is eat and listen."

"My beautician attended one of those things and almost went bankrupt. Anyway, I'm sorry I was so late. Augusta and I had our hands full with phone calls. Glad Saturdays are half days for me. And only twice a month. With Nate and Marshall at the AALPI conference in Scottsdale, we've been toggling between all sorts of things. Mostly conversations with clients who seem to think we're detectives as well. Hmm, maybe Augusta thinks so too, but I'm happy being the bookkeeper/accountant for Williams Investigations."

"You might as well be," my mother said. "With all the strange goings on in Sun City West. At least the snowbirds are clearing out and things should quiet down. And what's the AAL—whatever it is?"

"Arizona Association of Licensed Private Investigators. They hold it once a year in Scottsdale." I looked around the large oval table and realized I hadn't greeted everyone. Then again, the book club ladies were busy chomping on bagels and Herb Garrett, my mother's neighbor, and his pinochle-playing buddies were no slouches either when it came to chowing down. It was one of their favorite retiree pastimes in their senior community.

The waitress noticed I'd arrived and quickly took my order. *Quickly,*

I'm sure, before she got embroiled in conversation with them. Conversation? More like interrogation.

Why don't they have herring in onion sauce like they used to?

Find out why we don't have gluten-free everything bagels.

Tell them to add almond milk. Oat milk is too heavy.

Yep, another fun Saturday at Sun City West's favorite gossip spot. Even though the restaurant was across the road in Surprise, Arizona, on Route 60/Grand Avenue, folks referred to the place as their community's hangout. Usually I come up with excuses to avoid the weekly Saturday talk-fests, but with my boss and my husband at that conference, I acquiesced and joined the merriment.

I'm forty-something Phee Kimball Gregory, and Nate Williams is the one responsible for talking me into leaving my civil service position at the Mankato Police Department in Minnesota and joining his burgeoning detective agency in the Peoria-Glendale area outside of Phoenix, Arizona. Not only that, but he pulled some strings, resulting in Marshall Gregory joining the agency when he retired from the Mankato Police Department. Next thing I knew, Marshall swept me off my feet straight to the altar.

The fourth person in our agency is Augusta Hatch, a retired secretary for a tool and die company in Wisconsin, where she grew up back when Truman ran the country. And when she's not cleaning her guns or plucking feathers from a chicken, she's playing canasta.

My ancient grain bagel with egg and cheese appeared almost instantaneously, and as I bit into it the first complaints of the day flew across the table like Canadian geese on their way south.

Myrna Mittleson brushed some bushy curls from her forehead and looked around. "Can you believe that woman? How did she get on the committee to select the summer puzzle?"

"She volunteered," Lucinda replied. She pushed the sleeves of her plaid shirt past her elbows and leaned forward. "That's how anyone gets on those committees. But had I known Lettie Holton and Samantha Wiggins were going to chair it, I would have volunteered myself."

I studied the faces around the table hoping someone would clarify what was going on, but I should have known better. Instead, I waited it out until I could piece together the snippets of their conversations.

"Let me get this straight," I said. "All of you are upset about the choice for a giant puzzle in the library?"

"Not just a giant puzzle," Shirley Johnson explained. She reached for a butter knife and I noticed her nails were an iridescent teal that looked gorgeous against her dark skin. "It's our summer entertainment. The puzzle spans the length of the entire front room with over fifteen stations for people to work. It's like painting Picasso's *Guernica* but without the mess."

"The only downfall is that I can't bring Streetman." My mother crossed her arms and shook her head.

"That's a good thing, Harriet," Herb shouted from across the table. "No one wants a nipping, neurotic chiweenie in the library. That dog has more issues than the past decade of *National Geographic*."

"So it's a done deal?" I continued. "The puzzle, I mean. Not Streetman in the library, heaven forbid."

"It's down to three choices. Three horrible, despicable choices." Louise Munson turned to Lucinda and the two of them grimaced. "And for those of you who don't know what those choices are, let me be the first to inform you."

My grain bagel began to feel like a lead weight in my stomach as I waited to hear the horrible puzzle choices. I figured it couldn't be all that bad, but boy, was I wrong!

"The first choice," Louise said, "is called 'Snowy Blizzard,' and it's an all-white puzzle with speckles of gray. Apparently some nincompoop thought it would be 'challenging.'"

"That's not challenging, that's torture," my aunt said. "Thank goodness we don't have anything like that going on in the Grand."

"The Grand" was the new name for Sun City Grand, where my aunt and uncle lived. It was across the road from Sun City West, but to listen to my aunt, it sounded more like a private island in the Caymans.

I gulped. "What are the other choices?"

"Oh, honey, they're worse." Shirley smeared the butter on her bagel and took a bite. "The next choice is 'The Sandy Beach.'"

"That doesn't sound too bad. Beach themes are fun. Umbrellas. Swimmers. Waves."

"No," Shirley said, "just sand. Nothing but sand. Just like the snow one, only beige, not white."

"Oh."

"The third is the worst yet," she added. Then Gloria Wong, who was seated adjacent to Shirley, spoke up.

"The third choice is 'Depths of the Brain.'"

Herb all but spat out his Danish. "Whose brain?"

"Does it matter?" Louise glared at him. "Gloria is right. It's a hideous depiction of the inside of a human brain. Looks like someone's MRI. Honestly, who picks a thing like that?"

"Samantha Wiggins, that's who. The woman has a screw loose if you ask me."

It was the first comment Bill made, but not his last. For the next five minutes, he and Wayne grumbled about Samantha and the ridiculous puzzle committee.

3

"Isn't there something you can do about it?" I asked. "I mean, if everyone is miserable, won't the librarian step in?"

Heads shook in unison. "Nope. It's a library *committee* thing. That's different." Bill leaned back and stretched. "You know what I think, don't you? You can't fight City Hall but you can pee on the front steps."

Oh no. I'm afraid to see where this is going.

"Please don't tell me you're suggesting something that will get all of you in trouble."

"Not literally," he said. "Unless your mother brings that dog where he doesn't belong. Relax, it's just a manner of speech."

"Uh, yeah. I figured as much, but still—"

"Bill has a point." My mother furrowed her brow and poured herself another cup of coffee from the carafe on the table. "The summer puzzle is the major form of recreation around here during the heat of the day. Besides, it's a veritable gold mine as far as picking up the local chatter goes."

"You mean the local gossip?" I shot her a look.

"It's not as if we're stuck with our faces in our phones on Insta-Pot or whatever you call it. We're old school. We like things up close and personal."

Up close, personal, and spread like manure.

"The vote is next week. Written ballots that get dropped off at the library. And no cheating. Voters have to write down their rec card numbers for verification." Then she paused before clasping her hands with a loud clap. "I have a brainstorm!"

Oh heck no!

"The ballots get picked up at the library. All we need to do is substitute our own ballots with three different puzzles. What do you say? We suggested Thomas Kinkade's 'Hummingbird Cottage' but Samantha had the audacity to tell us it was juvenile. Then Cecilia thought a Ravensburger puzzle would be appropriate but Samantha and Lettie nixed that as well. So, switch out the ballots? What do you say?"

A chorus of "Count me in," "Go for it," and "Do it!" followed.

And, just like that, my mother opened the floodgates that would take an entire summer to contain. Unfortunately, none of us realized it at the time.

Then, out of nowhere, my aunt asked, "When does Marshall get back?"

"Tomorrow afternoon."

"Good. Then you can join us tonight for dinner at the Babylonian Gardens in Sun City. It's a lovely Mediterranean restaurant that Louis and I discovered a few weeks ago. Their tabouli with stuffed grape leaves is about the best I've ever had and your uncle is enamored with their tikka beef kabobs. All of us are going. It will be as if our brunch conversation never stops."

4

No, it will be as if the pounding in my head never stops.

"That's really nice of you to include me, but I made plans with my friend Lyndy this evening."

"Bring her along." My aunt shrugged.

And while Lyndy was used to the book club ladies and Herb's entourage, I didn't want to subject her to an endless evening of rumor-mongering and complaining.

"It's been so hot that we had our hearts set on an evening swim. Maybe another time." *Or decade.* "But thanks for the invite."

And like that, the conversation bounced back to the giant puzzle, where it remained for the next fifteen minutes. That's when Kevin woke up from his food stupor and scratched his head. "Lettie Holton. Is that the woman with the mustache?"

"It's not a mustache. It's freckles. They look like a mustache," Cecilia said.

"You could have fooled me."

I rolled my eyes and held my breath as the topic morphed into various kinds of makeup and concealers. Finally, my mother jumped from her seat and announced, "My Streetman must be getting hungry. Got to run. See you all tonight." Then to me, "I'll keep you posted on our switcheroo."

I started to reply but she was out of there like a flash. And like dominos falling one after the other, everyone followed suit, including me.

CHAPTER 2

The cool pool water splashed against the beads of sweat on my neck and I took a deep breath. "Best part of my day. Or evening, as the case may be. Too bad they don't offer food and drink service in here," I said to Lyndy as we leaned against the far wall in the deep end of Vistancia's community pool. "I'd be hard-pressed to leave."

"Got that right!" She shook the water from her dark curls and smiled. "Lyman's team has a game tonight or he'd be joining us. I'm surprised Herb didn't mention it when you saw him at brunch."

"He didn't get a chance. Everyone was busy fussing about the puzzle selection for the library, otherwise we would have been subjected to an endless discourse on slow pitches."

"The library puzzle, huh? I heard all about it from my wacky aunt this morning. She was furious. Said the lunatics who came up with the three final choices needed to have their heads examined."

"Get ready for this one—my mother and the book club ladies plan to swap out the ballots and replace them with duplicates that list three other puzzles."

"Uh-oh. If they get caught, they could lose their rec card privileges for the summer."

"Too bad that's not the case for her dog. All Streetman gets is probation from the dog park for his behavior."

"So what's the deal on those puzzles and why is it such an issue? My aunt wouldn't say."

I gave Lyndy the complete rundown and she was hysterical when I described the choices. "Frankly, all they go there for is the gossip, but I suppose working on something frustrating wouldn't appeal to me either."

"Yeah. My aunt said the big puzzle was the only thing that made hot summer afternoons bearable and that Mahjong Mondays can only do so much. Heck, maybe that puzzle committee will have a change of heart when they get all those complaints."

"Doubtful. From what my mother said, the two women are overbearing and used to getting their own way. Ironic, huh?"

We both laughed before nabbing lap lanes for the remainder of the evening. We agreed to meet for coffee after work in a few days and commiserate. That was before a barrage of bizarre events turned everything upside down in my mother's otherwise predictable community.

• • •

Like Lyndy, Marshall couldn't keep a straight face when he got home from his conference the following afternoon. I told him about the puzzle disaster and he chuckled. "I don't know which is worse, hon, your mother's brainchild or the puzzle choices. Hmm, come to think of it, it's the puzzle choices. Some of those people can't see an inch in front of them. They can barely navigate the streets, let alone decipher same-color puzzle pieces."

"Let's just hope this doesn't spiral out of control when the book club ladies pull their ballot switch."

What planet had I landed on? Of course it was going to spiral out of control. Nothing those women did was within the limits of normalcy. I just didn't realize it would spiral so fast.

At a little past eleven on Monday, Augusta couldn't wait to tell me that my mother had left me a message while I was out picking up donuts for our midmorning break.

"She said to tell you, and I quote, 'The fix is in.' Must be she got a good gambling tip."

"Nope. She substituted library ballots for the big summer puzzle choice."

Augusta removed her tortoiseshell glasses and rubbed the bridge of her nose. "Come again?"

I took a breath and filled her in on the latest Sun City West scuttlebutt. She shook her head and shuddered. "And this is why I live on county land. By the way, Nate and Marshall skedaddled out of here a few minutes after you. They've got full plates, but nothing out of the ordinary."

"Good to know."

That was the last time the word *ordinary* was used. Four days later, on Friday afternoon, my mother phoned to inform me that the librarian called a special meeting of all patrons to discuss a "disturbing occurrence regarding the puzzle selection for the summer."

"It worked, Phee. I can't believe it. First of all, we got Louise to make a new ballot. She's the queen of cut and paste, so she was able to take the original and redo it. Then we got Cecilia to distract the librarian on Monday and Myrna switched out the ballots. They got tallied on Wednesday and that's when the proverbial you-know-what hit the fan! So, now we have a special meeting on Tuesday night to discuss 'the ramifications of ballot tampering.' Good grief! It's not like the presidential elections, for crying out loud."

"I warned you, didn't I?"

"Don't be so dramatic. They'll re-vote. With better choices. Wait and see."

"I'll be sure to hold my breath. Just don't insist I attend."

Fortunately, I was spared an evening of whining and complaining, but I got the full rundown at eight fifty-three on that Tuesday night when the meeting ended. Only this time, it wasn't my mother who called. It was Herb.

"Is everything all right?" I asked him. "Is my mother okay?"

"Oh, she's fine. She told me to call you. She and the women were in a rush to get to the Homey Hut before they closed. It's strawberry pie night and they close at eleven."

"Uh, thanks for the heads-up."

"Don't you want to know what happened at the meeting?"

"Um, not necessari—"

"I'll tell you. It was a maelstrom. Chest pounding, sobbing, and shouting. And that was the library staff! The librarian had no choice but to take action herself. She nixed the three original choices as well as the ones the book club ladies substituted."

"So now what?"

"Apparently, it's too late to order another jumbo-size puzzle for the library, so she's going to contact the library at Sun City and see if we can borrow one of their puzzles from a prior year. No one objected."

"How could they? Didn't sound like there were other options."

"Anyway, I'm sure your mother will fill you in with the details tomorrow. See you, cutie!"

"Uh, yeah. Thanks, Herb. Have a nice night."

I did a mental eye roll and told Augusta about the call as soon as I got to work the next morning. She didn't sound too surprised. "One less thing to worry about, I suppose. Although, knowing that crew, they'll find something onerous about the new puzzle. Wait and see."

"I'd rather not."

"While you were driving in, I got a text from Mr. Williams. They picked up a colder than cold case and are now meeting with our favorite MCSO deputies."

"Sheriff's business?"

"Old sheriff's business. So old that Bowman and Ranston don't want to go near it, so they pulled the consultant card."

"Those deputies are too much. Still, the remuneration for contractual services is nothing to balk at. Did Nate give you the particulars?"

"The CliffsNotes version. About twenty-three years ago, a man disappeared from Sun City. No sign of foul play and the wife declared him dead after seven years."

"Don't tell me she had second thoughts and decided to track him down."

"Nope. Someone else did. A coworker who insisted the wife murdered him but couldn't prove it."

"And they waited over twenty-three years to let someone know?"

"The coworker was afraid she'd lose her job so she waited until she could collect her retirement."

"Oh, brother. Sounds fishy to me."

"Fishy or not, MCSO now has it in their lap, but not for long. It's a hot potato that's been passed to us. Murder doesn't have a statute of limitations."

"Um, didn't the sheriff's office investigate when the guy vanished?"

"Yep. And they concluded the man walked out on the wife."

"Guess the guys will have fun with this one. Re-interviewing people after twenty-three years may be a problem."

"Re-interviewing people after twenty-three minutes in that community may be a problem."

We both burst out laughing as I headed to my office for a morning of spreadsheets and figures. Two and half hours later, as I ambled into the workroom for a coffee break, my cell phone rang. Figuring it was Lyndy, I picked up.

"Phee!" My mother's voice was crisp and loud. "I've been trying the office phone but it's been busy."

"That's because this is a place of business. What's going on?"

As soon as those words left my mouth, I regretted it. For the next four minutes, my mother gave me the complete update about the puzzle. Yep, Augusta was right. It *was* going to be onerous. Between the puzzle nightmare and the colder than cold case, the summer wasn't exactly getting off to the relaxing start everyone expected.

I took a deep breath and waited for the salient details to surface. Too bad I couldn't drown them.

CHAPTER 3

"I got the details, Phee. I found out from Cecilia, who went to return a John Grisham novel to the library. She ran into Gloria, who overheard Samantha talking about the new puzzle. And here's the best part. We can hear her, too. Gloria's daughter showed her how to use her phone for videos so Gloria videoed people returning books and it picked up Samantha's voice. Imagine that! Anyhow, you'll never guess what that puzzle is."

Please. Let there be an earthquake or something.

"As I was saying, Gloria found out that the puzzle is a blown-up photo of a street in Sun City. A street in Sun City! Taken years ago. Before cell phones. That's it. A boring old street with people's houses. If I wanted to see that, I'd drive to Sun City."

"I thought you said it was the process and camaraderie that mattered."

"Not if our brains turn to mush. At least the other puzzles were challenging."

"This one could be challenging, too. You don't know that."

"Well, I'll find out on Saturday when they hold the big reveal."

"The big reveal?"

"Yes. They'll have photocopies of the completed puzzle for everyone to see. Then they'll draw numbers to see who gets to sort it out by section. Now do you understand why we couldn't do that ridiculous snow one or, heaven forbid, the brain?"

"Uh, sort of."

"It's simple. We study the photo and sort out the pieces by color so that everyone can work on a special area without getting in each other's way. It's only when we get close to the end that we put it all together. After that is the big celebration."

The moisture left my mouth the second she said "big celebration." I didn't have to ask. I knew what was coming. Another reason to indulge on fattening foods and hold a photo op for the newspapers. Even worse, a radio broadcast that featured my mother's weekly murder mystery program with Myrna and Paul.

I still cringe when I think about that combination cozy mystery and lake fishing show where the three of them speak over each other and no one gets a word in edgewise. How it remained a KSCW radio success was beyond me.

"Well, Mom, that sounds all fine and good but I've got to get back to work." *Or what's left of my coffee break.*

"I'll keep you posted."

For the next three days, I basked in glorious delight, not having to listen to my mother ruminate about the puzzle. Meanwhile, Nate and Marshall had a puzzle of their own with that cold case. They divvied up the interviews since both of them had other cases to deal with, but according to Augusta, those were relatively easy.

Then Saturday rolled around, and thankfully it was a work morning for me so I was spared coming up with an excuse for not joining the book club ladies for bagels. However, there was no excuse for me not to answer my office phone.

Oddly enough, it wasn't my mother or any of the women. It was Lydia Wong, Gloria Wong's daughter, and she sounded out of breath.

"Sorry to bother you, Phee, but I only have a few minutes before I'm needed in Imaging. Honestly, this hospital is understaffed. Anyway, I called about that ridiculous library puzzle. My mother said you joined them last Saturday so you know all about it."

"Uh, I know the women were upset."

"Oh, they're upset all right. According to my mother, someone named Samantha told them she had dibs on the brown and orange pieces when the puzzle gets sorted out today."

I tightened my shoulders and held them still before releasing the tension. "Uh-oh."

"Uh-oh is right. It's going to be a free-for-all over there. I'd head over myself but I have a full day. Is there any chance you can scope it out? Last thing any of us needs is for this to escalate into something awful."

"Trust me, it's already awful. I'm surprised my mother didn't call me. Usually she phones with the most picayune things."

"According to my mother, the giant puzzle box will be opened at one p.m. today in some sort of tradition. At least she didn't use the word *bloodbath*, but from what I hear, some of those women are barbarians when it comes to staking out their territory. I remembered you work half days on Saturdays so I'm hoping you can run interference."

Run interference? I'd like to run, period.

"Uh, yeah. I work every other Saturday morning. And sure, I'll check it out. I'd rather prevent something awful from happening than deal with the aftereffect or aftershock, as the case may be."

"You're a lifesaver, Phee. Text me later, okay?"

"Okay."

Augusta practically doubled over laughing when I used the word *bloodbath*.

"Lydia was serious," I said. "And I've seen some of those women in action at bingo games, and believe me, they're ruthless."

"Better you than me. What do they intend to do? Hoard the pieces?"

I shrugged. "Nothing would surprise me."

Ha! The scenario I faced at the library not only surprised me but left me speechless. It was a veritable war room, complete with an enormous table surrounded by strategists. Strategists who made brigadier generals look like kindergarteners at play. With heads bent down and a cacophony of sharp, irritated voices, I realized how right Lydia was.

"Section off! Section off!" someone announced. Then, "There are eight bags for eight sections. Two people per section. Take a seat. You can always move."

Then a man's voice. "Like hell we can. I was stuck at the end all last summer."

"Get over it, Carl. First come, first serve."

And this is summer relaxation.

I edged closer but made sure to keep my distance. The woman making the announcement continued. "Lettie will distribute the bags but do not open them. I repeat, do not open them. The librarian should be here any second to go over the rules. And let me offer my congratulations to those of you who are here for the grand initiation. Your names were randomly drawn by the librarian for this momentous occasion. All sixteen of you."

I crept toward the table and all but bumped into my mother's chair. Her highlights in shades of honey, caramel, and cinnamon were unmistakable. That, and the orange streaks that screamed "Adolescence is a state of mind."

Next to her were Gloria and Shirley with Louise a few chairs away. With their backs facing toward the table, no one had seen me. *Yet.* I imagined Cecilia, Lucinda and Myrna would get their turn at "mission control" the following week.

"No over-the-shoulder peeking!" a large woman sporting a sun visor shouted from across the table. All heads turned toward me and the gig was up.

"What are you doing here, Phee?" My mother crinkled her nose. "Don't tell me a crime's been committed. Are Nate and Marshall here too?"

"No crime." *Except me showing up. Thank you, Lydia.*

"I, uh, had some office errands to run and was near here so I thought I'd see what the puzzle unveiling was all about."

"You'll have to stand way back!" the large woman announced. "Way back. And no photos allowed. It's against the rules."

I smiled. "No problem. Curious, that's all."

Gloria, Shirley, and Louise all said hello to me before turning their attention to the librarian who had just arrived. Darcey Hartwell was the third one to assume the position since I was first summoned here to investigate a cursed book. And while library science is not considered a high-risk occupation, working in a senior community did present its own challenges. Not to mention the stress level.

Why doesn't that book come in large print?

I can't get the computer to find my book.

Why can't we drink coffee in here?

My sister can bring her dog into the library in Indiana. Why can't we?

Darcey cleared her throat, leaned over the table and adjusted her readers. "Welcome, everyone. As you know, we are about to begin the crowning star of our summer library recreation—assembling the big puzzle. And this summer, our very own library is going to be featured in *Senior Living* magazine to showcase this extended event. A writer and photographer will be here in a few weeks, once the puzzle gets underway."

"*Senior Living*? That's a major publication. How on earth did Sun City West get chosen?" Louise asked.

Darcey puffed her chest and smiled. "The Del Webb Communities are very well known and ours has an outstanding reputation. Plus, one of the editors happens to be my sister-in-law's brother."

"That explains it," someone said under their breath. Either Darcey didn't hear or chose to ignore the comment before continuing.

"Now then, there are eight clear plastic bags with puzzle pieces for each section. They are all carefully marked by panels. Once your team has removed the pieces for your panel, you are free to sort them. I would suggest looking for the edges first. Panels one, four, five, and eight have the side edges as well."

"We've done this before, Darcey," a tall woman dressed in a floral caftan said. "What we need is the photo of the puzzle so we can see what it is. It wasn't on the outside of the box like all the others we've done."

"That's because it was a special-order puzzle, not from a company like Disney or Masterpieces. It's got forty-two thousand pieces, that when completed, will showcase a street in Sun City, from days gone by. Hold on, I have a photo of the puzzle that their librarian emailed me. I'll be right back."

The second she walked to her desk, Carl spoke up. "A fine mess this is. And we have Lettie and Samantha to thank." He looked at Lettie but Samantha was absent from the unveiling. "If the two of you didn't come up with such ridiculous choices, we'd be doing a Disney puzzle, or better yet, a Ravensburger."

"What's done is done, Carl," a large woman said. "A puzzle is a puzzle. Match up the shapes and put it together."

"I know how to do a puzzle, LaVonda."

I did a mental eye roll and heaved a sigh of relief when the librarian returned.

"It's a rather small photo," she said, "but I took the liberty of photocopying it for everyone. Plus, we'll have extra copies at the desk for anyone who stops by to work on it this summer."

With that, she distributed the copies and rushed away as fast as she could. Too bad I didn't follow her lead.

CHAPTER 4

"These copies are all grainy," my mother said. "Where's the original?"

Someone passed her the photo and she studied it. "Looks like a plain old street to me. Oh my!"

"What? What did you see?" Shirley sat straight up.

"A rather large Buick. Too bad they don't make them like they used to."

Next thing I knew, thirty-two hands dove into the puzzle pieces that were dumped from the plastic bags, and for a few seconds it was absolute quiet. Then the shuffling and moving of pieces began as if it was a competition.

"You need to change seats with me, LaVonda," Lettie said. "I promised Samantha I would start sorting the brown and orange pieces and it looks like your bag is the one that has them."

LaVonda looked down at the pieces. "How did Samantha know that there would be brown and orange pieces? We just saw the photo today."

"She used to live in Sun City and most of those houses were brown and orange. She didn't want to do the sky or the ground."

Then Lettie said, "Everything was in its original bags. The puzzle was never opened. No one put it together in Sun City. It just sat there all those years. Imagine that."

"Oh, I can imagine it all right," Carl said. "Even those people in Sun City didn't want to put together something so mundane."

"Mundane or not, it's all we've got. Too bad we can't go back to our original choices." Lettie straightened her shoulders, oblivious to the collective groans that filled the room.

"Tell me," LaVonda said to her, "what's the deal with Samantha getting her way?"

"She always gets her way or she becomes a real prune."

"Prune?"

"I didn't want to say the word I really wanted to say."

"We can all guess."

At that point, I was ready to strangle Lydia. Still, I thought I'd better remain there for a few more minutes.

"Oh, for criminy's sake." Carl flashed a look at LaVonda. "Just swap seats so we can get going. What difference does it make?"

LaVonda groaned as if she was asked to walk up three flights of stairs. "Fine. You can have my seat."

Meanwhile, my mother and Shirley engaged in their own picking and choosing their puzzle bag.

"This one has some nice blue, Shirley. Probably the sky. Or maybe a house. Oh, and look! Some green. Let's grab it now."

"I need to sit next to Gloria," Louise announced to the large woman who was beside her. "Do you mind moving?"

The woman didn't say a word but got up and moved one seat over. I did a mental eye roll. It was worse than junior high. Then Louise motioned to my mother, Shirley, and Gloria. "Do you see who's at the far end of the table? It's the Bellowses. Drake and Norva. I'm glad we're at this end."

I looked at the couple and wondered what the problem was. The man was tall with salt-and-pepper hair and a matching goatee. He sported a bland button-down shirt while his wife, a hefty woman, shared the same sense of style with a beige frock. Then, he opened his mouth and my question was immediately answered.

"I'm handing out Clorox wipes to everyone around this table. We don't need germs. Please wipe your hands before you touch the puzzle pieces."

"We're not touching yours, Drake," LaVonda said.

"All of them get mixed in and I don't want to leave here having contracted a scourge."

"Just take the darn wipe and let's get going," someone said.

Drake passed the cylinder of wipes around the table as puzzle pieces were emptied onto the table. The woman with the sun visor leaned over the table, and with the woman next to her, gathered their pieces into a giant cluster.

"Look for edges, Betty-Jean. Edges."

"I know what edges are."

Just then, a rotund man burst through the connecting door to the computer room and shouted, "Has anyone seen our staple gun?"

"Shh!" was the collective response. The man approached the book checkout counter and repeated his question. Then he turned to our table and asked again. This time with more detail. "I'm replacing the old corkboard in the room. The staple gun was on a table in front of it last night."

The library aide, who maned the front counter, walked over to him. "We haven't seen it. If it shows up, I'll make sure someone lets you know."

"Thanks. Most likely it will have to be replaced. People walk off with all sorts of things. Harrumph. They think community property means it's up for grabs." He turned and walked back to the community room.

"Is that one of my pieces? It's got orange in it." Lettie eyeballed the person seated across from her.

"It was in my bag," the woman responded. "It's not as if the bags are colored-coded."

"We'll see about that."

At that point, I'd had enough. I put my hand on my mother's shoulder and whispered, "This was very enlightening. Have fun. I've got to get going." With a quick wave, I was out of there and made a mental note not to return any time soon. But how was I to know things would take a different turn?

When I told Marshall about it that night, he couldn't stop laughing. "I can just picture it, hon. At least it will be short-lived. June and July, right?"

"Uh-huh, unless it takes a tad longer. Then they have some sort of reveal, and who knows what that entails. Meanwhile, I'm positive my mother will keep me apprised day by day."

"Better you than me."

"Any progress on that cold case?"

"If you mean how the interviews are going, then the answer is slower than a three-legged turtle."

"That bad, huh?"

Marshall ran his fingers through his hair. "I interviewed three people, and let's just say that recalling details was not their strong suit. I mean, after all, it's been twenty-three years. Worse yet, their information contradicted each other. Nate and I haven't had a chance to compare notes and we've got more interviews in store."

"What about tangible evidence?"

Marshall shook his head. "I'm interviewing the coworker on Monday so maybe she'll be able to point us in the right direction. Meanwhile, we've got a nice day ahead tomorrow for just us. No interviews or puzzle parts."

I wrapped my arms around his neck and gave him a long hug. "Hallelujah!"

• • •

When Monday morning arrived, I had all but forgotten the tension at that puzzle table, but a midday phone call from my mother brought it all back to mind.

"Lucinda had a cold so I'm here at the library with Myrna, Cecilia and Herb. I took a quick restroom break and thought I'd touch base with you. The Bellowses are back and so is Carl. Oh, and Samantha. Don't let me forget Samantha. She's been a regular pill."

"Mom, I've got work to do. Just work on the puzzle and forget about the others."

"Easy for you to say. You don't have to listen to them."

Thank goodness!

And so it went for the next few days. A steady accounting of who said what, who did what and who was the most unbearable. On the days my mother wasn't there, she got the rundown from the book club ladies who were. Apparently, passing along secondhand information was deemed as accurate as FBI intelligence.

I also had the privilege of hearing all about the other players, including Celeste Blatt, the woman with the visor, and Keenan Alcorn, who was a recent transplant from the state of Washington. For the most part, I let it waft over me, but on Thursday, my mother sounded an alarm.

It was a little past nine and Augusta transferred the call to my office, but not before shouting, "Trouble in the bubble! Thought I'd warn you."

The bubble. My new term for Sun City West.

"What's up, Mom?" I asked.

"A threat, that's what. Although the librarian dismissed it as a disgruntled patron. But you know how those disgruntled people are. One minute they're waving their hands and shouting, and the next minute, they're waving a machete in the air."

"Come on. How many machete-waving people have you seen? The librarian is probably right. And what was the threat?"

"I'm glad you finally asked. When Shirley and I got to the library a few minutes ago, the Bellowses had already started assembling their pieces. Then Norva picked up a piece and shouted, 'Someone wrote a threat on the back side of my piece.' Sure enough, it said, 'Stop doing the puzzle.'"

I tried not to laugh. *Probably a local mental health professional who observed the crew at work.* "I'd hardly call that a threat. More like someone who wanted to stir up trouble. Just ignore it."

"Right now, everyone is turning over the pieces to see if more threats were made and Drake is spraying Lysol all over the place. Too bad there's no surveillance in the library itself. Only at the entrance/exit doors. Besides, the Bellowses got here early and didn't see anyone around the puzzle."

"Hmm. Maybe someone took a piece home yesterday, wrote that message and snuck it back before the Bellowses sat down. Just a thought."

"You may be on to something. I'll keep you posted."

"Terrific. Have a nice morning."

I shuddered as I ended the call and left my office for more coffee. Whoever wrote that message was either a jokester or had nothing better to do. At least that's what I hoped. Last thing any of us needed was more drama in our lives. The paid cases that came through this office were more than enough.

"Hey, Augusta, do you happen to know who the wife was in that cold case? With all that puzzle nonsense, I forgot to ask Marshall."

"Yep. Got the name right here. Let me pull it up."

She tapped her keyboard and leaned back. "Tisha Stoad. With an *S*. That's her married name. She could have gone back to her maiden name, you know. Or remarried. And if you're wondering, the men haven't located her yet. They were lucky to find anyone in the community who remembered the details."

"What about the missing husband?"

"Arthur Stoad. Retired from a printing job in Cleveland. Moved to Sun City when he retired. No children."

"Did the wife work?"

Augusta studied the screen and shook her head. "It doesn't say. Why the interest in this case? It's not exactly the most exciting."

"Just curious. Marshall said the interviews were taxing."

"Sure they were. Asking someone to remember the details of a movie they saw last week can be taxing."

I laughed and headed back to my office. Two hours later, when my eyes blurred from staring at spreadsheets, Lyndy called my cell number.

"Please tell me this is your break time," she said. "Or close to it."

"Close enough. What's up?"

"My lunatic aunt phoned from the library a few minutes ago. When she finished telling me the titles of the books she returned, she said there was a minor commotion at the puzzle table."

"What kind of minor commotion?"

"Apparently there's a nosy woman who doesn't work on the puzzles, but leans over to tell the people which pieces should go where. I guess it didn't go over too well when she actually moved a piece into place. Right in front of someone by the name of Samantha."

"Samantha Wiggins. She was on the original selection committee. What happened next? Did your aunt say?"

"Oh yeah. Samantha had a meltdown and threatened to have the woman arrested for tampering with community property."

I all but choked. "I don't think there is such a thing. Then what?"

"Oh, it gets better. The nosy woman leaned over again and pounded her fist in the middle of Samantha's puzzle pieces, scattering a few of them. Not a big deal according to my aunt, but you would have thought the woman bulldozed an entire village from the reaction."

"Wow."

"Yeah. The woman stormed out but not before this Samantha woman made a threat to get even for—are you ready for this?—destruction of property."

"What destruction?"

"One of the puzzle pieces chipped."

I tried not to laugh but it was impossible. "Want to swim tonight? Marshall will be tied up."

"Sure. Seven-ish?"

"Sounds good."

Summer swim nights in my community of Vistancia have been a high point for me, ever since I moved here a few years ago. And when Marshall and I got married, we stayed in Vistancia because the relaxed lifestyle fit us perfectly.

Lyndy wasn't just the first friend I met when I moved here, but she turned out to be my best friend. She was my age, widowed and working for a medical insurance company. She got introduced to Lyman, the captain of Herb's softball team, and has been dating him ever since. I keep expecting a wedding announcement but nothing moves quickly around here. I blame it on the heat.

Then, Augusta's voice rang out. "Your mother is on the line, Phee! Said there was a ruckus at the library."

Ruckus. Commotion. Disturbance. It never ends . . .

CHAPTER 5

My mother's version of the ruckus at the library concurred with what Lyndy's aunt had said, only longer. My head pounded when the call ended and I was thankful it was my break time.

I grabbed a chocolate croissant and was about to bite into it when Augusta asked, "Aren't you curious who the cold case tattletale is?"

"You mean the employee who was convinced the wife did her husband in?"

"Yep. Seems kind of fishy to me, waiting all those years. Job security my patootie."

"What are you saying?"

"It may be a setup. Maybe the guy is living happily in the Cayman Islands. Or, maybe the wife had an affair with the coworker's husband and she wanted to get even."

"Good grief! You're beginning to sound like Lucinda Espinoza, and you don't even watch Telemundo."

I clamped my teeth on the croissant and let the flaky blend of dough and chocolate melt in my mouth before I finished speaking. "I'll see what I can pry out of Marshall. We don't even know where that woman lives. Or *who* she is, for that matter."

"I do. I have it in my notes. Mr. Williams has me keep track of all sorts of things. Her name is Tabitha Stephens. Like the witch's kid in *Bewitched.* That's how I remembered her name. Must be her parents liked Elizabeth Montgomery."

"What else?"

"She worked for a commercial air-conditioning company in Phoenix that's now part of a huge conglomerate—Temperature True Industries."

"Oh, no. Not a huge conglomerate. Nate and Marshall will be up to their elbows with interviews."

"Got that right. Look at the bright side. They'll be out of the office all day tomorrow and we can catch your mother's radio show during break time without interruption."

"That's not the bright side. That's a tension-filled, stomach-churning waste of valuable time."

"And yet, you tune in."

"Only because I need to stay on top of whatever idiocy hits the airways and creates a maelstrom in the community."

Augusta burst out laughing. "I'm holding you to it. Tomorrow at ten. It's the Cozy Mystery Hour, not the combined fish and mystery book talk."

"Thank goodness."

It was incomprehensible but my mother and Myrna shared two radio shows on KSCW, Sun City West's local radio station. They got their start when the hostess of a cooking show went to Iowa for the summer to judge pies or pickles, or something or other, for the state fair. Sewing, maybe? Yes, sewing.

A slot needed to be filled and next thing I knew, Mom and Myrna went on the air with the *Booked 4 Murder Mystery Hour*. They were to discuss cozy mysteries but wound up discussing anything and everything that was remotely related to books, mysteries, or "local interest." A polite way of saying *gossip*. How they stayed on the air was the greatest mystery of all.

Then the combined show. I still get hives thinking about it. Local fisherman and resident Paul Schmidt had his own show—*Lake Fishing with Paul*. On one unfortunate day, the schedules got mixed up and the three of them were on the air at the same time. Talking over each other about quaint villages, bakeries, bait, gills, bass, plotlines and protagonists. It was a disaster. At least I thought so. The audience, however, didn't. They found it hilarious and next thing any one of us knew, it became its own show.

"I'll take over your interviews if you listen to my mother's radio show tomorrow," I said to Marshall when we got home.

"I haven't lost my mind. Not yet anyway."

Then, over Cobb salad and dinner rolls, he picked up where Augusta left off regarding Tisha and Arthur Stoad. By the time he finished, I was dazed. "Talk about putting on a fight show for the neighbors," I said. "And in front of their triple-pane front window, no less."

Marshall chuckled. "At least the noise wasn't audible. Just body language from their spats."

I tried to picture hands on hips, finger pointing, and a number of unmentionable gestures.

"I think I owe Augusta an apology. According to what you found out, those two give new meaning to the term *daytime drama*."

• • •

When I arrived at work the next morning, Augusta had the phone to her ear, where it stayed until a few minutes before ten. I didn't have time to tell her what I gleaned from Marshall.

"Sorry, Phee," she called out. "I've been scheduling those interviews for Mr. Williams and Mr. Gregory ever since I got in. "Come on, let's hightail it to the workroom. We'll keep the door open in case anyone walks in."

I plopped in a Green Mountain K-Cup and proceeded to our break room/workroom/multipurpose room. Augusta turned on the radio and motioned for me to keep still. The next voice I heard was my mother's.

"Good morning, everyone, and welcome to the *Booked 4 Murder Mystery Hour*, where Myrna Mittleson and I, Harriet Plunkett, will discuss anything and everything related to cozy mysteries. We also have a call-in time for listeners to ask us questions about anything cozy that piques your interest. Oh, goodness! Someone is calling us already. Myrna, pick up the phone and put it on speaker."

"Hello? Hello? Harriet, it's me, Gloria. I'm at the library."

"What's that drilling noise?" It was Myrna's voice.

"Maintenance is changing the lock to the little storeroom where they keep the puzzles. Someone tried to break into it last week, according to the librarian, so now the rec center is putting in a dead bolt. The guy just got here and fired up his drill."

"I don't think drills get fired up," my mother said. "Is that why you called?"

"No, actually, Cecilia and I wanted to know if you and Myrna would like to go out to lunch after your show."

"You're on the air, Gloria. And yes. I'll call you later."

I looked at Augusta and shuddered. "Oh, brother."

"Today we're going to discuss Tina Kashian's great summer read, *One Feta in the Grave*," Myrna announced. "Do any of you know the first line of chapter one?"

"There's a dead body!" the next caller shrieked.

"No," Myrna said. "Good guess, but the first line is 'It looks like a giant nose.'"

"Not the first line!"

"Yes. I have the book in front of me." Myrna was adamant.

"Not the book! The library! The Sun City West Library. The locksmith just found a dead body in the puzzle room. A woman!"

CHAPTER 6

Next thing we heard was screaming, screeching, and yelling. Then my mother was back on the air. "Who is this? Who are we talking to?"

"Celeste Blatt. I'm one of the puzzle workers. I was listening to your show on my earbuds when everyone left the table and ran to the front of the library. Someone screamed 'dead woman in the puzzle room.'"

"So she called my mother's radio show?" I whispered to Augusta.

"Apparently so."

Then Celeste continued. "I grabbed my phone to call the posse but tapped KSCW instead."

"Okay, call the posse and then call us right back."

Next thing I knew, my mother announced, "This is a developing story and we are the first to bring it to you on KSCW. Don't go away!"

"Oh, no." I was positive the color had left my face. "She's not KPHO, or any bona fide news station, for that matter. Developing story? The only thing she and Myrna will develop is a tangled mess."

Then Myrna's voice came across the airwaves. "I hear sirens, everyone. Stay put. In the meantime, let's take a look at the location for *One Feta in the Grave*. Tina writes about a lovely—"

"Are you there, Harriet?" It was Gloria's voice. "You're not going to believe this but when the locksmith opened the door to the puzzle room, a woman was lying facedown on top of an open puzzle box. I couldn't tell who it was and everyone is crowding around me."

"Elbow them and get a better look."

"It must be one of the library workers. The poor woman probably had a heart attack when she was sorting stuff. And no one knew because the door was closed to the room."

Then, more bellowing and Gloria ended the call.

"It's most likely a medical emergency that turned fatal," Myrna announced to the radio audience. "Of course, that's just the firsthand observation from one of the ladies at the library."

Seconds later, Gloria was back. "Forget the heart attack. I think she was murdered. Good thing I'm on the thin, petite side. I was able to squeeze through Carl and Lettie to get a better look. I could see blood on the woman's neck. It's all over the puzzle too. Guess they'll have to throw it away and buy a new one. Oh no!"

"What?" my mother shouted. "What now?"

"Deputy sheriffs arrived with the posse and they're moving everyone away from the puzzle room." Then, to what I presumed were the deputies, "All right, all right. I'm going."

24

"And there you have it," my mother said. "The live report about the body found at the library this morning. We will continue to keep you apprised of the situation as best we can. In the meantime, Myrna will talk about Ocean Crest, New Jersey, where Tina Kashian's mystery takes place."

"I think I'm going to be sick," I said to Augusta.

"Eat another croissant. It settles the stomach."

"I guarantee that in less than an hour, my mother will call and beg me to take Streetman out because she'll be on her way to the library once her radio show is over."

"And I guarantee that Bowman and Ranston will now shift gears away from the cold case to have our guys assist with a murder investigation, if it turns out to really be a homicide."

"Well, there's nothing to be done right now so I'm heading back to my office and the solitude of spreadsheets. I might as well enjoy the peace while I can."

"Ditto, here. I still have cold case interviews to set up but I'd hate to schedule them, only to turn around and cancel them. Hmm, guess I'll break the happy news to Mr. Williams. He can tell your husband."

I wasn't wrong about my mother phoning in a few hours to see if I would take "her little man" to the dog park, but she wanted me to go the following morning. And she was insistent.

"Phee, you know as well as I do that talking to Cindy Dolton is the only way we'll know more about that woman in the puzzle room. She has her eyes and ears glued to this community."

And her mouth wide open.

"Mom, the news stations will cover that unfortunate situation, and if it is murder, then I'm sure Nate and Marshall will get the salient details from the deputies."

"I can tell you right now what they'll get—'we have to wait until the toxicology results come in,' and 'the coroner's preliminary postmortem hasn't come in.' By the way, the women at the library said no one could get close enough to see who it was. They covered the body with a tarp and whisked her off on a gurney. Believe me, Gloria and Cecilia tried."

I'm sure they did.

"Let the deputies handle this. They know what they're doing."

More or less.

"You know as well as I do that time is of the essence when it comes to murder. For all any of us know, we could have a lunatic library hater out there, intent on doing away with us. Not to mention the fact we are going to be featured in *Senior Living* magazine. We can't miss an opportunity to showcase ourselves."

"You mean *yourself.* And slow down. All Gloria saw was some blood. The woman could have fallen and gotten injured. And those injuries, on top of a prior medical condition, could be what caused her death. So before you go off the rails about maniacal killers, wait until the facts come in."

"Exactly. That's why you need to speak with Cindy."

"Ugh. Will that put a lid on it for you?"

"Yes."

"Fine. Five fifteen tomorrow morning. I can't believe she's such an early riser."

"So is my Streetman. He'll be overjoyed to see you."

"Tell me now. Is he off park probation this time?"

"Yes. No amorous or other such incidents."

I propped my elbows on my desk and let my head rest in my palms. It wasn't as if I minded talking with Cindy. She was personable and helpful. It was Streetman who managed to spike my blood pressure. Still, it was better than my mother's nagging.

True to form, the evening news reported the incident at the library. It was nonspecific, just as my mother had said. Even Marshall couldn't provide more detail, only what Augusta already knew—he and Nate would be on the case should it be deemed murder.

"The deputies were able to get preliminary statements from the patrons at the library but nothing striking," he said. "Until we get a verdict from the coroner, Nate and I will plod on with that cold case as well as our other minor ones."

I stretched out on the couch and sighed. "I'll be plodding, too. Tomorrow. At an ungodly hour. With Streetman, no less. My mother's convinced Cindy Dolton has picked up enough intel to make it worth the trip. And before you say a word, she and the women are convinced it's a homicidal maniac driven to murder library patrons."

"We don't even know the actual cause of death!"

"Trust me. I told her as much but you know what I'm up against."

"Only too well. Have fun dishing the dirt. Or should I say, trying not to step in it."

"Aargh."

• • •

"Why is the dog's mouth all blue and gooey?" I asked when my mother ushered me inside the house at sunrise.

"Oh no! Don't tell me he got into that mixed berry pie I bought at the Farmer's Market yesterday." She rushed to the kitchen and then came back with a wet towel. "He's been quite naughty lately when it comes to sweets.

Especially jams and jellies. I can't leave anything laying around. He can get himself up on a chair and rifle through food on the kitchen table. I had to buy a whole new jar of raspberry jelly last week. Thank goodness the cat has no interest whatsoever."

She nabbed the little bugger and wiped his face. Then, she handed him to me.

"He'd better behave at the park. That's all I can say."

"You worry too much, Phee. He'll be an angel. An absolute angel."

So was Lucifer.

The usual cluster of white dogs and a few Boston terriers greeted Streetman at the gate when we got to the park. It was only a little past six and it was already ninety degrees with a high of ninety-nine expected.

"Phee!" Cindy called out and motioned me over to the fence where she stood. Her well-behaved little dog, Bundles, sniffed Streetman before moseying along the fence line. "Wow. That didn't even take a full twenty-four hours for you to show. Must be your mother and that book club of hers are really stressed out over that tragic discovery yesterday. Listen, you didn't hear this from me, but I know who it was."

"How? Nate and Marshall don't even know. Although I'm sure those deputies will call the office this morning. If it is foul play, they'll want the guys on the case for sure."

"My brother-in-law, Mike, was the locksmith who discovered the body and he got a good look at her wrist. She was wearing one of those colored coils that holds keys and stuff. It was purple and her little rec card was on it. Samantha Wiggins."

I gasped.

"Shh! Not so loud. No one knows. I promised him I'd keep it hush-hush, but since you're unofficially investigating, I figured that would be okay."

"Oh my gosh. Samantha. Not that I knew her or anything. Only by reputation. Well, reputation via the book club ladies. She was on the original committee to select a puzzle. Uh, that didn't go over well—but gee whiz—it was not a cause for murder."

"Yeah, I know. I mean, who kills over a puzzle selection? It had to be something else."

"Do you know anything else about her?"

Cindy shook her head. "Not much. Somewhat socially. She used to have a poodle but that was years ago. She wasn't married. I knew that because she belonged to the singles club. Maybe she was widowed, or divorced, or just a plain old man-hating spinster."

"Wow. That's a lot more information than anyone else has gotten so far."

I glanced to the far end of the park and watched as Streetman christened the mesquite tree before turning his attention to the date palm. *So far so good.*

"I've got to get going," I said, "once Streetman completes his business."

Cindy squinted and laughed. "I don't think you'll be waiting too long."

And then, the all-too-familiar shout—"Poop Alert! Poop Alert!"

"That's my cue!" I reached in my pocket, pulled out a plastic bag, thanked Cindy and hustled to tidy up and get the dog home.

I knew if I disclosed Samantha's name to my mother, it would be all over Maricopa County like a swarm of cicadas. Instead, I told her Cindy's antennae were up and that she'd keep me informed.

"Make sure you follow up, Phee." She picked up Streetman and nuzzled his face. "You know how full that woman's plate is. Following all the news in this community can't be *that* easy."

"Uh-huh."

"I'm planning on stopping by the library this afternoon to work on the puzzle. It'll be the hottest part of the day so it's a good time to be there."

"Are you sure it's going to be open?"

"It is. Whatever that forensic team did, they did it yesterday. I imagine the puzzle storage room is cordoned off but the rest of it should be wide open. If I find out anything, I'll call you. And you be sure to do the same."

She held out the dog for me to kiss and I all but gagged. I knew where his mouth had been. Then I raced out of there and headed for the nearest Starbucks.

So help me, they better not run out of espresso shots.

CHAPTER 7

"I know who the victim in the library was," I announced to Augusta the second I got in the door.

"They had it on the news? Mr. Williams didn't say anything when he got in. And, by *in* I mean in and out. Same with your husband. You missed them by about five minutes. They went hustling off to finish up those cold case interviews. Both of them are certain they'll be conferring on that library death if it turns out to be a murder. What did the news say?"

"Not the news. Cindy Dolton. And before you start laughing, it was one dog park trip that actually paid off. Turned out Cindy's brother-in-law was the locksmith who found her. The woman was Samantha Wiggins from that puzzle selection committee. Kind of bossy according to my mother. I can't believe it might have been an intentional act."

"Nice euphemism. But yeah, given the average age in that community, it could have been a heart attack. Or a brain aneurysm. You don't hear much about brain aneurysms but let me tell you, they're downright scary. Talking one minute and—pfft!—you're gone."

"Thanks for that cheery thought, Augusta. Anyway, until the preliminary postmortem is made available to the deputies, we'll just have to be on the wait-and-see list."

"More like wait until your mother calls and see what happens. Hold on! That's a fax coming in. Might be Samantha's postmortem."

Augusta walked to the fax machine while I made myself a dark roast K-Cup. She studied the two sheets of paper and handed them to me. "Trauma to the left external carotid artery. Puncture to the neck, consistent with pneumatic staple gun."

I stopped short of taking a sip of my coffee. "A staple gun? One thing's for sure. It couldn't have been self-inflicted. I mean, who does such a thing? Oh my gosh! A staple gun!"

"Yes, that's what the report says."

"I know. I know. But when I was at the library the other day, a man from the computer room came in and asked if anyone had taken their staple gun. He was putting up a bulletin board, or something like it."

"You think someone absconded with it for nefarious purposes?"

"I hate to speculate, and yet—oh heck—I'm getting as bad as the book club ladies. No, I don't think someone planned a murder with a staple gun. But it *is* quite possible someone borrowed the gun and then left it in plain sight, where someone else, in the heat of the moment, grabbed it and well, you know . . ."

"You've been hanging around those women way too much. Now, if you want my opinion, it was premeditated. The question is *why*. Wait! Another fax is coming in."

Augusta snatched it like the last chocolate chip cookie on a tray. She furrowed her brow and studied it for a second. "It's marked confidential from Bowman and Ranston. Well, someone has to read it in order to pass it along."

We both laughed. "Go ahead, I won't tell."

"You'll be reading it over my shoulder." Augusta adjusted her tortoiseshell glasses and moved the paper closer to her face. "Maybe we ought to hire Cindy Dolton. She was right. Says here the victim was Samantha Wiggins, age seventy-nine. Widowed. The sheriff's office is in the process of contacting next of kin. No information other than gender and age will be released to the public."

"Let me be the first to release some—Nate and Marshall will be on the case."

• • •

For the remainder of the day, I had to dodge questions from my mother and tell Lydia to do the same. Apparently Gloria Wong was equally persistent. To make matters worse, the unofficial scuttlebutt at the library pointed to Samantha. When she didn't show up to work on the puzzle, it didn't take long for word to get around that she had to be the victim. No doubt, putting puzzles together wasn't the only tangible feat for that crew. Armchair detecting was the other.

Never before did I breathe as big a sigh of relief as when the news channels announced her name that night. By then, speculation had gone rampant. Everything from mob business to an unhinged person on the loose.

And if that wasn't enough to get tongues wagging, another threat surfaced. This time, however, it was Lucinda who phoned to tell me. It was the following morning. Thursday to be exact, and my mother was at the beautician getting her summer cut and color. I knew because I had to listen to her go back and forth between "cool beige blonde" and "buttery blonde." I already knew the result. She'd get there and pick an entirely different color.

When I heard Lucinda's voice, I thought maybe she was helping my mother decide the color choice, but then she told me she was at the library and that they found a new threat on the back of another puzzle piece. She didn't want to disturb my mother at the beauty parlor and wanted me to know in case my mother called.

"This time the librarian took the threat seriously," she said. "She phoned the sheriff's office and they sent a deputy over to take the puzzle piece. One of the library aides traced the shape and said she'd get her husband, who's in the woodworking club, to make another two."

"Two?" I was totally confused.

"Yes. They wanted the first piece, and then we all had to stop and try to find it."

"Everyone's had their hands on it. I doubt they'll get fingerprints. Tell me, what did the second threat say?"

Lucinda cleared her throat. "It read, 'I told you to stop!'"

"That's it? 'I told you to stop'?"

"Yes. It didn't say what they'll do, but given what happened to Samantha, it's bound to be another murder. The librarian thinks maybe we should stop working on the puzzle until things settle down."

"How do the participants feel about it?"

"Carl and a few others pooh-poohed it, but Lettie was shaken up and suggested no one go into the restroom or any of the small materials rooms alone."

"That makes sense." *For once.*

"I've got to get back to the puzzle, Phee. If your mother calls you, have her call me right away. Say, do you think someone's waiting in the wings to knock off more of us? Myrna had Amazon expedite an order for the new Super Screamer. If you ask me, the old one is loud enough."

"Uh, just be careful. And cautious. And don't let your imaginations go haywire." *Like that's going to happen.*

"Okay. Good talking to you."

"Same here."

"Hey, Augusta," I called out when the call with Lucinda ended. "Any word yet if Nate and Marshall are being called in to investigate Samantha's death?"

"As a matter of fact, I just got off the phone with Deputy Ranston. That's the one who resembles a Sonoran Desert toad, right?"

"Uh, yeah."

"Good. Need to keep them straight. Anyway, they want Williams Investigations on the case. He said he'd call Mr. Williams on his cell phone with the details."

I rolled my eyes. Once word got out to my mother, there'd be no peace.

"Any word on next of kin? They had to be notified or the news wouldn't have provided her name."

"Oh, they were notified all right, according to that deputy. And you won't believe who it is—Forrest Frost Wiggins, her son. But you probably know him from those late-night infomercials for Restoration Youth Gummies."

"Forrest Frost? *That* Forrest Frost who promises to turn our bodies back a decade?" *And proof Samantha was not a man-hating spinster.*

"That's the guy. According to Deputy Ranston, he's Samantha's only surviving relative. Lives in the Biltmore area of Phoenix. Must be Restoration Youth Gummies have paid off."

"Hmm. If his was the body that was discovered in the puzzle room, I'd surmise it had something to do with that gummy business. But it was his mother. Unless she was partnered up with him."

Augusta shrugged. "We'll know soon enough."

"It's odd that those cryptic puzzle-piece messages implore everyone to stop what they're doing."

"Maybe there's something in that puzzle they don't want anyone to see."

"Like what? A street in Sun City? More than likely, someone wants the library space for another purpose. And I doubt those threats have anything to do with Samantha's demise."

"Guess our guys will find themselves digging up the dirt on that woman. If I didn't think Mr. Williams would pitch a fit, I'd phone Rolo Barnes to get started. But I value my job so I'll just wait."

As it turned out, Augusta didn't have to wait long. Nate phoned her from Chandler, a good hour or so away, where he and Marshall had tracked down Tabitha Stephens at the corporate headquarters for Temperature True Industries. At least they were making headway on the cold case, which was more than I could say for Bowman and Ranston and the hot case. Then again, I wasn't privy to everything.

"I was right about Rolo," Augusta said when we caught up during an afternoon break. "I had to send him a fax, pull out a burner phone, and make an offering to the gods."

"Yeesh. At least he hasn't put in any more layers to his communication requirements."

"No, but he's on a new diet. Intermittent fasting coupled with apple cider vinegar infusions with tart cherry and olive oil. It's supposed to increase lifespan and cut body fat."

"Sure. It'll get those gag reflexes going like crazy."

"Crazy. Good word for it. And Rolo, too."

Looney or not, Rolo Barnes was the best cyber-sleuth on this side of the Mississippi and possibly the other. He was the one the professionals went to when they hit a dead end. He used to be the IT specialist for the Mankato Police Department when Nate, Marshall and I worked there, but he decided to open his own business and has been thriving ever since.

His very demeanor gave the word *quirky* a whole new meaning. He preferred to be paid in kitchen gadgetry and refused checks with certain number sequences. I still shudder when I think about payroll back in Mankato.

The FBI, CIA, and Homeland Security were amateurs when it came to Rolo. He took deep dives into the dark web and had connections that would make hardened criminals shudder. A black look-alike for Jerry Garcia, Rolo had no problem when it came to the opposite sex. Women seemed to be drawn to him like felines to catnip. Go figure.

"Sounds like Nate isn't wasting any time looking into Samantha, either." I studied Augusta's face for a reaction.

"He knows what's coming. He and your husband are going to be pulled in two directions, but my guess is that the cold case will go into a deep freeze until this recent situation is resolved. Heck, Arthur Stoad's been in the deep freeze for over two decades. What are a few more weeks?"

"I suppose. Then again, if those deputies get antsy, Rolo will need to pull out another shovel and dig around for him."

"Better hope you're using that word in a figurative sense." Augusta chuckled. She reached into her desk drawer and pulled out a small box of chocolate chip mini-cookies. "Here, try one. Only eleven calories."

"You're counting calories?"

"No, but if anyone asks, I'm eating a health food."

"These things are the size of a dime."

"Take a handful. It's the only way you can taste them."

I crunched a mouthful of the hard-as-a-rock cookies and swallowed. "When you said *dig*, you don't think a body will show up after all those years, do you?"

In spite of the fact no one was in the office, Augusta darted her eyes to the left, and then to the right. "For Tabitha Stephens's sake, a body better turn up. Or a murder weapon with Arthur's DNA on it. Otherwise, what real evidence does she have for making the accusation of murder?"

"Unless she did it and she plans to point the finger at the wife. We've seen stranger things around here."

At that time, we had no idea how strange things would get, but in retrospect, we should have been prepared.

CHAPTER 8

With one bona fide dead body and one not-so-silent accuser signaling that there's another one to be discovered, Nate and Marshall had seen more of Bowman and Ranston in twenty-four hours than they had the prior month.

Meanwhile, I had my own issues to deal with on Friday. Mainly the book club ladies and my aunt. At a little past seven the night before, my aunt Ina called to inform me that she had "put out feelers" in her community regarding the murder in my mother's.

"What kind of feelers?" I asked.

"Oh, the usual. The social club women, the art club, the literary society, and the gourmet club."

"You have a gourmet club?"

"I live in the Grand. Of course we have a gourmet club. And a wine-tasting club."

I rolled my eyes and waited for my aunt to continue speaking. "And I asked your uncle to do the same with those musician friends of his. In fact, he'll be playing that saxophone of his next Saturday for a wedding at the Biltmore. Very fancy-schmancy."

And close to Forrest's place.

"Thanks, Aunt Ina. That's very thoughtful."

"I'm always here to help."

If only it was just Aunt Ina. But—oh no—her call was followed by Cecilia, who asked if I thought the women should "step it up a notch" and buy tasers in addition to the Screamers. I vehemently replied, *"No!"*

Then Shirley, who's usually the voice of reason, phoned to ask if there was some way Gloria could get Thor, her Great Dane, classified as a service dog so he could protect them at the library. I couldn't spew the words out fast enough. "Thor? He's such a fraidy cat! And yes, he's huge, but he's a huge coward. You'd be better off with Streetman." I said it acerbically but Shirley thought I was serious and told me she'd speak with my mother. Then she ended the call before I could choke out another syllable.

All in all, last night was strained. At least there was some normalcy at work.

I printed out the monthly invoices to mail and gave them to Augusta so she could put them in envelopes. Thankfully, most of our invoices were now emailed so that cut down on postage and time.

It was a little past ten and the men had left the office well over an hour ago. Sometimes they split up the county cases but other times, like these, they worked in tandem. Meanwhile, my stomach rumbled and I looked over the leftover pastry items we had in the workroom.

"I'm ducking into the donut shop," I said to Augusta as I charged out the door. "French cruller, bear claw, apple fritter or otherwise?"

"Bavarian cream and an Old-Fashioned."

"On it!"

When I returned with the goodies, she handed me a Post-it and said, "From your mother. She called."

I snatched it and read it aloud. "Spoke to Shirley. Took your advice. Ordered a bandana for Streetman." Then I widened my eyes and looked directly at Augusta. "What else did she say? I'm almost afraid to ask."

"Oh, it's pretty clear-cut. She intends to have him wear an emotional support animal bandana since the library allows emotional support animals."

"Emotional support? People will *need* emotional support after a half hour with that fur bundle of neurosis. My mother can't be serious. And if she thinks for one second that Streetman will provide protection, she'd better think again." I pressed my fingers into my temple and closed my eyes. "For everyone's sake, Nate and Marshall had better find Samantha's killer in record time."

• • •

By the next morning, two things had become apparent: For starters, the sheriff's office and Williams Investigations weren't the only ones on the case. The puzzle solvers and my mother's book club had decided to join forces to catch "the maniacal staple-gun-wielding killer" before he or she messed up their opportunity for notoriety. I didn't dare tell her that *Senior Living* might choose another community as a result of said notoriety.

In addition, Drake appointed himself the next Monk, complete with a month's worth of Lysol and Clorox wipes.

"What does he plan to do?" my mother complained. "Spray the killer to death?"

She phoned me the second I walked into my office. Then used the next thirty to detail their "action plan."

"You are not detectives." I tried to keep my voice soft and low. "You are not deputies. And your dog is not a service animal. Sorry, Mom, but every time you and the ladies stick your noses into ongoing investigations, it ends with a disaster. Stick to armchair investigating if you must."

"Right now we're dealing with a colossal nightmare. Do you have any idea what forty thousand puzzle pieces spread over a huge table look like? It's taken days to sort them. Now, we're being asked by the librarian to turn them over so that the forensic people can make sure there are no threats on any more of them."

"Technicians."

"What?"

"Forensic technicians."

"They're people, aren't they?"

"Never mind."

"Goodness, Phee. It's a 'hurry up and wait' situation. We hurry up and then we wait. Meanwhile, Herb decided to call his own powwow to plot our next move. Something about not getting upstaged by Carl. Apparently there's some history from when Carl used to play pinochle."

I remembered Herb's last powwow. "Can you talk him out of it? Let the deputies handle it."

"I don't think so. He used words like *sitting ducks*. Besides, you know how Herb is. We'll never hear the end of it if Carl winds up to be the one to crack the case."

"Crack the case? You don't even have a case to build."

"That's where you come in. Herb's called a meeting at the men's club and wants the book club ladies to join them."

"When?"

"Monday, right after you get out of work. We're ordering pizza."

"Wait a minute. Who said I was going?"

"I thought you understood. We need your expertise. I promise it will be a short meeting. The men will stuff their faces, come up with a few wacky ideas, and then turn it over to us women to figure out."

I knew Marshall had a full schedule, including evenings, so I agreed. "Have Herb order a giant meatball sub for Marshall. I'll bring it home for him. The men's club has a refrigerator where it can stay while we meet."

If nothing else, I thought I could hold back the reins. But I was only kidding myself. Once those women get an idea in their heads, it's like extracting a tooth.

CHAPTER 9

I walked into Sun City West's Men's Club on Meeker Boulevard Monday evening just as the delivery guy from Uber Eats pulled out of the parking lot. Herb had reserved the conference room with a giant oval table, which now housed stacks of pizza boxes.

"Get some of those boxes open, Bill," he said. Then he waved to me. "Hi, cutie! Grab a seat and help yourself."

I perused the room and all of the book club ladies were there, including their newest member, Gloria, and my aunt Ina. Naturally the pinochle men showed up in full force once they knew pizza would be served.

Seconds later, paper plates and napkins were distributed along with bottled water and cans of soda. "Once we stop eating and start talking, we need to keep our voices down. We don't want anyone to overhear us," Myrna said. *This, coming from perhaps one of the loudest women in the county.*

"It's not like we're undercover agents," Louise said. She bit the bottom triangle from her pizza and reached for a napkin. Then she looked at Herb. "Well, what's your plan?"

He got up, closed the door to the room, and cleared his throat. "The deputies are probably looking into the staple gun that killed Samantha. Trace evidence and all of that." Then he eyeballed me. "Your boss and your husband are going to get stuck interviewing anyone who has a pulse."

"What does that leave us?" Shirley looked at Cecilia, who was seated next to her, then at my mother.

She leaned forward, placing her chin in the cup of her hand. "We begin by stalking her son. Forrest Floor or whatever his name is. They mentioned it on channel 10. Or was it channel 5?"

"It's Forrest Frost," I said, "and don't use the word *stalking*."

"Fine. I'll go with the more conventional—*Looking into.* How's that?"

I nodded.

"Herb's right," Wayne said. "Half these murders turn out to be domestic situations. Money, greed, latent psychological issues, anger, jealousy—"

"We get it." Myrna took another slice of pizza and bit into it. "But someone, please tell me. How do we do that?"

"We know where he works," Lucinda announced. "It's that gummy ball company and it happens to be located on Cotton Lane between Surprise and Buckeye. Where all those Amazon warehouses are. And if you want to know how *I* know, it's because Cecilia and I drove down that way to get to a parish event last year. Cecilia refused to get on the highway. I kept telling her the 303 isn't really a highway, but —"

"It has more than one lane." Cecilia loosened a button on her blouse. "That makes it a highway."

Herb propped his arms across the table and boomed, "Enough with the side chatter. We need to articulate the plan."

Then a few voices. "What plan?"

"Snoop around the warehouse and strike up conversations with the workers. Find out if there was bad blood between Forrest and his mother."

I literally felt my chest pound. "That's a horrible idea. First off, you can't just walk into those places. They have security. And even if you got in, it's a horrible idea. Really horrible! The last time this crew was in a warehouse, Streetman wreaked havoc!"

"What do you suggest?" Bill grabbed another slice of pizza and chomped into it.

"That we leave Restoration Youth Gummies alone. I'm sure the deputies will speak with Forrest to determine if he had a motive to murder his mother. Which, I doubt."

"I'm not so sure, Phee." My mother smiled. "Not everyone enjoys an idyllic relationship."

"But they don't go around committing murder. Okay, fine. How about if a few of you pay him a condolence visit. Bring food or something. With all the snooping you do, I'm sure you've already determined where the guy lives."

"It's in Phoenix," Shirley whispered. "But that was all I could see while the library aide was away from the counter."

"Huh? Come again."

This time it was Myrna who answered. "They keep the volunteer information on an old Rolodex on the counter. It's got their emergency contacts with phone numbers and addresses. In case someone falls or something."

"So you looked up Samantha's?"

"It wasn't as if Shirley broke into the library or anything," my mother said. "She was gathering vital information. Too bad she didn't gather enough. We don't have the complete address for Forrest."

I shrugged. "Maybe one of the library staff will give it to you."

"They're not allowed to, but don't worry. I may have a plan."

The minute she said that, I could feel my pulse quicken. "What kind of plan?"

My mother dismissed me with a wave of her hand. "I haven't gotten that far. But no worries. We'll get Forrest's address."

"Paying a condolence call is a clever idea," Louise said. "I can bake my oatmeal cookies."

Herb elbowed Wayne and I read his lips—"Nearly cracked a tooth on them."

"That's wonderful!" I gave Herb the "eye" and continued. "Remember, a simple and short visit. You'll get a sense of his relationship with his mother without resorting to anything that could get you in trouble."

If only . . .

I left the pizza powwow feeling somewhat victorious. I had thwarted a plan of action that surely would have spelled disaster. Unfortunately, my plan turned out to be much worse. It wasn't so much the condolence call, but rather the means and manner of finding out where Forrest lived.

• • •

"You suggested *what?*" Marshall asked when I told him what had ensued at the get-together. He had just finished eating the meatball sub and enjoying a cold bottle of Coke.

"It was the best I could come up with. Herb wanted them to barge into the processing plant for Restoration Gummies. Can you imagine?"

"Yes. In vivid detail. Hey, I know that proper investigations take time and that those pinochle players and book club ladies are short on patience, but honestly, they need to trust in the authorities to solve this. Armchair sleuthing is one thing, but they take it to a whole new level."

I had visions of the ladies descending on Forrest's house like seventeen-year locusts in a corn field.

• • •

The following evening Augusta and I had just turned off the printer and shut off the lights in the office. Nate and Marshall were at the posse office in Sun City West finalizing some details with Bowman and Ranston regarding Tabitha Stephens. At least one case was moving along.

"All set?" Augusta asked. She walked toward the door when the phone rang. "Drat. It'll ruin my evening if I let that call go to the answering machine. Hold on."

I glanced at the street and pictured a lovely evening in Vistancia's pool with Lyndy when I heard, "Sorry, Phee. Hope this doesn't ruin your evening. It's your mother."

"I'll close up. One of us might as well get out of here while we can."

"Sure?"

I nodded and took the receiver from her. "What's up, Mom?" I asked.

"We have a situation here at the library. Can you drive over and take Streetman home?"

"Isn't the library closed by now? And what's the dog doing with you? Don't tell me you snuck him in there."

"Technically, the library *is* closed. Just drive here and take him home. Please. Shirley and I need to stick around for a while. It'll go faster when Cecilia and Gloria get here."

"What will go faster? What are you talking about?"

"I told you. We have a minor situation."

"Does it involve the dog?"

"In a roundabout way, yes."

I closed my eyes and shuddered. "Just tell me. Are you supposed to be in there right now?"

"In a manner of speaking, yes."

"Tell me what's going on or you'll have to take the crowned prince home yourself."

"Fine. But not a word to Marshall."

"I'm listening."

"You know how we needed to get Forrest's address, right? Well, they took the Rolodex off the counter and it was impossible to extricate it from the desk drawer where they had it stashed. So, Shirley and I stayed late and hid in the ladies' room so we could have a look-see when everyone left."

"And?"

"I happened to have Streetman with me in a dog sling carrier that I got on Amazon."

"And he got out, didn't he? Please don't tell me he peed on the lower bookshelves."

"No, not that."

"Then what? Spit it out."

"When I walked past the table with the giant puzzle, he got out and landed on it. Then he ran all around it and knocked most of the puzzle pieces on the floor."

"Oh my gosh! That's over forty thousand pieces!"

"There are still some of them on the table. The other twenty thousand are strewn all over the place and Streetman thinks it's a game chasing them. That's why I need you to get over here and get him. Shirley and I have to pick the pieces up and try to reassemble the puzzle a bit before the library opens tomorrow. Cecilia and Gloria will be a big help when they get here."

"I can't believe this. I really can't believe this."

"Are you coming or not?"

"Fine. Good thing Marshall is at a meeting."

"We put a small pebble in the back door by the tower stairwell. You can get in that way. Luckily Wayne remembered the security code from when he did some woodwork here last year and they had to install an alarm system."

"So Wayne knows what's going on right now?"

"Wayne, Herb, Bill, Lucinda, Myrna—"

Terrific. The Greater Phoenix area.

"But only Cecilia and Gloria are coming, right?"

The silence at my mother's end of the phone said otherwise. Once again I closed my eyes and shuddered. Then I locked the office door, took a deep breath and headed to my car.

CHAPTER 10

As I started the engine, a text came in from Marshall: *Stuck here with B & R on staple-gun report. Will grab something to eat. Please do same. Xoxo*

I texted back: *Will do. Xoxo*

My mother told me to park at the pickleball courts so no one would get suspicious. I prayed that the lineup of cars I joined were pickleball players and not her friends, but I knew otherwise. Especially when I realized they were all Buicks except for one.

The lights were dim when I slipped through the library's side door and made sure to wedge the little stone that held it open back in place. "I'm here," I said, keeping my voice low as I walked down the corridor into the main room.

Sure enough, the floor was covered in puzzle pieces. Shirley, Cecilia, and Herb were on their hands and knees picking them up while Myrna, Bill and Wayne sat at the long table and tried to put them together.

"I'm not having any luck," Myrna said to Bill. "Think of something."

"Like what? Setting fire to the place? Face it, you gals are going to have to own up to this mess."

"Speaking of mess, have any of you seen my mother or the dog?" I asked.

Bill pointed to the back of the library. "Past the mystery section toward the reading rooms. The dog has a mouthful of puzzle pieces and refuses to give them up."

As Bill had said, the little nipper stood his ground as my mother tried to coax them out of his mouth. "Oh, good! You got here, Phee. See if you have any better luck with Streetman. I tried giving him a doggie treat but he refused."

Next thing I knew, he squirmed under the media center display and plastered himself against the back wall.

"Maybe wait it out," I said. "Long enough for me to grab a sandwich at Arby's and bring him back something more enticing than those dry dog treats."

"Eat fast," was all my mother said. "And get lots of ketchup on his food. He goes wild over it."

I was out the door and in my car before she had a chance to change her mind. But when I returned, things had changed. And not for the better.

"Streetman's still crouched under that media display," my mother said, "and now he's growling if anyone goes near him. You know how possessive he gets. But that's not the worst of it."

"You mean there's more?"

"Shh! Yes. Shirley just remembered it's Tuesday night."

"So?"

"In twenty minutes, the Weight-Watching Women are going to have their meeting. It starts at seven thirty. The club president has a key so they'll use the main entrance. That means we have to scoop up all the puzzle pieces and lure the dog out before they get here."

"Okay, but it's impossible to put the pieces back."

"Well, not now. We'll do it when the meeting ends and the women leave."

"By *we'll*, you better mean *you*, because I'm heading home once I get Streetman out from under that display. I got him a roast beef sandwich. With plenty of ketchup like you asked."

With that, I bent down and waved the Arby's treat under his nose. In a nanosecond, he rushed out and I grabbed him by the collar. He was too busy eating to object and my mother was able to nab him and tuck him back in the tote carrier.

"Leave now, Mom, before he gets away again. I'll stick around and help stack the pieces back on the table."

"Can you get the ones he dropped under the display?"

I reached underneath and swept up a handful of the puzzle parts. "I think that's it." Then I studied the pieces. "Um, some of these are chewed up and all of them are wet and slimy."

"Maybe no one will notice."

Fat chance.

To the absolute delight of everyone, my mother and her ball of neurosis exited the library. "As soon as you're done, come to my place," she said to everyone. "We've got to get back in here to arrange the puzzle once that meeting ends."

A cascade of groans followed. Then Herb asked if my mother had any food at her place. When she mentioned the freezer, he told her to forget it. "We'll hit Curley's bar when we're done. You women can join us or go to the Homey Hut for pie. Your choice."

Then a few voices said "pie" before they continued to scavenge for puzzle pieces.

"How much more time do we have till those women get here?" Lucinda asked.

"Twelve minutes," Myrna replied. "Just put the pieces on the table for now. They won't notice. They'll be too busy weighing themselves and lying about what they've eaten. I should know. I used to belong to that club."

I tried not to laugh as I scooped more puzzle pieces into my hands.

"Five more minutes, in case anyone wants to know." Wayne pushed his chair back from the table and looked down. "I think you've got them all. Come on, let's get out of here."

He didn't have to ask again. And while it wasn't quite a stampede, I had to admit, I'd never seen that crew move so fast in the few years that I'd known them.

Miraculously, we were able to exit before the weight-watching women arrived. I hightailed it to my car and drove home just as the sun set in my rearview mirror.

It was still early so I phoned Lyndy and met her at the pool. It would be another hour or so before Marshall would get home and I needed to reenergize myself in the cool water. Besides, I needed to share the evening's insanity with someone, and what better choice than Lyndy.

"Hey, stranger," she called out from the far end of the pool. "You just missed the crowd. We've got the whole place to ourselves." Her brown curls glistened in the solar lamplight as I tossed my towel and jumped in.

"What a circus! I don't know what's worse—my mother's lunacy or that dog of hers."

"Nothing like family lunacy. My aunt phoned a few minutes ago. She saw a throng of people leaving the library after hours and phoned the posse. Said she thought it was a roving gang up to no good."

I all but spat up pool water. "It was a roving gang all right—the book club ladies and the men."

Lyndy was all ears when I told her about the puzzle fiasco and my mother's attempt to find Samantha's killer.

"And it's not over. Not by a long shot. They've got to sneak in later to try and put the puzzle pieces back to the point where people won't notice. Good luck with that."

"You going?"

"Oh, heck no! I've done enough. I had to buy Streetman a roast beef sandwich at Arby's to lure him out from under a media display. Nope. They're on their own."

In retrospect, maybe I should have gone back, but who could have predicted what would happen.

It was past nine when the ringtone from my cell phone made me jump. I had just pulled the lightweight sheet back from the bed and prepared to crawl in.

"If it's your mother, I say we move to Madagascar." Marshall was already on his side of the bed and scrolling through his phone. That was a no-no according to sleep experts, but that never stopped him from catching those z's.

I looked at the caller ID. "Darn. It's her. So help me, she better not have another *situation*."

Her voice was soft but clear. "We're not alone."

"Who? Alone where?"

"In the library. I told you we had to go back."

"Everyone?"

"No. Only Shirley, Myrna, Lucinda and me. The men are probably still at Curley's. Gloria had to get home to let Thor out and Cecilia, Louise—"

"It doesn't matter. Simply tell me what's going on."

My mother's voice got even lower and I strained to hear her. "We waited until the weight-watching ladies left. They used the front door so we were able to get back in the building from the side door. The dimmers were on so we didn't mess with them. We spread out around the table and that's when we heard a creaking sound. Like a door opening from the computer room side of the building. So right now, we are all under the table. Even Myrna, who practically had to contort herself."

"Do you hear anything right this minute?"

"Yes. Shh! It's a man and a woman. They're getting closer. I'll keep the phone on and you can hear them for yourself."

I put my phone on speaker and held it out for Marshall. Sure enough, the man and woman were clearly audible. Unrecognizable voices, but audible.

The woman spoke first. "This can't be obvious. Let's take a few of the pieces that are completely colored and get out of here. I'll be in big trouble if someone finds out I got ahold of a key to the place."

"Uh, that's not going to be so easy. Look! The table's a big mess! What the heck happened? You think someone beat us to it?"

"Someone must have. Did you tell anyone?"

"I'm not the one with the big mouth. Let's get out of here. I have a feeling we're being watched."

"What about the pieces?"

"We don't have time to turn them all upside down and look. Whoever got here first left a big enough mess. It'll slow things down but now it'll call attention to the matter. Something like this has to be subtle so no one notices."

"I think it's too late for that."

"I'll think of something. Come on, we're out of here."

The silence at the other end of the call was nerve-wracking. Finally, my mother spoke. "Someone is trying to sabotage the puzzle and prevent it from being completed. And I have a darn good idea why!"

CHAPTER 11

"What on earth for?" I could hear shuffling as my mom, Shirley, Myrna, and Lucinda got out from under the table.

"The summer showcase readers want the whole place to themselves. Good golly! They can read anywhere. Ever since the library decided to award prizes to the people who read the most titles from their list, they've petitioned to eliminate the puzzle and install recliners."

"So you really think they'd go as far as to break in and remove puzzle pieces?"

"You have no idea how territorial some of these people are, Phee. And don't get me started on that adult coloring book club. They wanted the big table too. Herb overheard one of them say they were going to color a giant Mona Lisa."

"Great. The Louvre will be ecstatic. Look, you need to leave now. Seriously. Before who-knows-what happens."

"Don't worry. Myrna doesn't like missing the ten o'clock news. When we get here tomorrow, we'll act as shocked as can be."

"Wonderful plan. Good night."

I put the phone on the nightstand and turned off the lamp. "That was pretty weird, wasn't it? Imagine, trying to steal puzzle parts in order to commandeer a table."

Marshall adjusted his pillow and stretched. "Unless it wasn't that, after all."

"Then what?"

"Who knows? Lately nothing surprises me in that community."

• • •

Augusta greeted me Wednesday morning with two words—"Mission accomplished."

I gave her a quizzical look and waited for a response.

"Not me. Your mother. She left a phone message a few minutes before you walked in. She said, 'Tell Phee mission accomplished. We got Forrest's full address.'"

"Oh my gosh. Forrest! With all that puzzle nonsense, I forgot the real reason they snuck into the library."

"You okay, Phee? You have a funny, spaced-out look on your face."

"Just thinking. My mother and her entourage snuck into the library after hours to get the address for Samantha's son. They think he knows more than he's letting on."

Augusta patted her bouncy bouffant hair. "And they're going to snoop around his place while someone distracts the guy?"

I nodded. "That was the ill-conceived plan. Until last night's roadblock."

"I'm making myself a cup of coffee. Tell me everything while I wait for the K-Cup."

When I finished, she shook her head. "Just when you think you've seen or heard it all . . ." Then she broke up laughing. "What's your mother going to say about the chewed-up puzzle pieces?"

"Next to my aunt Ina, my mother's a pretty good actress. She'll act dumbfounded and deny knowing anything about it."

"For her sake, and yours, I hope her performance is Academy Award–worthy. Hold on a second! Got an alert on my phone. I subscribed to Apple News. This better be good. I don't want to hear about the Kardashians."

"I can't blame you."

"It's a real alert, Phee. A 5.6 earthquake hit early this morning in Palm Springs, California. It was either the Banning Fault or the Garnet Hill Fault."

"Talk about serendipitous. This is fantastic. Did your alert mention aftershocks?"

Augusta nodded and took a sip of her coffee. "Uh-huh. Said they could be felt all the way to Gila Bend."

"Works for me. My mother can extend it a few more miles to Sun City West."

And like that, Mother Nature provided the book club ladies with an out. What she didn't provide, however, was information on who the prying couple was or why they needed to remove puzzle pieces. I knew it would be only a matter of time before that little matter got under my mother's skin, but in the meantime, she and her friends were on to "Plan Forrest" and a condolence call.

"Marshall and I barely had time to speak this morning," I said. "Did he mention his agenda? Or Nate's, for that matter?"

"Sure thing. Mr. Williams drove to Chandler to have a chat with Tabitha Stephens and your husband is about to do the same with Forrest Frost. Guess working in tandem has taken on a new meaning. Better hope no more bodies crop up."

"Swallow those words!"

The remainder of the day moved at a steady pace. Not boring, but not frenetic either. At a little past three, my mother phoned to tell me they decided to bring baked goods from Boyer's Café to Forrest's house in lieu of flowers.

"When? And who?"

"Tonight. Just Shirley, Gloria and me. Myrna is much too loud and clumsy. She won't be very good at snooping and sneaking. Cecilia is way too timid and refuses to open drawers. Louise can't leave Leviticus home in the dark and Lucinda has a bunco game."

"Can't Louise turn on a light for Leviticus? Or cover his cage?"

"He's a temperamental parrot. And she's very doting."

I rolled my eyes. "I suppose Aunt Ina is tied up."

"When isn't she tied up? She has a quatrain poetry meeting tonight. Whatever *that* is. Honestly, the Grand has clubs none of us would imagine."

"Um, didn't you say you wanted to gage Forrest's reaction and not pry around his house like cat burglars?"

"We need to make progress. Besides, Gloria is quiet and petite. She'll be transparent."

Transparent. Until she knocks something over.

"What is it you're looking for?"

"A reason for Forrest to commit murder. Chances are he's got a hefty insurance policy on Samantha. For your information, two sisters in Boise did their mother in. It was on *48 Hours*."

"Stick to the original plan, will you? If Forrest was responsible, Nate and Marshall will find out. By the way, how did the puzzle solvers react when they discovered the mess on the table?"

"The main library room was closed for the morning. The librarian posted a sign explaining that an aftershock from the California earthquake had unsettled a number of puzzle pieces and that things had to be rearranged and put back in place."

"By who?"

"Drake and Norva Bellows. I have no idea why she asked them."

"Uh, did you find any chewed pieces that Streetman might have taken home?"

"Only one and I'll slip it in tomorrow."

"Don't get too carried away at Forrest's house. Okay?"

"Honestly, Phee. You act as if a horde of vandals is about to enter the man's residence."

"A horde of vandals might be more preferable. At least they'd be pillaging for food and the like."

"You can be as snippy as you like, but believe me, once we find evidence of intent, you'll change your mind."

"As long as Forrest doesn't find evidence of your intent!"

CHAPTER 12

"What's up, hon?" Marshall asked when I studied my cell phone as we watched the news. We had cleared the table and put the plates in the dishwasher. "You keep looking at your phone."

"Aargh. My mother's paying that so-called condolence call to Forrest tonight. Along with Shirley and Gloria."

"I'm sure they'll be fine."

"Wish I could say the same. My mother's convinced he's hiding something and she intends to scope things out. The ladies are getting tired of waiting for results from the official investigation into Samantha's murder. And the men are getting tired of listening to the ladies."

"I'm sure if she gets into a jam, you'll be the first to know."

Regrettably, I wasn't. That honor was bestowed on Paul Schmidt of all people, and he, in turn, called us.

"Hey, Phee. It's Paul. How fast can you drive to PetSmart?"

"Huh? What for?"

"Replacement swordtails. Just found out they're on sale until nine tonight. It's a tropical fish. I'd do it myself but I'm on my way to the Outdoor club's evening barbeque. I'm bringing the trout. So, are you familiar with swordtails?"

"I know what they are. My daughter had some when she was twelve. What I don't know is why you want me to get them."

"To replace the ones that died. Your mother thought I might have some at my place, but I have a saltwater aquarium. I didn't know your mother had tropical fish."

"She doesn't."

"Hmm. She called because your aunt knocked into the fish tank and it cut off the oxygen supply. Hey, are you still there? The line got quiet."

"I'm here." *I'd like to be in Oz or even Narnia, but I'm here.* "Uh, okay. I'll deal with it. Enjoy your barbeque."

"I intend to. And tell her to make sure the fish adjust to the change in temperature."

It was actually the furthest thought from my mind, but not for long. As soon as the call ended, I texted my mother: *Give me Forrest's address. Paul called. Why is Aunt Ina there?*

My mother texted back: *Gated community in the Biltmore. They let us in. Gloria's sciatica acted up so I called Ina. Said she'd skip the poetry meeting. Too bad I forgot how clumsy she can be. Did Paul mention the fish incident?*

Yes! Now what? I texted.

Shirley is showing Forrest photos of her teddy bears. Ina just got the aerator or whatever you call it to work, but most of the fish are belly up. We snuck into his office. It's next to the guest bathroom. We have to hurry up in here.

I stood, dumbfounded, looking at the screen on my cell phone.

"Is everything all right?" Marshall asked.

"Not exactly. My mother's snooping around Forrest's office, my aunt murdered his tropical fish, and Shirley is talking him to death."

It was the first time I saw my husband double over with laughter. "I probably shouldn't be laughing, considering what may happen next, but honestly, didn't they think things through?"

"For sure. That's what got them into this mess. They've been reading too many cozy mysteries and watching way too many movies on the Hallmark Channel and BritBox. Now I'll be biting my nails until I hear from my mother later tonight."

I paced around the house, tidying everything in sight because I couldn't sit still. Meanwhile, Marshall grabbed his iPad and pulled up his notes on Forrest. A short while later, my mother called from True Food Kitchen where she, Shirley, and my aunt stopped to eat a late dinner.

"This place is wonderful, Phee," she said. "They have the most amazing flatbread dishes and—"

"Forget the flatbreads. What *exactly* happened at Forrest's house? And it's a good thing you didn't do any more damage. Wait until he discovers you killed his fish."

"Those things have a very short shelf life. And besides, we were discreet. Ina didn't shriek when she knocked into the tank."

I shuddered. "Please tell me you didn't make a mess in his office. I know how my aunt pokes around in dressers and drawers. I watched her when she was at Uncle Louis's house before they got married. So, did you find anything worth mentioning?"

"A motive for murder. That's what we found. And I even took a picture of it on my phone. Hold on. I'll text it to you. Herb showed me how."

In the background, I could hear my mother speaking to Shirley and my aunt. "I'm showing Phee what we found. Oh, look! A cute photo of Streetman and Essie on the couch. It was before he ripped off the floral vest."

I shook my head at Marshall and sighed. "She better not go through the entire dog photo gallery."

A second later, her text came through. Three photos in all. The first was my aunt's rear end in front of a four-drawer file cabinet. I rolled my eyes and swiped to the next one. This time it was a copy of a two-hundred-thousand-dollar insurance policy on Samantha Wiggins with Forrest Frost Wiggins named as the sole beneficiary. The company was American Guardian Life Insurance and it was dated five years ago.

I swiped to the third photo and that's when my eyes nearly bulged out. "Marshall! Check this out. Samantha was a major stockholder for Prosaic Puzzles. That's one of the largest manufacturers according to the book club ladies. And get this! Forrest was the beneficiary for those stocks. Although that doesn't exactly scream *motive*. But it may be the reason she wanted those awful puzzle choices. Most likely they were Prosaic Puzzles."

"I heard you, Phee," my mother said. "Look closely. She had a controlling interest in the company. It screams motive to me."

"Well, don't scream it to anyone else. Marshall will share your unauthorized findings with the deputies, but keep in mind, they can't act on them. Besides, most people bequeath their estates to relatives."

"He was a partial relative."

"What do you mean?"

"Forrest was Samantha's stepson. Didn't I mention that? She never adopted him when she married her late husband. And if you want to know how I know, it's because Cecilia and Lucinda told me. The husband went to their church."

"That doesn't necessarily spell out motive."

"No, but—Oh my, the salmon salad looks exquisite! I'll talk to you later, Phee."

And with that, the call ended and I stared wordlessly at Marshall.

"I know, hon. It takes a while to process stuff like that. The snooping. The fish tank disaster. The insurance policy. The stocks. And the fact Forrest is the stepson. That's a lot to digest in a matter of minutes."

"No, what will be hard to digest is the fact none of those women will be able to keep that information to themselves."

I hate when I'm right. But I knew the minute my mother, my aunt, and Shirley uncovered what they deemed to be ironclad evidence of murder, it wouldn't take long until it unfolded like a badly written soap opera in Sun City West. And while the "we won't breathe a word about it" ladies managed to huff and puff the gossip, another tittle-tattling circle emerged.

• • •

"My looney aunt heard the most disturbing news on her CC & R walk this morning," Lyndy said when she called me at work on Thursday. "She was doing her usual, jotting down violations, when she ran into someone who told her that a credible rumor was spreading about Samantha's murder."

"A *credible* rumor? In this community?" I glanced away from my computer screen and rubbed my eyes. "What rumor?"

"That Samantha's murder wasn't going to be the only one."

"Based on what?"

"That whoever killed her mistook her for someone else."

"Did your aunt say how this person knew?"

"Oh, yeah. When it comes to that stuff, my aunt is very thorough. She said the Sun City West Gab-About Group gabbed about it at breakfast this morning. One of the women stopped into the posse office to drop off a cell phone she found and she overheard a deputy tell another deputy that 'once they find out it was a case of mistaken identity, it will get everyone's hackles up.'"

"That could be anything."

"*You* know that, and I know that, but since the hot topic is that murder, it will be hard to convince them that the deputies were discussing anything else."

"Oh, brother. At least I'll be prepared when my mother gets wind of it." I then proceeded to tell her about last night's fish debacle with the Snoop Sisters. "I'll say one thing, Lyndy. Your aunt is certainly persistent."

"Not my aunt. Lyman. When he and that softball team unwind, they're worse than fourteen-year-old girls."

"Oh, no. I'm afraid to ask."

"He went to the Outdoor club's barbeque last night and got an earful. Give those guys a few beers and you'd be surprised at what spews out of their mouths."

Probably Paul's trout.

I held still and waited for Lyndy to drop the other shoe.

"Someone named Carl was seeing Samantha but she dumped him. The men think his pride was wounded and he got even. According to Lyman, Carl once lost it when someone named Drake pitched a fit because Carl left a used tissue on the table."

"Drake, huh? Has to be the same guy. I watched him hand out wipes the first day of the puzzle. Could be that little event escalated, but I didn't notice any more tension than usual that first day of the puzzle reveal."

"Maybe Samantha did something to aggravate Carl even further. Then you could add another suspect."

"You're getting as bad as the book club ladies."

Both of us broke up laughing, but when the call ended, I added Carl's name to my murder map and an off-centered notation on Drake.

CHAPTER 13

Around midmorning, when Nate and Marshall emerged from a client meeting, I let them know about the presumed Carl-Samantha relationship as well as the source.

"We'll look into it, kiddo," Nate said and chuckled, "but those men are as bad with rumors as the women. No offense."

"None taken. They give new meaning to the word."

Marshall gave my shoulder a squeeze as he stepped toward the Keurig. "I'll add it to the list. We got a call from a Celeste Blatt, who apparently works on the puzzle every year with a friend of hers—Betty Jean Wiseman. She thinks Samantha was killed because she was about to 'spill the beans' on someone. Most likely, it's another piece of gossip, but that's where we're headed—to the library for a little chat with her."

"I hope you don't run into my mother."

He laughed. "We won't. When I said *library*, I should have said *vicinity*. We're actually meeting in the interior courtyard by the welcome center. Facing the pool. Celeste didn't want to be spotted."

"Oh, brother. She's not trading government secrets."

"No. Worse. Tales from the crypt."

"Don't say that out loud, Mr. Gregory," Augusta said from her desk. "Some of those women will take you seriously. You know how they are about ghosts and spirits."

"Don't remind me."

"You have that antsy look about you," Augusta said when the men headed out.

"It's midday and any minute now I expect my mother to call with an update about the puzzle. She was going there to work on it. The Bellowses were asked to piece together as much of it as they could before it was made available to the community members to continue."

"Seems reasonable. No sense bringing in everyone. They'd only step on each other's toes."

"Oh, I'm not worried about that. They're weeks away from that *Senior Living* article, and by then there'll be plenty of progress on the puzzle for a photo op."

"Then what?"

"The Bellowses. It was a man and a woman that I heard via my mother's phone when she hid under the table at the library with Shirley, Myrna, and Lucinda. It could have been the Bellowses who snuck in to steal some puzzle pieces. I need to hear their voices to see if they sound like what I remembered from the ones I heard on the phone. Drat! Too bad they didn't have a distinguishing accent or even a drawl."

"Let me guess. You're going to ask your mother to record them."

"Covertly. All she'd need to do is put her phone on video and let it do the rest. How difficult could that be?"

"You tell me. It's *your* mother."

"This is one task she should be able to accomplish without fanfare."

I plopped in a French Roast pod, and as soon as it was ready I headed off to my office to prove I was right. Regrettably, I wasn't.

"You want me to record the Bellowses? I don't know how to do that." My mother had just gotten out of the car when she answered my call. "I'm late as it is, Phee. I promised Cecilia and Lucinda I'd be here ten minutes ago but I caught every darn light between Limousine Drive and Meeker Boulevard. Every single light!"

"Look, it's basically the same process you did when you were under the table speaking to me."

"I didn't record you. I held out the phone so you could hear the voices."

"Same idea. Pretend you're taking a video of the dog. You do that all the time."

"Now you want me to video the Bellowses?"

"No. Don't video anything. Put the phone on the table. As if you were waiting for a call or text, but first set it up as if you were going to video something. Then push the little red video icon."

"I know how to do that, Phee. I video Streetman and Essie all the time."

"I know. I know. That's what I just said!" My eyes had gone past rolling and spun in my head. "The video will pick up their voices. I'll see if they sound familiar. And you do the same. You're sitting at the same table. The Bellowses could very well be the ones from last night."

"What if they are? Never mind. I'll let Cecilia and Lucinda know. We'll set a trap."

Oh no! Not one of her traps.

"No trap. Don't do anything. Just record them. No traps. No action plans. No nothing. Got it?"

"I wasn't born yesterday. Oh, Lucinda's getting out of her car. Hang on." And then, "Lucinda! Phee wants me to video the Bellowses. Hold on. I'll tell you all about it." Then back to me. "I've got to run. Talk later. Bye."

"It's going to be a disaster," I said to Augusta as soon as the call ended. "A complete disaster."

"And that surprises you?"

The truth was, it didn't. But what happened at the library later that afternoon certainly did. In retrospect, it may have sped up the investigation into Samantha's murder, but that would be like saying dropping a carton of eggs on the kitchen floor sped up the floor-cleaning process.

It made it inevitable, but at what price?

• • •

An hour and a half later, Nate and Marshall straggled in, each of them with a giant Polar Ice Drink in their hands. I was on my way back to the office with some invoices when I heard Nate's voice.

"It's what? The beginning of June and already it feels like mid-July." I turned and saw him take a red bandana from his pocket and wipe his forehead.

"How'd it go with Celeste?"

They winced simultaneously.

"Apparently armchair detectives are more common in Sun City West than we thought," Marshall said. "Celeste believes Samantha's killer was either 'the puzzle nuisance' who leans over the table and puts together pieces that 'are in someone else's possession,' or someone who knew that Samantha was privy to classified information."

"Classified information? As in government secrets, or *classified* as in which candies will be placed in the vending machines?"

At the sound of the word *candies*, Augusta looked up from her desk. "My money's on the vending machine."

"It would make things easier." Marshall took a large gulp from his drink. "Celeste said that during Margarita Night a few months ago, Samantha told her that she knew about a local business that falsified its data to get more customers. Said it was a prominent business, too, and one that everyone would know."

"Let me guess. She didn't mention the name."

"You guessed right," Nate said.

Augusta leaned over the desk and looked directly at us. "They have Margarita Night in Sun City West? It's a thing?"

"Margarita Night, Martini Night, Wine Night, you name it. Lyndy was the one who told me. She found out from her aunt, who snoops around people's recycling and sees the empty alcohol and fixings bottles."

"Like I've mentioned a million times," Augusta said, "I'm glad I live on county land and not in a development."

"If you ladies are done chatting, we've got to get back to work. There may be some validity into what Samantha knew." Nate finished his drink and tossed the giant cup into the trash.

"Wait!" I held out my hand like a crossing guard. "What about the nosy puzzle woman? The one that Samantha said she'd file charges against for destruction of property? You know, the chipped puzzle pieces?"

"I think we can safely eliminate that one," Marshall said. "Seems really far-fetched to think someone would commit murder over something so petty. And yeah, we always say 'People have been known to kill for less,' but in this case, I can't imagine anything less."

"While we're doing question-and-answer, I have one too." Augusta pushed her chair back and stretched. "I never found out how it went with that conversation you had with Tabitha Stephens on Wednesday, Mr. Williams. Did you email me notes? Please don't tell me you left written notes on the back of a taco bag like last year."

"Sorry, Augusta. Been pulled in so many directions, it escaped me. I'll forward you my notes."

"Can you tell me the abridged version?"

Nate took a breath and pinched the back of his neck. "Tisha Stoad sold the house and hadn't been heard from since. According to a neighbor, who read it in the local paper, she had Arthur declared dead seven years later. I figured we were busy enough, so I asked MCSO to track down that article. Sure enough, it was in the paper, but scant information."

I widened my eyes. "Husband declared dead, huh? And the wife missing. Another possible murder?"

"Not according to Tabitha. She's under the impression Tisha is somewhere right under our noses."

"Or six feet under."

"Wasn't she supposed to have some sort of evidence?" Augusta loosened the sides of her glasses.

"Yep. And that's why Tabitha's back on our docket for Saturday morning. She chipped a tooth and had to leave for a dental appointment so we cut our meeting short."

"Better than bagel time with Phee's mother." Augusta went back to her computer screen and the men retreated to their offices. Following suit, I moseyed back to my office, expecting to settle in with the pile of invoices. Instead, I took a call from the librarian at the Sun City West Library and sat with my hand over my mouth for a good two or three minutes after the call ended. Then, I rubbed my eyes and reached inside my desk drawer for a Tylenol.

CHAPTER 14

"Did you say what I thought you said?" Augusta asked.

"Oh, yeah. That was Darcey Hartwell, the librarian. My mother asked her to call me. Get this—something went wrong with the fire alarm/sprinkler system at the library and the sprinklers that were above the puzzle table all went off and drenched the area."

"Not the entire library?"

"Fortunately, no. The sprinkler system was installed in sections according to Darcey."

"Why didn't your mother just call you?"

"Because she rushed out the door, soaking wet, and yelled for Darcey to call Williams Investigations to let me know what happened. Not that I can do anything about it, mind you, but still, you know how she is."

Augusta made a chortling noise. "Do you think it was sabotage?"

"I'm beginning to wonder. First those threatening notes and then the two people, possibly the Bellowses, who tried to remove pieces. The question is, why? Why doesn't someone want that puzzle to be solved? It's a boring photo of a street."

"Maybe they just don't want the library to be showcased in that magazine. People can be downright strange."

"True, but we didn't find out about *Senior Living* until after the first incident."

"Like I said, people can be strange."

"If everything got drenched, it may mean kaput for the puzzle. Wood swells up and they'd never get those pieces back together."

"Maybe it's for the best, Phee. That whole endeavor was sounding more and more nightmarish each day." Augusta stood and walked to the counter where a freshly opened box of Entenmann's chocolate donuts beckoned her.

"True, but now I'll have to listen to her and the book club ladies whining and complaining that their summer entertainment was gone."

Too bad I was only partially correct. The women whined and complained all right, but not because the puzzle pieces were ruined. That would have been too easy. Thanks to someone's quick thinking, they were salvaged.

Carl had insisted that trash receptacles be placed behind the table so the crew wouldn't disturb everyone getting up and down to throw wrappers and such away. Not wanting to argue, Darcey had done exactly that.

According to my mother, who phoned an hour later, all of the puzzle pieces were unharmed. Everyone at the table immediately slid the pieces into the trash containers so they wouldn't be destroyed. Unfortunately, that meant starting over again. And this time with a time clock.

"Early! They're coming early! The magazine people!" she shrieked into my ear. "We've got to put that puzzle back to where it was before that idiotic sprinkler system went off."

At least she didn't mention sabotage, but I knew it was only a matter of time.

"Um, are they closing the library for mopping up?"

"They're closing now and will reopen an hour late tomorrow. The rec center sent one of those mop and vac crews with the big machines. None of the bookshelves got wet. Only us. And by us, I mean Shirley, Lucinda, Gloria, Cecilia, the Bellowses, Betty-Jean, Celeste, Lettie, Carl and some newbies. I was soaked, Phee. Soaked! Honestly, doesn't maintenance ever check anything?"

"Do you think you'll be able to get the puzzle assembled to the point where that magazine will be able to showcase it?"

"You sound like Lettie Holton. Talk about unglued. I never saw anyone move their hands so fast across a table to get those puzzle pieces into the trash baskets. Then again, your aunt Ina's pretty quick moving mah-jongg tiles across a folding table. One flick and boom—Bamboos, Dragons, Flowers—hard to keep up."

"Okay, then, I need to get back to work."

"Too bad you'll be working tomorrow. You could have helped us."

Not on your life.

"Yeah, a real shame. Bye, Mom."

Augusta thought it was a premonition that the puzzle needed to be scrapped, considering how many starts and stops they had. And, remarkably, she wasn't the only one. Suffice it to say, Nate and Marshall chimed in on it as well when I caught up with them later.

"Sometimes it's better to call it quits than beat a dead horse," Nate said. It was late in the day and I almost wondered if he was referring to Arthur Stoad's alleged murder. He and Marshall had spent the day meeting with realtors and bankers regarding the sale of the Stoad property and possible whereabouts of Tisha.

"Between one actual murder and one speculative one, we're certainly doing a lot of pavement pounding." Marshall pulled the tab from a can of Coke and took a drink. "The heat doesn't help either."

"Any progress on Samantha's death?" Augusta asked.

"A regular potpourri of possibilities, none of which are solid enough to deem viable. Bowman and Ranston said they'd dig deeper into the claim about a business that falsified records and left us with 'the puzzle nuisance,' Samantha's love liaison with Carl, and of course the recent evidence that Phee's mother managed to pull up at Forrest's house."

"Did we ever find out if Samantha partnered up with her stepson? That restorative gummy business has quite a following. Lyndy checked it out on Facebook and even considered buying some. My mother and her merry band of outlaws didn't dig up anything about it in his home office."

"Nope. Too busy suffocating tropical fish." Augusta burst out laughing and I struggled to keep a straight face.

"No proof one way or the other," Nate replied. "Meanwhile, our plate is overflowing as it is."

"No worries. I'll pick up extra donuts tomorrow." Augusta winked.

• • •

Friday morning started out fairly routine with Nate and Marshall gumshoeing, for lack of a better word, and me settling in with invoices and spreadsheets. As for Augusta, she was in the midst of ordering supplies for the next quarter. Client appointments had been scheduled for midday so things remained quiet until my mother graced us with her latest library puzzle update.

"Take the call, Phee!" Augusta shouted. "It's your mother."

"From now on, I'm only taking calls from the Pope!" I shouted back. Then I picked up the receiver.

"You won't believe this, Phee. Darcey called a special meeting of the puzzle solvers to discuss the situation."

"I thought everyone was called on board to put the pieces back."

"Yes, that, too. Darcey set up the meeting for tomorrow at ten. It's a Saturday so we should get a decent turnout."

"I'm working." *Please tell me I'm working.*

"You worked last Saturday, didn't you? I can't keep up. Besides, Bagels 'n More introduced two new churro bagels. They're on special. One is the gourmet kind with apple filling and coffee cake crumbs on top and the other is, well, a churro bagel."

"Good to know. I'm sure I'm working."

"Phee, Darcey wouldn't have called a meeting unless it was something that had to do with either the murder or the fact that strange things are happening in the library. Shirley and Lucinda will be convinced it's paranormal and the men will tease the daylights out of them. Besides, what better opportunity to eke out developing information as well as picking up on who's hiding what. Put those investigative skills to work."

Much as I hated to face it, she was right. I did have a penchant for putting clues together, but I'm no investigator. Still, she dangled the right carrot and I agreed to attend.

"The meeting only. Not churro time at Bagels 'n More. I have chores at home."

"Fine. The meeting only. Did I mention they also added skinny bagels? Half the calories."

"Again, good to know."

CHAPTER 15

At a little past nine the next morning, I drove to the nearest Starbucks and fortified myself with a triple-shot-venti-vanilla latte. If I thought I could handle a quadruple shot, I would have ordered one. I tried not to let my imagination go too haywire as I envisioned the library meeting. True, it was to discuss the "puzzle situation," but I'd been to enough of those meetings to know that they inevitably morphed into something more agitating. This one was being held in the lecture hall adjacent to the bowling alley because they expected more attendees than the small library conference room could hold.

When I pulled into the parking lot, I prayed that the bulk of the cars belonged to the morning bowlers. Sadly, I was wrong. With the snowbird exodus and the early pool hours, the lanes were practically empty. I had parked on the tennis court side and cut through the bowling alley so I had an up-close and personal look at the bowlers. No one I recognized, but then again, I was only familiar with Gloria's team.

The lecture hall, on the contrary, was bulging at the seams. I didn't realize that assembling the summer puzzle was of such magnitude as to command a crowd. So much for discreetly nabbing a seat in the back. All of those were taken. It was worse than high school and college lecture rooms where everyone hid in the back.

With no other option, I took a seat in the empty front row and tried not to turn around lest I make eye contact with anyone. That was before Myrna spotted me and broadcast it across the room. "Harriet, Shirley, Louise, Herb! Phee's here. Someone let Lucinda and Shirley know when they show up."

Next thing I knew, she bumped against me and sat. "Can you believe this crowd? I should have figured as much. That puzzle runs all day long and lots of folks try their luck as if it was a casino. Not like the regulars who are really committed to the outcome."

I nodded. "I suppose the hotter it gets outside, the more people it attracts."

"Absolutely. I mean, how much swimming can you do before you prune up and can't distinguish sun skin from wrinkles? And forget about pickleball, tennis and golf in this heat. Unless it's at five in the morning. Even my beloved bocce ball becomes unbearable."

A whistling sound caught our attention and I looked at the stage. Four chairs were spread out with water bottles on the rectangular table facing the audience. Darcey adjusted the microphones when Myrna jabbed my elbow.

"It's for the puzzle committee. There're only four of them now that Samantha's no longer in the picture."

As I was about to reply, my mother and Shirley positioned themselves on the other side of me and Herb tapped my head from behind and leaned over my shoulder. "Hey, cutie. I see they dragged you into this mess. Take notes. Might come in handy."

I recognized Lettie Holton as well as Celeste Blatt and the Bellowses onstage as they took their places at the table. Large placards with their names were positioned in front of them, although I'm sure most of the people in attendance knew them.

A few seconds later, Darcey walked to the podium on the left and cleared her throat. Again, Herb tapped my head. "Looks like a parole board."

"Shh!" Myrna spun around.

"Good morning, everyone," Darcey said. "For those of you who don't know me, I'm Darcey Hartwell, the librarian at Sun City West. Thank you all for coming. It shows just how committed our community is to our library-media center and all of the extraordinary programs we sponsor."

"Committed. That's the word for it," Bill said. I didn't realize he was seated next to Herb, but it figured. Those men were glued to the hip when it came to cards and gossip.

Then Darcey went on. "As you are aware, the showcase program of the summer, our giant puzzle, has met with a series of unfortunate incidents."

"That's putting it mildly," someone shouted. It was followed by "Just call a spade a spade. The puzzle's been a welcome mat for murder."

Darcey's posture went from relaxed to rigid in a nanosecond. "I'm referring to the puzzle process. The horrific homicide is an entirely different matter and is left to the sheriff's office and their investigators. Now then, regarding our puzzle, I have asked the puzzle committee to address the concerns we have, elicit comments from the audience, and come up with a solution as we move forward. And now, I will turn the meeting over to Lettie Holton, our remaining chair."

Lettie took a sip of water and moved the mic to her mouth. "Thank you, Darcey. As most of you know, this year's summer puzzle has been fraught with challenges. Recently, the sprinkler system had a malfunction, and had it not been for quick thinking on the part of the participants who thought to move the pieces into the trash, we would not have been able to salvage it. Prior to that, we experienced threatening notes and the aftermath of that earthquake."

"Oh, Lordy! The puzzle is cursed!" Shirley gasped.

Lettie peered into the audience. "Please refrain from commenting until we get to the public participation."

Celeste jumped in before Lettie could continue. "And while I don't believe in curses, I do believe someone or more than one person doesn't want us to complete that puzzle."

"So what are we supposed to do in the library? Just read?" It was a man's voice but I wasn't sure which man. "If I wanted to read, I could do that in my throne room."

I didn't think it possible, but I cringed and rolled my eyes simultaneously.

"What are you suggesting?" Herb yelled out. "Scrap the puzzle because you think there's some loco out there who managed to set off an earthquake?"

The audience broke up laughing but Lettie wasn't pleased. She pursed her lips and glared at Herb. "What I am suggesting is this: We go back to one of the original puzzles and complete that one instead. 'Snowy Blizzard' might be a good choice. It will offer a mental escape from the heat."

"It will offer a headache," Myrna called out. "What's the big deal about starting over?"

"I have to take Lettie's stance on this," Norva Bellows said. "It's quite upsetting and a bit too coincidental. Besides, we need to showcase something for *Senior Living*."

At that moment, Darcey returned to the podium. "Please allow me to interject if you will. The library has a number of easy-to-assemble community puzzles that we can choose from. Larger, fewer pieces. The group would be able to put it together in no time. Last year we loaned one to the Willow Creek Elementary School and they loved it."

The grumbling that came from the audience was hard to ignore. Along with the comments that were flung like mud.

"Are you insinuating we're kindergarteners?"

"We're seniors, not senile."

"I have a PhD. Don't insult my intelligence."

"I'll tell you where you can stick those larger pieces."

Finally, Lettie spoke. "Those responses were uncalled for and unsolicited."

"Then call for them," Bill shouted. "My rear end can only handle so much seat time."

Lettie faced the audience and shrugged. "Fine. Please raise your hands if you'd like to offer a comment or if you have a question."

In the next few minutes, the same comments were restated and regurgitated. Finally, Drake Bellows threw his hands in the air. "Got the message. Give it up, Lettie. We'll dump the puzzle pieces back on the table. What's this? The second or third time? Anyway, we'll start over. It's what everyone wants. And as far as I'm concerned, everything that's happened is coincidental. Time to get over it."

Again, Darcey leaned into the mic at the podium. "That being said, I will speak with the recreational center administration to extend library hours for the next week so we can keep a round-the-clock crew working on the puzzle. And by 'round-the-clock,' I'm suggesting seven thirty a.m. until ten p.m."

"Works for me," Herb whispered to us. "Curley's Bar is open until one thirty."

I watched the puzzle committee members and noted their body language. Lettie scowled, Celeste looked down and fidgeted with her bracelet while the Bellowses appeared nonchalant, as if they didn't have a care in the world.

Darcey's hands, now fists, hung at her sides as she stood like a sentry. Finally, she took the mic and said, "Thank you all for attending. As your librarian, I am happy to oblige. Nevertheless, should there be another suspicious incident involving that puzzle, I will use my administrative power to replace it. That's all. Have a wonderful day!"

"Lordy, if that doesn't top the cake, I don't know what does." Shirley stood and nudged my mother forward.

"Speaking of cake, let's head directly to Bagels 'n More before those specialty churro bagels disappear. You know how people are when new menu items are added. Too bad Phee can't join us." Then to me, "Are you sure? Housework can always wait."

Am I hearing her correctly? "Housework can always wait"? Since when?

"Okay, fine. But only for a quick cup of coffee."

If I had to be honest with myself, I wanted to know more about Forrest's house and if his Restoration Youth Gummies company had anything to do with his stepmother's demise. I knew it would be conjecture, but underneath the drama and exaggeration from the women were little pearls of information that needed to be strung.

CHAPTER 16

Bagels 'n More was bustling, even though most of the snowbirds had left town. It was lunch hour and my mother was right. There was a full line waiting to try the new churro bagels.

"I'll nab us that big round table by the window," Myrna said. She stomped off as if she was staking a claim for a gold mine. We followed her but not at breakneck speed.

The table held eight, but we were able to squeeze in a ninth. Only Gloria and Cecilia were absent from the ladies' group and only Herb and Bill were there from the pinochle crew.

"Was it my imagination or did Lettie want to put the kibosh on that puzzle?" Louise asked. "She was really cagey."

"Maybe she's on the take from one of the library clubs. They're all clamoring for room space. I wouldn't be surprised in the least." Lucinda picked up the menu and perused it.

My mother furrowed her brow and shifted in her seat. "Don't any of you find it odd that Lettie didn't offer a moment of silence for Samantha? Usually they do that sort of stuff."

"Maybe she and Samantha were on the outs," Louise said.

Much as I wanted to keep my mouth shut, I didn't. "I was there on the first day and it appeared as if they were chummy. In fact, Lettie told LaVonda to move her seat since Samantha wanted to be where she could sort the colorful pieces."

"Might not mean chummy." Bill helped himself to the coffee carafe on the table. "Could be Samantha intimidated her. Some of those women are like bull moose. And my apologies to the bull moose."

Myrna started to speak but the waitress seemingly appeared out of nowhere and put out a new carafe.

"Coffee anyone?" I recognized her as the one who normally got stuck with my mother's table and I made a mental note to leave her a good tip.

Seconds later, coffee cups were filled and surprisingly, orders were taken in record time. I attributed it to the fact that the new churro bagel special was half price and included the coffee. Herb and Bill ordered two each but the rest of us opted for one. The menu listed it as having a whopping four hundred and seventy-five calories and that was without cream cheese.

"Um, speaking of 'Snowy Blizzard,' that was the Prosaic Puzzle Company, right?" I wiped my lips with a napkin and took a sip of coffee.

"All three of those horrendous puzzles that are supposed to enhance the mind come from that company," Lucinda said. "And guess who held a controlling interest?" She looked at my mother and Myrna, who nodded like bobblehead dolls.

"We found that out when we paid a call to Forrest, her stepson. Shh! No one is supposed to know." Myrna reached for half-and-half and poured it into her coffee.

"Everyone knows now," Bill said. "They heard you in Iowa."

"Hilarious as always, Bill."

I moved my head so everyone looked my way. "Forget Prosaic Puzzles for a minute. I'd like to find out if Samantha had anything to do with her stepson's company. Williams Investigations was unable to find out. Not yet, anyway."

"If Williams Investigations hasn't been able to find out, how do you expect us to?" My mother topped off her coffee and looked directly at me.

"Because none of you have boundaries. Unlike investigative agencies and law enforcement that have to follow certain rules and protocol. All I'm asking is that you keep your eyes and ears open. Not barging into places that are off-limits or worse yet, stalking someone."

A series of groans followed but they dissipated when the waitress arrived with our food.

"We'll be working overtime on that puzzle, you know," Louise said. "Then again, it's getting so hot that spending time in a nice air-conditioned library is fine by me."

"More like spending time gossiping and gabbing." Herb took a giant bite of his gourmet churro bagel and for a minute resembled one of the Chipmunks.

"You men do a good job yourselves," Louise shot back.

"For goodness sake, it's not gossiping. It's senior socialization and it's recommended by all the health care agencies." My mother raised her head as if she was Sanjay Gupta.

"I wouldn't call it therapeutical, Mom, but yeah, sometimes it comes in handy."

• • •

At a little past four, when I returned from a quick dip in the pool, Marshall staggered in. "Dry heat, my you-know-what. It's only dry because the sweat evaporates proportionally to new perspiration."

I laughed. "New scientific explanation?"

"Nah, just grumbling. Anyway, Nate and I got the evidence from Tabitha. We knew she was a coworker of Arthur's who lived a few doors down from them, but it seemed her hobby at the time was photography. She was in the Sun City Photography Club."

"Oh my gosh! Are you saying she has actual photos of the murder?"

"She has photos, all right, but not exactly ironclad evidence of murder. It seems one of her club assignments was to take pictures of her neighborhood."

"And?"

"She took digital photos of a suspicious, *her words*, white van in front of Tisha and Arthur's house two days before the wife reported him missing. The good news is that the file was date-stamped. Remember, this was twenty-three years ago. And Tabitha's camera, like most, had that feature."

"Did it show the time?"

"The time, yes, but not the time zone. And it would show without designating a.m. or p.m. That feature wasn't introduced until 2016. Trust me, Nate and I had a fast learning curve on that one."

"Why did Tabitha think the van was suspicious?"

"There was a magnetic sign on the side of the vehicle that read *Sudsy Dudsy Cleaners*. The garage door was open and Tisha, along with a husky male, were in the background rolling one of those large trash cans down the driveway. Whatever was in the can was extremely large and covered with either a dark plastic bag or a tarp. Hard to tell."

"A body? Arthur's body?"

"*That*, or her laundry. Could have been quilts for all we know. Tabitha said she never heard of that company and most people took their bulky wash to a local laundromat. The cleaners didn't come to them. It's definitely not enough to arrest someone on suspicion of murder. Plus, we have no idea where Tisha resides at this juncture in time. Couldn't garner the information from the local realtors. For now, those photos are case file information. They could be used in conjunction with other evidence, provided we uncover it."

"I guess it's better than nothing."

"It's a start. We'll chat again with the former neighbors and show them Tabitha's photos without mentioning her name. See if it jogs any memories. We'll also do some digging to find out if there ever was a Sudsy Dudsy Cleaners."

"Sounds like a plan. A plan in need of concrete evidence." I walked to the fridge and grabbed two Powerade drinks.

"Speaking of evidence, Bowman texted us. They found out how the sprinklers at the library were tampered with. Surprised it took them a few days. Most likely it wasn't a priority because a third-grader could have figured it out. There's a valve a few feet from the main water shutoff to the library. Actually, a few valves since the sprinkler system was installed in different areas. Anyway, someone just turned the valve and opened the waterline. Woo-Hoo! Shower time in the library."

"Stop laughing. My mother got soaking wet. I'd only laugh if Streetman got showered."

"You're worse than I am. But here's the clincher—someone would have had to know *which* valve to turn."

"An inside job?"

"That's my take. Meanwhile, it's in Bowman and Ranston's laps."

"Laps, huh? Hope they can swim."

This time it was Marshall who rolled his eyes.

CHAPTER 17

Marshall and I were stretched out on the couch at a little past eight when my mother's call interrupted our quiet evening.

"I'm with Shirley and Gloria. We decided to take the dogs to Panera Bread and sit on the patio."

"Let me guess. Streetman did something deplorable and you need us to bail you out."

"Don't be ridiculous. The little prince is under the table enjoying his cheese sandwich. But that's not why I called, even though he looks adorable. The three of us got to talking and I had an epiphany about getting the puzzle pieces done before *Senior Living* shows up. Shirley thought we should run it by you."

Already this sounds like a doozy.

"I'm listening." I held the phone so Marshall could hear her as well.

"The librarian handed out those awful grainy photos of that street and it's impossible to work out the puzzle without knowing what we're looking at. So we decided to take a little field trip to Sun City and see if we can find the street."

Marshall poked my elbow and whispered, "Tell her Sun City is huge. Not like Sun City West."

I nodded to him before I spoke into the phone. "Do you have any idea of how large Sun City is? It stretches from Olive Road to Beardsley. That's what? Fourteen or fifteen miles? You'd be spending more time than Lewis and Clark—" I caught myself and realized that this could be a great distractor, taking them away from other, more troublesome schemes. "Um, then again it would give you something to do. Maybe even find a nice coffee shop as you tool around."

"Exactly. But we won't have to traverse the entire development. The one thing that was clear on the photo was a tall tower from one of the churches. It was behind the houses. All we have to do is find the church with that tower and cross and we'll be in the neighborhood. Then we'll check out the streets around it and see if anything remotely resembles the street in the photo."

"You *do* realize that the photo was taken years ago and the houses have been updated. Plus, those little trees are forests by now. And most churches have towers with crosses."

"It's a start, Phee. The houses may have been updated, but the spacing between them wasn't. Phase One in all these developments has the most

69

space. By the time they got to Phase Three, homeowners were lucky if they had three feet between the houses."

I couldn't very well disagree with her logic, and neither could Marshall.

"Just to clarify," I said, "you, Shirley, Gloria, and the dogs are going to drive around looking for a match. No trampling on people's property, or worse yet, letting the dogs out. Right?"

"Honestly, Phee. I'm not ten years old. But if, by happenstance, we come across someone of a certain age who may have lived there at the time of the photo, we would most certainly engage them in conversation."

"Why? Why in heaven's name would you do that?"

"To find out why they made a puzzle out of that street. For all we know, there could be a mystery behind it. At least that's what Myrna and your aunt thought. I mean, why else would anyone in their right mind take a photo of a boring street and turn it into a giant puzzle?"

My eyes spun inside my head. "Not everything is a mystery. Besides, isn't Samantha's murder a mystery enough?" Then I caught myself. "But, yes! Yes! You're right. Focus on that puzzle. You never know. The deputies and our guys will deal with Samantha's death." I was literally yammering in an attempt to prevent my mother from deciding to stick her nose into that murder. "Tell me. When do you plan to take the little sojourn into Sun City?"

"Tomorrow. And Cecilia will join us once she gets out of church. The other ladies are tied up. We figure we'll eat lunch at BoSa donuts. That way we can have snacks in the car."

And probably Streetman helping himself to them.

"Okay, just stick to your original plan. Track down the street. No need to complicate things any more than they already are."

"The puzzle solvers will be ecstatic when we find a match. At least we'll know what we're looking at. You can't say that about 'Snowy Blizzard.'"

"No, I suppose not. Have a nice night, Mom."

Then I turned to Marshall when I ended the call. "You don't think we have any real cause for concern, do you?"

"I'd be lying if I said no, given their track record, but this plan sounds pretty innocuous."

Sadly, it wasn't.

• • •

Sometime in midafternoon the following day, while Marshall and I were outside grilling hamburgers, his phone rang and I heard every word of his side of the conversation.

"Yes, this is Marshall Gregory from Williams Investigations . . . I see. Yes, I am most definitely acquainted with them . . . They what? . . . That close to the houses? . . . I understand. Tell me, were there any complaints about a small, snappy dog?" He flipped the hamburgers with his free hand and rolled his neck. The minute he said "small, snappy dog," I knew my mother's plans had birthed a new life. I stood still and listened to the rest of his side of the conversation.

"That's good, I suppose . . . Uh-huh . . . Three of them with cell phones and one driver who stayed in the car . . . Yeah, I suppose it *is* a first. Six calls to your office. Sure. What? She said she was intimately acquainted with Deputies Bowman and Ranston?" Then Marshall burst out laughing and I didn't know what to think.

"I know. Got to hand it to Mrs. Plunkett. She knows how to embellish a description . . . Uh-huh . . . I agree. Odd choice for a giant puzzle. What? . . . No kidding . . . Yes, I'll speak with them as well. Thanks for phoning me. Have a good afternoon if you can."

"Oh my gosh! What did my mother do? Was that the Sun City Posse?"

"Indeed it was." Marshall gazed at the grill and then back to me. "Seems your mother and her partners in crime decided that driving around wasn't enough so they pulled the car over on one of the streets and three of them got out to take photos with their cell phones."

"In and of itself, that doesn't sound too concerning."

"It is if you walk on private property and aim the phone directly at the house. The six people who phoned the Sun City Posse Office reported that, and I quote, 'a sketchy crew of women were casing their houses for a possible burglary.'"

I bit my lip and gulped while Marshall continued to speak. "That's not all. And here's the hilarious part. Your mother told the posse that Bowman and Ranston could vouch for them. Said they'd worked with that office before."

"In what capacity? Oh good grief! Now what?"

"No worries. The posse officer said he'd speak with them about boundaries and asked if I'd do the same. Also said he heard some wonderful things about Williams Investigations. He phoned me to verify the ladies' information before sending them on their way."

"I'm sure my mother will have another version when she gets home later."

"I'd be surprised if she didn't. Come on, we might as well see if these hamburgers are as good as Herb said they'd be. He developed a new barbeque sauce and we're his guinea pigs. If it's anything like the last sauce it'll be incredible."

As nightfall approached, Marshall proved he was right on both counts.

Herb's sauce was magnificent and my mother phoned with her version of the afternoon's "annoying events."

"Sorry to call so late, Phee, but the ladies just left. We decided to order a pizza and wings and unwind from our productive day of puzzle street sleuthing."

"Is that the new name for trampling over people's lawns and taking photos?"

"Who told you that?"

"The Sun City Posse Office placed a courtesy call to Marshall. Hmm, I wonder where they got his name from . . ."

"Fine. Fine. I wasn't going to mention it, but now that you've brought it up, our car was approached by one of their posse cars and we were politely asked to follow it to their office a few blocks away. It was no big deal."

"Thank goodness. What were you thinking?"

"We needed house details to make sure we found the right block. I'm certain we did. It's on Brookside Drive off of Del Webb Boulevard. We could see the church tower in the back. We tried two other blocks where you see the tower but the houses on Brookside seemed to match the photo."

"Wonderful. Maybe you'll all be able to make a dent in that puzzle before the magazine people show up."

"That's not the best part of our outing. After we got done with that nonsense in the posse office, we drove back to that block."

"Really? You wanted to tempt fate?"

"No, Cecilia was certain she dropped her car keys in front of one of the houses. Of course, as it turned out, she put them in the console cup in my car but she forgot. Anyway, when we got to the house where she thought they were, but weren't, a man came out to see what was going on. We got to talking and it turned out he's lived on Brookside Drive for over thirty years. That meant he was around when someone took that photo that became the puzzle."

If my head spun when she started to speak, it was in full-tilt by the time she finished.

"So, like I was saying, Phee, the man's name is Sherman and that photo became the big puzzle when it won some contest way back then. 'Capture Your Hometown' or something like it. He remembered thinking that if that photo was the winner, he hated to see the other entries."

"That was it? A photo contest?"

"There's more to it. Sherman was convinced someone paid off the judges to select it, although for the life of him he couldn't think of 'a darn good reason.' And get this—he was one of the people who worked on the puzzles. Said it was a pretty close-knit group."

"Sounds about right."

"That's not all. Once the photo was made into a puzzle, it sort of disappeared and was never assembled. They found it hidden away somewhere in the library. Rumor had it that the puzzle was so awful, no one wanted to work on it, but Sherman had another idea. He was convinced someone hid it on purpose and not because it was a boring puzzle."

"Please don't tell me he thought it was cursed. The book club ladies have been down that road so many times that they've worn grooves in it."

"This time could be different."

"Doubt it."

"Cecilia, Gloria, Shirley and I are going to share our cell phone photos with the puzzle assemblers tomorrow. We've got lots of catching up to do."

"I do, too. And by that, I mean sleep. Night night, Mom."

CHAPTER 18

"Casing out the houses, huh?" Augusta couldn't stop laughing the next day when I told her about my mother's exploits. It was a little past ten and the men had been working with MCSO at their office since eight.

"Marshall said the deputies were able to acquire Samantha's financial and business records. Our guys and Ranston are scouring them. I think they're scoping out the possibility of the rumor that she was about to 'spill the beans' on a local business. That could be motive for murder." I tore open a small bag of mini-pretzels that Augusta had added to our snack tray on the counter. "We know she was a controlling stockholder for Prosaic Puzzles, but that's a major conglomerate. Then again, it could refer to her stepson's restorative gummy business. More than one person met their demise when their family business turned sour. Anyway, the guys are looking into it. If anyone's doing any bean spilling, it would be for a local business, don't you think? And those gummies are as local as you can get. They're right here in the Valley. But think about it, why would she turn on her stepson?"

"Like you said, Phee, families do all sorts of despicable things. Don't you ever watch *48 Hours*? Still, I don't think Samantha had eyes on those restorative gummies. Tell you one thing I do know. I always watch *Sunday Morning Futures with Maria Bartiromo* and yesterday I learned that Prosaic Puzzles is about to do a belly flop. Maybe Samantha knew about it and those were the beans she was about to spill. Or the can of worms she was about to open. What's that expression? Oh, yeah. 'The bigger they are, the harder they fall.' Especially if the bean spiller falls into money." She chuckled and held out her hand for a few pretzels. "Mr. Gregory got a call about a local business from . . . hmm, let me check my notes. All those women in Sun City West . . . It's hard to keep them straight." Augusta shuffled through some papers and grinned—"Celeste Blatt, but that's all my note says."

"Could be it was a closer connection than a business."

"Close enough so that someone would zonk her with a staple gun?"

I shrugged. "Samantha either knew something that she shouldn't or enraged someone to the point of violence. Face it, using a staple gun doesn't exactly cry out premeditated murder. More like grab something in a fit of anger."

"Anyone in that puzzle crowd have anger issues?"

"Drake has obsessive cleanliness issues and Carl was the dumped suitor, but that's as far as I know about them."

74

"Forget Drake. The woman wasn't suffocated with a Clorox wipe, but the week is still young."

"Shh! Bite your tongue. They're still working on that puzzle and sometimes murders come in twos."

"Ha! And you tell me I'm the morbid one when it comes to things like that."

I dumped the remainder of the pretzels in her hand and smiled. "Face it, we're both bad."

"Nah, we're both cunning, astute and clever."

"Put it on a business card." I laughed as I took a bottled water from our supply and meandered back to my office. "Let me know if you hear anything."

"I'll raise a flag."

At a little past noon, Marshall returned to the office, a giant Polar Cup of Coke in his hand. Seemed it was his and Nate's latest summer indulgence. I had just finished off a Noosa yogurt in an attempt to eat healthy when I heard his voice and asked, "What did you find out?" I left my desk and stuck my head out.

"Simply put, I found out that Ranston had a part two for the morning. Once we were done perusing Samantha's financials, he insisted we revisit the scene of the crime. Call it my lucky day. I got out of the library before your mother coaxed me into joining her and some of the ladies for lunch."

"They were working on the puzzle, I presume."

"If that's what you call it."

"What do you mean?"

"Lots of arguing. Ranston and I stuck our heads in and out of the puzzle room at least half a dozen times."

"Now I'm curious, Mr. Gregory. What was this week's dilemma of the day?" Augusta asked.

Marshall leaned against the file cabinet and chugged his drink. "Harriet and Cecilia were there, along with Shirley. They were ecstatic to show the photos of the notorious street that they took yesterday. Too bad it wasn't received well by Lettie Holton."

"'Wasn't received well'?" Augusta furrowed her brow.

"You heard me. And I heard Lettie. Her voice practically boomed. At first she insisted it was cheating to use those cell phone pics, but she later said that there was no credible evidence that the photo was really the right one."

"My mother told us that a man who lived on that street said it *was* the street."

"And Lettie said the man was most likely 'too aged' to know the difference. That set off a few heads at the table and the librarian had to be called over there twice to quiet them down."

"I wonder why she was such a stick-in-the-mud about it. You'd think she'd be elated. They could finish that monster of a puzzle in less time. Plus, they'd make headway for that magazine article." I motioned for him to give me a sip of his drink and he handed me the Polar Cup. "Unless . . . oh my goodness. I'm surprised I didn't think of this right away. Maybe Lettie wants to sabotage that puzzle so they'd be forced to use 'Snowy Blizzard.' But why? It wasn't as if she had anything to gain with that all-white puzzle. Samantha was the one who was a major stockholder in the company. And the company produced a zillion puzzles. 'Snowy Blizzard' wouldn't have made a difference one way or another."

Marshall lifted his hands in the air and shrugged. "Could be Lettie had a vested financial interest in Prosaic Puzzles, too. We're not really sure of her relationship with Samantha. Maybe Samantha talked her into buying stocks. That does happen. Anyhow, Lettie wasn't the only stick-in-the-mud. Ranston was a real trip to the moon. Fussier than usual. Walked in circles. Reviewed the timeline at least five times before going over the forensic report with me."

"And?" I widened my eyes.

"We reached the conclusion that the killer didn't sneak up on her."

"But the coroner's report made no mention of defensive wounds."

"That just indicates she might have known the perpetrator. And that person overpowered her. Samantha was on the slight slide."

"Wish I could say that makes it easier to find the culprit, Mr. Gregory, but some of those women are built like Russian tanks. And don't get me started on the men."

Marshall and I should have been stunned by Augusta's comments, but after a few years we'd grown to expect it.

"There's more," he said. "The door into the puzzle room makes a creaky sound. Not quite mechanical, more like the hinges needing to be oiled. If Samantha was working quietly, she would have heard someone enter. More reason to believe she knew her killer. The big question is motive."

"What did you learn from the financials? Maybe that points to a motive." I shrugged.

"A good bulk of her income came from stocks, so if Prosaic Puzzles were to go under, she'd go under as well. But that would give her cause to take action, not the opposite way around. It had to be something else. Something personal, we think."

"Carl? Romances going down the drain are always personal. Then there's Lettie. If what you say was true about Samantha talking her into purchasing stock and the stock tumbled like her romance, that could be a darn good motive. Oh, and while I'm on a roll, Samantha could have been embroiled with her stepson's gummy business."

"Not that we could determine. Forrest's still on the suspect list, though. The fact he's about to cash in on her insurance policies is a motive for murder. I hate to admit it, but we have your mother to thank for that tidbit of information. I just hope it doesn't become an obsession of hers. Sneaking around and playing detective."

"Oh, it will. Trust me. It will."

No sooner did I utter those words when the office phone rang and Augusta held it out for me. "It's your mother, Phee. I'm getting a sixth sense."

I took the phone, unaware it was on speaker, and offered the usual Williams Investigations greeting. My mother's voice was on the other end. "What? They have you answering the phones?"

Augusta smirked and put her hand over her mouth.

"She's away from her desk. What's up?"

"Did Marshall tell you we saw him as well as that short, snarly deputy at the library? Too bad he couldn't join us for lunch. Bagels 'n More ran a special—barbequed brisket on a hash brown bagel."

"He just walked in. What's going on?"

"Ask him to tell you about Lettie. She was obnoxious with a capital *O*. You'd think she'd appreciate the effort we took to find the street, but no, she acted as if we were the ones who committed a crime. Anyway, that's not why I called."

"Go on."

"Shirley had a brainstorm while we pieced together a few puzzle corners. We're going back to Sun City for another chat with Sherman. He gave us his phone number and told us we could call him if we had more questions."

"He was just being polite. Leave the poor man alone."

"He could be sitting on a wealth of information."

"What wealth? It's a puzzle. A big puzzle of a street."

"I think he knows more."

"Listen, you don't know this man. Call him if you must, but don't go over there. Maybe meet him for coffee or something."

"We can meet him in Sun City and you can join us."

"Me? What? Why me?"

"Because you know the right questions to ask."

"About what?"

At that point, Marshall gave me a nudge and mouthed, "Tell her yes."

"Look, Mom, I'll have to call you back. Got work to do. But I'll think about it, okay?"

"So it's a yes?"

Marshall nodded and mouthed again. "Yes."

"Fine. Yes. Talk to you later."

"What on earth was that about?" I asked him as soon as I hung up the phone.

"Yes, Mr. Gregory," Augusta chimed in. "I want to know too."

"All right, ladies. Here goes. If Bowman, Ranston, Nate and I manage to keep those book club ladies away from Samantha's murder investigation, things might go faster. Whenever they meddle, we have to untangle things. And while it is true they manage to dig up information in the most uncanny way, they also leave those abysses so wide open for one of us to fall into."

"Guess that says it all, Mr. Gregory. I agree. Phee should go and poke her nose into it."

"Thanks, Augusta. Next time, I'm handing the phone back to you."

CHAPTER 19

"Look at all those adorable dogs on the patio," my mother said when we opened the door to the Starbucks in Sun City Tuesday evening. "If I thought my Streetman could handle the heat, I would have brought him."

"You can barely handle Streetman. For once you made the right decision to leave him at home." We stepped inside and walked toward the counter. "Is that Sherman off to the left in the corner? The elderly man with the gray Sun City Kiwanis shirt?"

My mother turned her head. "That's him, all right. I'll walk over. Can you get me a vanilla Frappuccino but no whipped cream? I'm watching my weight. Shirley and Gloria should be here any minute. Cecilia's home. She doesn't like to leave the compound after six."

"Poor night vision?"

"Everyone I know has poor night vision. That's not it. Your aunt Ina calls it 'the Bubble Complex.' It's where people don't want to leave their comfort zones when nightfall comes. She attributes it to early man before they mastered fire, but it's a bunch of hoo-ha if you ask me."

Just then I heard Shirley's voice and turned to see her and Gloria head toward us. My mother gave them a quick wave and was at Sherman's table before I could blink.

"Goodness, Harriet was in a hurry," Shirley said.

I laughed. "She's probably afraid he'll skip out on us before she can wheedle out any decades-old puzzle information."

"It appears as if she's wheedling now."

I glanced over. "Wheedling, talking, whatever it is, she's doing it."

With our orders placed, we introduced ourselves to Sherman and pulled over a few more chairs, creating our own compound in the corner.

"I haven't had this much attention in, well, frankly, I can't remember." Sherman took a sip of coffee and continued. In the dim evening light, he appeared to be in his late sixties or early seventies, so when he said he was eighty-three, we were taken back. He still had a full head of gray hair and very few wrinkles.

"I'm not one for all those fancy coffees," he told us. "Just regular with cream is what I'm used to. Anyway, I'm surprised there's such intrigue with that puzzle. Harriet told me that one of the women on your puzzle committee was found dead in the library. I read that in the paper. A homicide of all things. I doubt it was related to the puzzle, although I must admit there were times all of us wanted to do away with the puzzle selection people in Sun City, too. You can't imagine some of the atrocities they selected."

"Not any worse than 'Snowy Blizzard.'" Gloria went on to describe the all-white nightmare that made Sherman laugh out loud. "Has to be one of those Prosaic Puzzles. They're supposed to create more brain pathways. It was a real big deal back in the day. No wonder your committee didn't have much luck foisting them off."

"No offense," my mother said, "but that street puzzle isn't much better. And with our grainy photo, we're having such a hard time figuring out what goes where."

Sherman placed an eight-by-eleven envelope on the table. "I thought you might need some help so I brought these. Feel free to take cell phone pictures. It's our street taken a number of years back." He fanned out the colored photos and the women immediately pulled out their phones.

"This appears to be a photo of people in the library. It's 2002. I can read the calendar in the background," Shirley said.

Sherman reached over and picked up the photo. "Forgot it was in here with the street pictures. The street pictures go back further. We were all so enamored with the neighborhood, all we did was barbeque and take pictures."

"And the library?" I asked.

"That's a posed photo of the 'Puzzle Putters.' That's what we were called back then. Mostly women, but there are three or four of us men in there, too."

My mother studied the picture and passed it to Shirley and Gloria. "The blonde woman to the left of the heavyset man with the mustache in the second row looks somewhat familiar."

"Don't recognize her," Gloria said. "But people change."

"Lordy, that's a nice way of saying we're getting older." Shirley chuckled.

"Let me have a look." Sherman took the photo and moved his head back. "Darn it. I should have written their names on the back. I think that's Patricia or Tisha or something like that. She was one of the puzzle bosses. Not a heavyset man, although I can understand why you thought so." Then he laughed. "She lived on this street, too, only further down."

"Is she still around?"

Sherman shook his head. "Nope. Sold her house and moved. I think her husband got a job in another state, but maybe that was someone else. It's hard to keep these things straight after twenty or so years. I do know it was about the same time as that street puzzle got underway. Not many of those people in the photo are still around. Some moved, others went into assisted living, and the rest . . . well, they've moved on, too, if you know what I mean. Lots of new folks on this street. Young ones. Fifties and sixties."

"That's the same in Sun City West," my mother said. "A whole passel of Boomers."

Sherman studied the photo again. "Hmm, that's Henry Longmire standing between those two women, whose names escape me. Henry was one of the handymen at Sunny Skies Mortuary on Del Webb Boulevard. Now, he's enjoying the good life of retirement, I suppose. And look, that's Alfrieda something-or-other. She was quite chummy with Patricia-Tisha or whatever her name was. That is, whenever she wasn't batting her fake eyelashes at Henry. Wish I could tell you more but mostly I just went there to do the puzzles."

"Um, yes. Getting back to the puzzle," I said, "do you think its disappearance was an oversight or something deliberate?"

I had barely finished my question when Sherman jumped to answer. "Deliberate."

"What makes you say that?"

"Because it would surface, and then—poof!—nowhere to be found. Then it would resurface again but it would be too late for doing it. By then, another puzzle was chosen. If we didn't know any better, it was like a silly game of cat and mouse."

"Well, those photos of yours should certainly help us out a lot. We need to get that puzzle halfway done before photographers from *Senior Living* show up. Our library puzzle was selected for the magazine," my mother said. "Of course, none of us has a clue as to *why*, but we're not questioning it."

"No," Gloria said. "What we're questioning is why *some people* are doing everything they can to make sure we don't get to complete it." Then she looked at my mom and Shirley. "I'm sorry, but it's the truth."

Sherman tilted his head and was about to say something when Shirley beat him to it.

"What Gloria is saying is that we've received threatening notes, and an actual attempt to destroy the puzzle with a flood."

"What?" Sherman pushed away from the table and straightened his back.

"We thought it was a sprinkler malfunction but it turned out someone tampered with it." I tried to downplay my response with less drama in my voice but it didn't make any difference. Sherman rested his chin in the palms of his hands, elbows firmly planted on the table. "You said the other choices were Prosaic Puzzles?"

I nodded. "Uh-huh. Why?"

"It wouldn't be the first time that company paid off people to undermine competitors' products. They were given a slap on the wrist in a few courts back East but they never resorted to actual threats or destruction of property. But I bet their gloves are off now. Heard the company is going belly-up. It was on the news."

"Belly-up or bought out by another company?"

"It doesn't matter, does it?" my mother asked. "If that puzzle company is behind the shenanigans at our library, through some mole of theirs, then we have to sniff them out."

"Whoa! That's not what Sherman said." I looked at him as wide-eyed as I could. Thankfully he understood what I was up against.

He sputtered and muttered, "What I meant was, well, in general. In general companies like that do things like that. No need to go to extremes. I'm sure whoever is behind those puzzle incidents, it's for a specific and personal reason."

My mother was steadfast. "Fine. Then we'll ferret out the person and personal reason."

I rolled my eyes in the back of my head and prayed someone, *anyone*, would send me a text message or call me so I'd have a good excuse to bolt out of there.

"There's one more thing," Sherman said and we all held our breath. "It's probably nothing with nothing, but when I was in our Sun City Library the other day, a few people were grousing at our librarian because we weren't selected for the puzzle feature in *Senior Living*. A regular bunch of hens. Pardon the expression. And one of those cluckers insisted we take the puzzle back."

"Take it back?" Shirley moved a palm to her cheek. "Do you think that person is sabotaging us?"

Sherman shook his head. "Nah. Doubt it. That would mean too much work. Besides, it would take away valuable chitchat and tale-spinning time."

I all but dropped the Grande iced latte I held in my hand. Apparently this guy would blend seamlessly into Herb's crew, but I imagined he had his own cadre of yammering senior men.

We thanked him for his time and my mother invited him to see the finished product. That is, if it ever got finished. As the four of us walked to where our cars were parked, she nudged Shirley and asked, "Do you think you could make one of those murder maps we always see on the Hallmark Channel? One of the big paper ones. Not the glass ones they have on *NCIS* or *FBI*. Although, I'm sure the glass arts club could come up with something."

"A murder map?" A knot formed in my stomach. "And don't tell me it's for your own edification. I know you better. First, you'll fill in that map with all sorts of names, regardless of any credible information. Then you'll begin a snoop-fest, the likes of which I don't want to think about."

"Honestly, Phee. We can't afford to wait on our rumps for those deputies to move from Point A to Point B. The way I see it, we now have two viable possibilities regarding the puzzle sabotage."

"*Possible* sabotage."

"Fine. *Possible.* But most likely real sabotage."

I threw my head back and waited for her to continue.

"It's quite feasible that someone in Prosaic Puzzles did it, or, like Sherman mentioned, a disgruntled and jealous Sun City resident. So disgruntled that they badgered their librarian to get the puzzle back."

"That's an awfully wide net for ferreting out suspects, Mom."

"Not if we divvy up assignments."

"Divvy up assignments? This isn't a class project."

"Well, when you put it *that* way. Hmm, maybe we should shift gears and pry around about Samantha Wiggins. After all, that's a bona fide murder, not sabotage, as the case may be."

Rats! She's got me cornered. That's the last thing Nate and Marshall need.

"Forget what I said. Why stop now when you've made so much progress? Besides, those deputies will be focusing on the murder, not the other situation. You'll be able to find out who's behind it (*or not*), and make sure the Sun City West Library has its five minutes of fame."

"Phee's right," Gloria said. "We can research Prosaic Puzzles right from home."

Shirley nodded. "And I'd love to create a murder map. I can sketch murder weapons as a lovely backdrop. And I'll get Lucinda to join me. She's in the scrapbooking club. They do all sorts of cutesy paper designs."

"Wonderful." I gave Shirley a thumbs-up. "Cutesy murder weapons. Scrapbooking. Sounds like a plan."

"Absolutely." Gloria and Shirley approached Gloria's car and she hit the fob to open it. "After all, there's no danger working from home."

"As long as all of you don't go blabbing everything to everyone." I was adamant. "Stick with internet research and leave it at that."

Who was I kidding? I might as well have told them to repaint the Sistine Chapel.

CHAPTER 20

"You did the right thing, hon," Marshall said as we drove to work together. He didn't have a late night so we took his car. "Keep that book club as far away from the murder investigation as possible. Let them poke and pry into puzzle drama and whatever deep, dark secrets it may uncover." Then he burst out laughing. "Sorry, but it's like a bad episode of *Desperate Housewives.* And before you say a word, lots of us in the force watched it."

"I wasn't going to say anything. And yeah, you're right. Tell me, what's on your docket today?"

"Following up with Tabitha's neighbors on the off chance they noticed anything and meeting with two new clients. Her photos were worth considering, but without solid evidence we can't move forward. Similar day for Nate, only he has a meeting with the coroner regarding some anomalies."

"Anomalies? I thought Samantha succumbed to that staple gun."

"That was the cause of death, but the scenario tells us she knew her attacker so it was less likely the attacker snuck up on her and overcame her. Then the coroner discovered something insidious during the full autopsy that required lab analysis. It may provide us with a more complete picture."

"I'm glad my day will be less puzzling. No pun intended."

He chuckled. "Want to grab some donuts for the office? There's a BoSa drive-through on the way."

"Go healthy. Apple fritters, apple filling, and anything with nuts. Augusta decided that's how she would get her fruits and protein."

"Oh, brother."

• • •

"This is fantastic!" Augusta beamed when Marshall put the donut box on the counter. "Thanks. Wish I had fantastic news for you, but I don't. Ranston called. Bowman got bit by a spider last night when he reached inside his mailbox. At least it wasn't a brown recluse or a black widow."

"He actually checked?" Marshall's eyes couldn't have been wider.

"Checked? He probably asked for ID and blood type." Augusta took a napkin and wrapped it around a double-nut bear claw.

"Is he okay?" I asked.

She shrugged. "The hand swelled up like a balloon. His doctor told him to remain home all day and keep it on ice. Also to use Benadryl on it. Apparently there's no anti-venom for spider bites. When I took the call this morning, he sounded even more miserable than usual. Of course, it really doesn't make a difference as far as note-taking and reports go. Ranston's the one who does all that. Anyway, Bowman was supposed to be at that coroner meeting so I suppose it'll be Ranston. Half a dozen of one, six of the other, if you know what I mean."

"Yeah. More work piled on." Marshall chuckled. "It should make Nate's day. By the way, is he in his office?"

"Yep. New client. Background check for a 'suitor who attached himself to the client's elderly mother.' At least it was in person and not the internet." Then Augusta looked directly at me. "How did your clandestine meeting with the man from Sun City go?"

"Sherman. And it wasn't clandestine. Not at Starbucks. Boy, was he chatty. Showed us photos of his street so that the ladies would have an easier time assembling that puzzle once they snapped pics with their phones."

"What about those sabotage attempts on the puzzle. Did he have any idea why that would happen?"

I shook my head. "He made some educated guesses. Possibly a disgruntled person, but the book club ladies already had that one nailed. However, he mentioned companies that do all sorts of things to drive away their competitors."

Augusta crinkled her nose. "From what you told me, the puzzle was a street picture. Not exactly another company."

"True, but *if* another company wanted to get into the limelight, especially since *Senior Living* would be featuring the puzzle, they might stoop to anything to reclaim their spot. Yikes! That means 'Snowy Blizzard' could reappear."

"No," Augusta said. "That means someone on that puzzle crew wants Prosaic Puzzles back. Who would benefit?"

I bit my lip and looked at Marshall. "Samantha. But she's dead."

"Who else?" Augusta raised her brows.

In that second, Marshall elbowed me. "Guess that's something for your mother's klatch to latch on to."

"Very punny."

"And it's only morning. I haven't warmed up yet."

"There's something else," I said. "Of course, it could be nothing with nothing, but Sherman mentioned that while the puzzle was in the possession of the Sun City Library, it kept disappearing and reappearing. That's why it was never completed there. Or *started*, for that matter. Most likely, it kept getting shuffled around in storage, but he thought otherwise. He believed it was deliberate but hadn't a clue as to why."

Augusta looked up from her donut. "I'll send a post to Rod Serling."

"The two of you are really too much this morning. I'm off to the sanity of my office." Marshall winked.

I smiled back. "Good thinking."

• • •

"I'm surprised your mother hasn't called," Augusta said when the two of us split a calzone for lunch a few hours later.

"Shh! Not so loud. You'll incur the wrath of fate. She's probably stewing over that puzzle now, along with Lucinda and Louise. They agreed to work on it today."

"Oh, then I guess we have more time until the latest update rolls in."

As it happened, the update didn't *roll in*, it flew in when my mother phoned to tell me that Lettie tried to sneak off with puzzle pieces, even though she claimed they stuck to her arm when she leaned over to work on it.

"I don't care what cockamamie excuse she made," my mother said, "the puzzle pieces literally dropped off of her arms when she went to leave."

"Huh?"

"You heard me. Lettie said her arms were sweaty from the humidity in the library and the pieces stuck to them. A likely excuse."

"I, uh—"

"And that's not all, Phee. When we showed everyone the cell phone pictures of that street in Sun City, she pooh-poohed it and said we had no real proof. Then, three seconds later, she added that we shouldn't use those pictures because it would be tantamount to cheating."

"Um, maybe—"

"Cheating? The woman has lost her mind. What does she think this is, a ninth-grade math quiz? Do you want to know what I think? I'll tell you. It's all about sour grapes. And that's because we didn't select one of her precious brain puzzles from Prosaic. Which brings me to my next conclusion."

Dear Lord, how many conclusions can she reach?

"What's that, Mom?"

"Lettie Holton is working for Prosaic Puzzles. And you know what that means."

"Um, actually, I don't."

"And you call yourself an investigator?"

"What? I don't call myself—Oh, never mind."

"We need to investigate that woman. She could be on the payroll for that company. The mole we mentioned. Or maybe Samantha talked her into purchasing lots of stock like she did. There's only one way to find out."

"Doing the internet research that you, Shirley and Gloria mentioned last night?"

"Oh, heck no. Who's got time for all that? We find a way to get into her house and do what we do best."

Trespass, break and enter, bring Streetman, create a disturbance . . .

"Don't!"

"You didn't let me finish. Lettie always works on the puzzle from nine to noon on weekdays. I'm not sure about Saturdays. Anyway, Louise was positive she has a house cleaner from Dusting Damsels. We'll find out and use that as a pretense for getting inside the door when it's just the housekeeper. We'll come up with some excuse. You know . . ."

"Oh, trust me. I know. And my answer is still a solid *no!*"

"Listen, if it turns out she's a major stockholder for that company, she could be protecting her investment. And ruining our debut in *Senior Living.*"

"It's not a debut. You're not performing in a musical. It's a magazine article."

"A *showcase* article."

I sighed. "Look, I may have another option for this. Let me get back to you. And in the meantime, promise me you won't do anything that will require posting bail."

"Don't be ridiculous. I'd be with Shirley, Cecilia, Gloria, Lucinda or Louise. It's not as if I was with your aunt Ina."

Oh, sure. That makes me feel a whole lot better.

"Everything okay, Phee?" Augusta asked when I stepped into the break room for a Coke. "You look battle-worn."

"Not as battle-worn as Rolo is about to be. It's either that or a permanent parking spot in front of the Fourth Avenue Jail."

CHAPTER 21

"Any more investigators working with Nate?" Rolo asked. "I really should know so I can stay informed."

"Very funny. And no, this is more of a personal request."

"I'm listening. Don't worry. No one else is."

"I wasn't worried. This involves my mother."

"Oh, great. Now *I'm* worried. Don't think I'm not aware of her exploits. Or your aunt's, for that matter. Now what?"

"My mother and her friends are convinced that the giant puzzle they're working on at the library is being sabotaged so they have launched their own investigation of sorts."

"Mon Dieu. I'm adding French expressions to my repertoire. And that's French, too."

"Uh, yes. I know. Anyway, they believe a key motive involves the purchase of stock from Prosaic Puzzles. Specifically, they need to know if a woman by the name of Lettie Holton is a major stockholder. Can you find that out?"

"Can I tie my own shoelaces? Of course I can find that out. Anything else?"

"Just one. Find out if she was ever employed by that company."

"Okay. I've got a few things on my plate but I'll put a rush on it."

"Thanks, I appreciate it."

"No worries. A new IKEA catalogue will be coming out soon."

"Terrific."

True to his words, Rolo put a major rush on it because he got back to me three hours later, and it wasn't the answer my mother would have expected.

"Nope. Lettie Holton who resides on Desperado Drive in Sun City West does not own stock in Prosaic Puzzles. And, to go one step further, I checked her IRA and Prosaic Puzzles is not one of the companies they invested in. As for employment with Prosaic Puzzles or any of its subsidiaries, she wasn't. She was a former dean of students, and before that, an English teacher in Lowell, Massachusetts."

"Can you tell me if she's a stockholder in any other major company?"

"She's not. Other than her Wells Fargo bank account and the one she has at Desert Blossom Credit Union, there's no other monies showing up. By the way, I couldn't resist taking a deeper dive or it's no fun. No criminal records or court cases. Looks like the classic retiree who moved out west to get away from the snow. Hey, this was only a cursory look so let me know if you need more."

"Oh, it's cursory enough. No sense wasting more time. Just send me an invoice."

"Will do. Complete with a photo. Diets with Keto overtones are incredibly nuanced."

And expensive.

The minute I got off the burner phone, I called my mother. No sense waiting for her to come up with a disastrous and unneeded plan. My dumb luck, she'd returned to the library. Myrna had called her because Herb and Bill decided to work on the puzzle and were getting "really annoying."

What else is new?

"I'll be quick, Mom," I said. "I wanted to save you some time so I called Rolo Barnes."

"Lettie owns stock, doesn't she?"

"As a matter of fact, no. She doesn't. No stock in Prosaic Puzzles or any of its smaller businesses. In fact, no stock at all. Only bank accounts. And she never worked for them. She was a former English teacher and dean of students in Massachusetts."

"I should've suspected as much. The way she comports herself and corrects everyone. I think it's embedded in them."

"Uh-huh. Well, I have to get back to work. Have fun with Myrna and the guys."

"We've moving to the next phase—the Weight-Watching Women and the Summer Showcase Readers. Both of those groups would stop at nothing to boot the puzzle out of there and take over the space. Herb wants us to have a little powwow so we can strategize."

"Another powwow? Those powwows of his don't accomplish anything except gorging on junk food." Then I thought about what Marshall had said about keeping my mother away from the real investigation. "On second thought, you can eat and think at the same time. Go for it."

"That was a fast change of mind."

"Yeah, well, someone has to figure out what's going on with the puzzle tampering, and who better than you and your friends?"

"Why are you being so acquiescent? What are you hiding?"

"Nothing. Nothing at all."

"Okay, I'll let you know the details so you can join us."

"What? I didn't plan on taking part in Herb's powwow. I'm still twitching from the last one."

"Phee, you know as well as I do that those men can never focus, and for some reason they ignore us. You'll have better luck. If we don't find out who's behind the puzzle meddling, it will only get worse until they get what they want."

"And when will this summit take place? More importantly, where?"

"I'm not sure but I'll let you know or I'll leave a message with Augusta."

"Okay. Enjoy your day."

• • •

I wasn't sure which would be worse—the powwow or the actual outcome. In retrospect, both of them were equally disturbing, beginning with Herb's conclave. The group decided to meet Thursday night so as not to waste valuable "investigative" time. And they picked a venue that I would have never expected. At least not for the men. It was the outdoor patio at Handel's Ice Cream Shop in Surprise, home of forty-five rotating flavors.

"How can I be expected to make a choice?" Myrna's voice carried over to the parking lot at a little past seven and I heard her loud and clear. It was followed by, "Then buy two or three. Ice cream is healthy."

"I'm here, everyone," I said as I took a seat around a huge rectangular table, the likes of which I hadn't seen since summer camp. With the exception of my aunt, who was in Sedona for a retreat with my uncle, the entire passel of seniors was there. Amid the throngs of teenagers and crying babies, they stood out like ketchup stains on a white blouse.

"Look, Shirley," Cecilia said. "They have double fudge with nuts. Oh, and wait! They also have chocolate chip with macadamia nuts and blueberry fudge swirl."

"I'm getting the triple cone," Bill said. "Chocolate, vanilla and strawberry."

My mother poked his elbow. "That's absolutely boring. You could get those flavors at the supermarket. Try mint matcha with dark chocolate flakes, or cinnamon roll swirl. Maybe even banana cream pie or salty caramel truffle."

"You try those. I'm getting chocolate, vanilla and strawberry."

I looked at the time on my cell phone and sent Marshall a quick text: *Could be here until midnight.*

He texted back: *Bring home a quart of coffee chocolate chip.*

I replied: *Done*

The deliberations for ice cream took much longer than the actual "plan" to find the mastermind behind the sabotage. Finally, the crew decided to go to their usual playbook and infiltrate the organizations.

"Myrna," Louise said, "you could stand to lose some weight. Why don't you join the Weight-Watching Women and dig up the dirt."

"You're not exactly Twiggy, you know. If I join, then you're coming with me."

They bantered back and forth until Lucinda volunteered. "I've been meaning to shed those last ten pounds. I'll do it if Cecilia does."

"Cecilia is as skinny as a rail," Herb announced. "Heck, I'd do it but it's a women's group."

Then Myrna kicked his leg. "Since when has that stopped you?"

And on and on it went until finally my mother volunteered but, like everyone else, she also had a caveat. "Phee needs to come with me. These things work best in pairs."

I all but fell out of my seat. "First of all, I work during the day. And second, I'm not a resident. I can't belong to any of those clubs."

"Lordy, I'll do it, Harriet." Shirley sat upright and pinched her shoulders back.

"Good," Herb said. "Now for the Summer Showcase Readers. At least no one has to weigh themselves. One or more of us will slip seamlessly into the group and pry. Who wants to volunteer?"

Dead silence. Well, dead silence with the exception of a toddler pitching a tantrum a few yards away.

"I can do that," Cecilia said. "It doesn't sound too difficult."

Herb looked at the rest of the men but no one made a move. "Fine. I'll join too. But only if I can pick my own books. I like C. J. Box, William Kent Krueger and Nick Petrie. None of those romances for me."

"It's a summer reading," my mother said. "Not like a book club. More like a reading marathon. Besides, you'll be there to ferret out information on the club members."

The next few minutes were spent glued to our cell phones to look up the meeting times for the groups. The weight watchers met twice a week for weigh-ins, pep talks, recipe sharing and occasional programs. The readers met Saturday mornings as well as Tuesdays and Thursdays.

"They start at nine, Herb," Myrna said. "Bring a book and blend in seamlessly. I'm not worried about Cecilia. She'll be fine. She knows how to be quiet."

Herb shot her a look. "At least someone does."

Then Cecilia spoke. "I get the reading part, but if we're so busy turning pages, how are we going to poke and pry?"

"Be creative." Simple enough words coming out of Lucinda's mouth, but the reality was a far cry different.

CHAPTER 22

"Do either of you ladies use perfume?" Nate asked Augusta and me the next morning. I had just finished copying some invoices and was about to return to my office.

Augusta immediately sniffed the air. "Certainly not. I use a good old-fashioned oatmeal soap and whatever deodorant is on sale. Why? Is there a noxious odor I need to be aware of?"

"Don't look at me," I said. "I rarely use perfume. Body lotions, yes, but not perfume. Too heavy and too expensive. Toilet water is cheaper but the scent can linger and change."

"Whoa!" Nate raised his hands in the air. "That's way too much information. I was merely trying to ascertain if you were familiar with certain scents."

"Why?" We both asked simultaneously.

"Because a text arrived from the coroner regarding that anomaly. It was sent to me, Marshall, Bowman and Ranston. Residue from a particular perfume was found in the liquid part of Samantha's eyes. He gave a technical term but liquid works for me."

"The spray probably got into her eyes, Mr. Williams. Some women go really heavy with that stuff." Then she looked at me. "You were in the library that first day. Did it smell like a French bordello?"

"No. It smelled like a library." I looked at Nate. "Did the lab find traces on her clothes?"

"Oddly, yes. But only on the collar of her blouse."

"Like I said," Augusta continued, "she probably went overboard spraying it around her ears. That's where women spray that stuff, Mr. Williams."

Nate's jaw dropped but Augusta kept talking. "I don't think anyone's ever been murdered with perfume. Unless of course they drank it."

"Marshall and I believe it was the distractor our murderer used in order to stun Samantha and then go for the staple gun. We don't think it was Samantha's perfume."

Augusta fluffed her hair. Something she did whenever she needed time to think. "No one's in the office right now. Can you reenact it? Phee and I are visual learners."

"What?" I looked at Augusta, eyes bulging out of my head. "Visual learners?"

"Look," Nate said, "I'll make it simple, but no acting. I'm not Robert De Niro."

Without wasting any more time, he explained that whoever entered the puzzle room most likely caught Samantha's attention because the door creaked. "To do the deed, he or she had to temporarily stun Samantha, and what better way than with a spray of burning perfume to her face. Once incapacitated, Samantha became an easy victim. All the killer had to do was grab her and press the pneumatic staple gun to her neck, where it severed a carotid artery."

"You should have reenacted it, Mr. Williams. That's what they do on all those crime shows."

"Oh my gosh, Augusta, you sound like my mother. She's been getting to all of us." Then I looked at Nate. "I suppose MCSO wants to identify the perfume and find a match? Don't let that get out to my mother's friends. She'll bring Streetman to the library as if he's on a hunt. No telling what he'll do.

Nate nodded. "It's a long shot. I'll give you that much, but I thought you and Augusta might be somewhat familiar with perfume scents."

"Don't tell me they were able to extract it?"

"Amazing, huh? Welcome to the twenty-first century. Of course, hundreds of those scents overlap."

"What kind of scent?" Augusta propped her elbows on her desk. "Roses? Honeysuckle? That's a popular one with older women. Gardenia? Or was it fruity? That's a new thing. Then again, given the clientele, I'd go with floral."

"For someone who doesn't use it, you seem to have quite the handle on it." Nate walked to the mini fridge and grabbed a Coke.

"I always get stuck watching those ridiculous infomercials when I'm at the dentist's office. Surprising the stuff you pick up. Now they've got full body deodorant for places no one ever wanted to talk about in public, much less showcase them in a commercial."

Nate nearly dropped his Coke. "And again, too much information, but yes, the forensics lab is looking into transferred fragrance and its implications. It's trace evidence but that doesn't mean the perfume would be identifiable. However, it would be a start if any of the puzzle solvers were perfume or cologne users. I'm not discounting the men."

I opened my mouth but the words came slowly. "Uh, so, um, I guess you'd need someone who sat or currently sits at that large puzzle table to discern who's wearing it and who's not."

"Exactly."

"Looks like your mother is going to be in business, Phee."

I glared at Augusta. "My mother, her entourage, and the remaining members of Noah's ark."

"Hey, kiddo, I wouldn't ask if it wasn't needed on this case. Besides, after that last incident with the dog knocking over puzzle pieces, I'm sure she'll think twice about bringing him."

Fat chance.

"I suppose you want me to broach the subject with her."

"Either that or Ranston will. Peculiar enough, this was his brainchild."

"That figures."

"So you'll do it?" Nate winked.

"Do I have a choice?"

"Look at the bright side." Augusta flashed a wide grin at me. "At least you don't have to be the one sitting at that table."

"No, I have to be the one listening to the one who'll be sitting there sniffing out the evidence with her crime dog."

Nate patted me on my back and chuckled. "MCSO has to play by the rules, but thank goodness we can improvise."

"I might as well get it over with," I said as I walked back to my office. "No doubt Mrs. Pollifax will gladly accept the assignment."

"Who?" Nate and Augusta asked.

"The famous housewife-turned-spy in Dorothy Gilman's books. Heck, even I'm familiar with her and I don't usually read spy mysteries."

"As long as you get your mother to take on that role, we'll be closer to an outcome."

Or a breakdown.

I tried to formulate the words in my head before I called my mother. I had to keep the situation low-keyed for fear she'd go overboard. Finally, after ten minutes of mulling it over, I came up with, "Our office simply wants your observation, that's all, Mom. Nate and Marshall will take it from there."

My sentence, along with a complete explanation of the situation, was crystal-clear and well-rehearsed when I made the call. Unfortunately, I wasn't prepared for her selective hearing.

"Too bad you just sprung this on me, Phee. Only Shirley and I will be at the library this morning. But she's got a good nose. You know who else has a good nose, don't you? Although I hate to picture him in close proximity in the library."

"Don't say it—Paul Schmidt!"

"The man can sniff out a green bean in a pile of lettuce."

"He can also empty a room in five seconds."

"Fine. We'll only enlist his help if all else fails."

"Good! Very good."

"Tell me what you want me to do."

I explained everything in detail but I forgot one thing—the puzzle people varied each day. Even the regulars didn't work on it constantly. That meant my mother would have a longer sojourn sniffing out the clues. Figuratively and literally.

"Remember," I told her. "Just write down your observations. Don't engage in any conversation that would raise suspicion."

"I'm not your aunt Ina. Speaking of which, she and Louis plan to stay longer in Sedona. Something about chakras. I can't keep up with all those fancy foods."

"It's not a food. They're focal points for meditation."

"Oh, brother. Only your aunt would base a vacation on that."

"Let me know if you're able to discern anything today. Remember, be discreet and subtle."

"I'm meeting Shirley in forty minutes. That'll barely give me enough time to call the women. The more of us who attend tomorrow, the more noses we have to find that trace element or whatever it was."

"Trace evidence. And all you're doing is finding out who uses discernible perfume. By the way, thanks. The guys appreciate it."

"When we uncover the killer, they'll really appreciate it."

And with that, she ended the call, leaving me to wonder *exactly* what she planned on doing at the library today and tomorrow.

CHAPTER 23

"I can't believe no one's discovered this place at night," Lyman said as he shifted from the pool to the hot tub. He and Lyndy joined Marshall and me for a late-night swim that followed a quick Mexican bite at Pollo Loco near our house.

"It's a Friday night," I said. "Most of the younger families are trying to get their kids to sleep and the families without kids are probably at the sports bars."

"Sure is a far cry from Sun City West." Marshall followed suit and joined Lyman in the hot tub. It was a clear night and the crescent moon shone above the palm trees.

"Yeah, it's after eight. Lights out for everyone," Lyndy said and laughed. "I know for a fact my aunt is in bed by seven thirty. Of course she's up at four, but still . . . seven thirty."

"After a day with those ballplayers, seven thirty sounds pretty good." Lyman motioned for Lyndy and me to join them in the hot tub. The jets were super strong and the water temperature read a hundred and three degrees.

"One more lap," I said and took off as Lyndy slid over the rope and into the hot tub. When I finished my sidestroke and got into the hot tub, the conversation had shifted to the investigation into Samantha's murder.

"Lots of scuttlebutt from the softball team, but mostly speculation and embellishment." Lyman wiped his brow with the back of his hand and leaned against the wall. "Although, one rumor keeps popping up like a weed."

"What's that?" Marshall edged closer to Lyman even though no one was around.

"Something about her involvement with her son's restorative gummy enterprise."

"Hmm, we looked into it but couldn't find anything. Maybe it's time for a deeper dive."

"Only if it's in a giant bowl of ice cream. What do you say we go back to my place and dig out the rocky road?" Lyndy flashed a giant smile and Marshall and I agreed to go over there once we got out of our swimsuits.

"Might as well enjoy it now," he said. "Just think, in thirty or so years, this will be past our bedtime."

"What do you think?" I asked Marshall two hours later when we crawled into bed. "Think there's any validity to the gummy business as a motive?"

"I'll have Rolo poke around, but so far all we know is Samantha's involvement with Prosaic Puzzles. Maybe your mother's antennae will pick up on that as well tomorrow."

"Only time will tell. From what I hear, all of the puzzle aficionados will be working their tails off to get that thing back to the starting point. It takes hours to sort out and none of them are going to be all that thrilled to do it over again. Still, that's what they voted for when the librarian gave them other options."

"It's those generations—Greatest and Boomers. They have an amazing sense of purpose and work ethic. Unlike the younger ones who want a fast fix for everything. Oh my gosh! I'm beginning to sound like Herb and Bill."

"As long as you don't act like them, we'll be fine." I leaned over and planted a sweet kiss on his lips. After that, it was lights out, even though it was well past seven thirty.

• • •

"Boy, am I glad I'm working in the office this morning." I tossed the lightweight sheet from my body and raced to the shower. "I'll be quick. Only rinsing off and brushing my teeth."

Behind me, I heard Marshall yawn. "No hurry. We've got plenty of time. I've got a few minor things to deal with before I meet with Ranston in your mother's territory. We're going back to Samantha's house to see if there was evidence she used perfume. It wasn't on our radar prior to the lab report."

"I'm sure we'll be hearing from my mother regarding the perfume. I only hope she and her friends don't raise too many eyebrows in the library, especially if the murderer is among those working on the puzzle. By the way, any idea when Bowman will be back?"

"That spider bite was Wednesday and it takes a few days. It's anyone's guess, but I wouldn't be surprised if he joined Ranston and me today. Bowman's not one to sit on his haunches."

• • •

We took two separate cars to work since Marshall's day would be far more complicated and much longer than my half day. When we arrived, Augusta greeted us by announcing, "Herb called from the library to tell Phee that, and I quote, 'the Summer Showcase Readers are wound up so tight the rubber band might break.'"

"What's that supposed to mean?" I looked at Augusta and then at Marshall, who burst out laughing.

"What? What's so funny?"

"Just a guess, hon, but I think Herb must have done something to disturb the peace."

"That was my take, too, Mr. Gregory," Augusta chimed in. "I could hear people in the background shushing him."

"Terrific. I'd better phone him. What about my mother? Did she call too?"

Augusta shook her head. "Not yet. Give it time."

"Ugh."

"Bowman and Ranston are looking better and better." Marshall squeezed my shoulder and headed to his office and I walked to mine.

With my computer booted up and a fresh cup of coffee in my hand, I returned Herb's call.

"What's going on?" I asked.

"Keep your voice low. These people are super sensitive to sound. *Any* sound. One person even complained that I breathed too hard."

"Herb, I'm on the other end of the phone. They can't hear me."

"Don't bet on it. Cecilia's handling it much better."

That's because she doesn't yammer away.

"Okay, tell me what's going on."

"Hold on. I need to step outside."

A few seconds later, he was back. "I moseyed around to see what people were reading and made a list of the folks with books that lend themselves to sabotage."

"Just because someone's reading a novel about espionage doesn't mean they're the one tampering with the puzzle."

"It's a start. Boy, are these guys super sensitive. The way they reacted, you'd think their reading material was a government secret. Two of them turned their books over and told me to 'find my own book.'"

"You showed up without a book?"

"It's a library. I figured I'd find something. And as a matter of fact, I did. Well, not *something*, more like finding something out. That's why I called."

"What? What did you find out?"

"There may be another attempt to knock that puzzle out of commission. While I pretended to be interested in *Where the Crawdads Sing*, which, by the way, was not about insects in the South, I overheard one of the women, who was rooting through the stacks, whisper to another woman that 'they better get it over with quickly so as not to lose momentum.'"

"That could have been anything. And why on earth did you pick *Where the Crawdads Sing*?"

"The author is Delia Owens and I was seated near the O section."

I rolled my eyes and shook my head at least three times as Herb continued.

"Do you or don't you want to know why I think a new sabotage is imminent?"

"Fine. Why?"

"Because the other woman whispered back, 'we need to take them by surprise,' and then the first woman said something about library integrity. That sounds like a thumbs down to puzzles if you ask me."

"Hmm. You may be right. Did you get a good look at them?"

"They were in the stack behind the O's. I moved some books around and tried to take a photo with my phone but all I got was a narrow space and a close-up of a floral blouse. I figured they'd return to the quiet area but they didn't."

"Find my mother and let her know. She's probably working on that puzzle right now."

"Nope. That's why I called *you*."

"Are you sure? She and the book club ladies were on the scent of—never mind. They probably went out for coffee or something."

"I didn't see any of them but I'll check again. Just thought someone should know."

"Right. Keep me posted. Thanks, Herb."

"No problem, cutie."

Just then, I heard an alarm go off on the other end of the phone. "Herb? What's going on?"

"Fire alarm. I don't smell anything. Rats! It's probably one of the rec center's planned drills. Who reads those announcements? I better skedaddle out of here before one of those picky showcase readers reports me for lollygagging."

Or word usage.

CHAPTER 24

A half hour went by and Herb didn't call back. I figured he located my mother and the next step would be some sort of disastrous plan to trap the puzzle-tampering culprits. *If only.*

Instead, Cecilia called me. Her voice was usually soft but this time it was breathier than usual. "I hate to bother you at work, Phee, but the most awful thing happened. Oh, dear. I don't mean to worry you. Your mother's speaking with one of the deputies right now. A young one."

"Deputies? What's going on?" *Please do not tell me she brought Streetman and he sunk those little teeth of his into someone's ankles.*

"We were all trying to color-code the puzzle pieces and sniff around, if you know what I mean."

"Uh-huh."

"What a mess this time around. Anyway, Myrna and Louise insisted they needed a break and Lucinda said she was really hungry so we all decided to make a quick stop at DQ and get back to the library."

"And the alarm went off?"

"How did you know?"

"Herb called and I heard it. He thought it was a fire drill."

"That must have been after we left because we didn't hear it. We only found out about it after."

"After what?"

"After we got back and discovered someone really messed up some of our puzzle pieces this time. Those scoundrels! Oh, and Gloria asked the librarian about the fire drill but it wasn't a fire drill. Someone pulled the alarm. And I know who!"

"Who?" I was beginning to feel like I did when my daughter was back in middle school and I had to eke information out of her. But even Kalese was more coherent.

"Why, the person or persons who messed up our puzzle pieces. That's who."

I took a breath and let it out slowly. "Messed up how?"

"They dripped glue on some of them. Luckily, we got back before the glue hardened. Shirley had nail polish remover in her bag so we used it. It removed the glue but it also removed some of the paint, leaving just the puzzle pieces. I suppose we can figure out where they go from the shape, but if we were going to do that, we could have stayed with 'Snowy Blizzard.' Which reminds me, did you know DQ has two new Blizzard flavors—malted milk chocolate chip and caramel chip."

I hardly knew which of her thoughts to respond to first so I didn't. "Um, is that why my mother is talking to the deputy?"

"Yes. All of us are. He's taking statements."

"But no one was there when it happened." Then I remembered Herb's encounter in the book stacks. "Cecilia, ask the deputy to speak with Herb. He overheard something that could be important."

"Sure. Oh my goodness, I forgot the real reason I called."

Oh no! There's something else?

"What's that?"

"Herb is driving me crazy. He doesn't understand what silent reading is all about. I don't think I can do this anymore but I don't want to disappoint your mother. What do I tell her?"

"What you told me. It's nothing she's not already aware of. They've lived across the street from each other for years. They're like fixtures in each other's lives."

"Hmm, I hate to disappoint people. Don't say anything. I'll go on Tuesday. Maybe we'll be able to find out what we need."

"Great. You're a good sport, Cecilia."

"I try."

When the call ended, I got back to my spreadsheets, where I remained for the next two hours. By then, Nate returned to the office and rapped on my door. "I caught the false alarm alert from the library. Can't tell if it was an accident, a prank, or sabotage. The puzzle solvers are insistent it was the latter, according to Marshall and Ranston. Too bad I missed all the fun. I had a full docket of things to deal with."

"Did they find perfume at Samantha's house?"

"Nope. Only organic seaweed concoctions for skin. But they did turn up something rather questionable." He stepped inside my office and closed the door behind him. "You can share this with Augusta, but if clients walk in, we need to be discreet."

"What did they find?"

"A notebook with a long list of items she was in the process of selling on eBay and Craigslist."

"That's not so odd."

"It is when you write a goal amount and equate it to bills and money owed."

"Huh? I thought Samantha was well off."

"Her deceased husband, Forrest's father, was. But according to Rolo, who looked into it, Samantha was left very little in his will. She had her house but that's only because the deed and title were for Joint Right of Survivorship. All she had were her school pension, Social Security and stock in Prosaic Puzzles."

"You're saying she was bankrupt?"

"Not bankrupt, but financially stressed. That eliminates greed as a motive. You can't pull out money from a pauper. Which brings us back to our original premise—her murder was personal. Am now looking into her relationships with neighbors, etcetera."

"I'm sure my mother and her friends are as well. Only blatantly. With everyone they come across. And trust me, they're not done with the perfume angle."

"Neither are we, kiddo."

• • •

The remainder of the weekend was quiet, giving Marshall and me a chance to recover as the growing heat in the valley sapped more of our energy each day. Usually June temperatures run in the high nineties but we've been hitting the hundred and fives for days in a row. Thank goodness we had the community pool or both of us would have languished until November.

Unfortunately, I had the bad habit of taking my cell phone with me to the pool and placing it on a lounge chair in earshot of the water.

"Don't answer that!" Marshall called out that Sunday evening. "Pretend you don't hear it! Let it go to voicemail."

"Fine. Voicemail it is."

Ten minutes later, the phone rang again. And ten minutes after that. Finally, I couldn't take it so I got out of the water and walked to the chair. "It's my mother. I should have figured as much." I played back the voicemail but all she said was "Call me, Phee. Call me as soon as you get this message."

Marshall swam closer to me. "What's up?"

"Can't be that serious because she wasn't hysterical and the dog wasn't barking in the background. Probably a last-minute invite to join her and that crew for dinner."

Marshall ran his thumb across his neck as I returned the call.

"Oh, good! You got my call."

"I got all three of them, Mom. What's going on?"

"Lucinda called. She and Cecilia attended some church social this afternoon and you'll never guess who was there—that annoying woman who leans over the puzzle and tells people where to stick the pieces. Unless she grabs them from the pile and puts them where she wants."

"Did they get her name? Nate wanted to ask her some questions."

"Josephine Langostino. Like those small lobsters."

"Crustaceans."

"That's what I said. Lobsters. Anyway, she attends their church but only for major holidays according to the other women who knew her. Your boss can thank Lucinda and Cecilia."

"I'm sure he will. Tell me, do you and Shirley plan on infiltrating the weight-watching women tomorrow? You said Monday is one of their meeting days."

"Shirley plans on fasting all night so her weight will be lower, but my metabolism won't allow it."

"You mean your appetite won't allow it."

"When you reach a certain age, Phee, it's good to have some extra pounds on your body. In case you incur a serious illness."

"I'll keep that in mind. Um, let me know what you find out tomorrow at the meeting. What time is it?"

"Nine thirty in the reading room. Shirley and I will be homing in on their conversations."

"Whatever you do, refrain from making remarks about anyone's weight-loss journey."

"What about the horrible recipes they share? Like baking a cake with applesauce instead of butter and sugar? Or worse yet, using string beans instead of chicken livers in a pâté."

"Just refrain and take notes."

"Shirley and I will be close-lipped."

Until one of them steps on the scale.

CHAPTER 25

"**M**r. Williams says thanks for texting him that name last night. He got in super early and is already tracking the lobster woman down." Augusta retrieved a K-Cup of dark roast from the Keurig and added sugar.

"You're as bad as my mother. A langostino isn't a lobster. Or a shrimp."

"No, but this one could be a killer. Maybe she and Samantha had some ugly business between them and that's why the woman doesn't sit at the table like everyone else."

"Or maybe she's just quirky."

"Oh, before I forget, you got a message from Paul."

"Again? Now what?"

"He wanted you to know that he and Mini-Moose fished at Lake Pleasant last evening and ran into the Bellowses from the puzzle group. They were just returning from a dinner cruise and he overheard them talking about Samantha and Carl."

"That's not unusual. They used to date until she bid him adieu."

"Dumped him. And according to what Paul overheard, it was because she had her eyes on Drake, of all people. The Bellowses were arguing about it. And that's not all. Paul heard Norva say, 'It's a good thing she's six feet under or you'd be the one pushing up daisies.'"

"Whoa. The jealous wife. We hadn't considered that motive."

"I always do. Crimes of passion are the worst. You'd be surprised what these cherubic housewives can do with a filet knife."

"The first thing I'm going to do is let Nate and Marshall know."

"I already texted them. No sense wasting valuable time and no sense gutting one fish when you can gut two."

"Aarugh. By the way, I'm expecting a call from my mother. She and Shirley are going to be flies on the wall at the weight-watching women's meeting this morning. That group may be the one sabotaging the puzzle so they can have the big room."

Augusta broke out laughing. "The weight-watching women, huh? And they need more space? That's hysterical."

"Space for their weigh-ins and their meetings. Not for—oh, goodness, you're terrible, Augusta."

She grinned and sipped her coffee.

Oddly enough, the entire morning went by without a peep from my mother. It was the first time in days that I was able to work without interruption. Then, at eleven forty-five, Augusta ended my bliss when she shouted, "I thought your mother would never call. She's on the line."

"Thanks," I called back as I took the call.

"It's me, Phee." I rubbed my temple and mumbled something as my mom spoke. "Shirley and I went to the weight-watching women's meeting and got an earful. Way too much to tell you on the phone. So Myrna, who joined us for coffee, said we should all go out for lunch at Cheddar's, which is near you. But I think the reason is because they give you free cinnamon buns while you wait for your order. So, have you eaten lunch yet? If not, we'll meet you in a half hour. Or we could eat and come to your office and—"

"Cheddar's in a half hour is fine." I couldn't spit the words out fast enough. Last thing Williams Investigations needed was the three of them yammering nonstop.

When I got off the phone, I asked Augusta if she wanted me to pick up a take-out order and she immediately replied, "Two orders of Wisconsin cheese bites. Reminds me of home."

Thirty minutes later, my mom, Shirley, Myrna and I were seated in a booth by the window in a quiet part of the restaurant.

"Okay," I said, "what did you find out? Do you have reason to believe someone in that group is sabotaging the puzzle?"

"Lordy, yes." Shirley looked up from the menu. "More than one of them complained that they needed the space and didn't like being crammed in the back reading area. Goodness. Even the quiet readers don't like being crammed in there. The chairs are right on top of each other."

"But did anyone say anything directly?"

Shirley looked at my mother. "Did you get the name of the woman in that polka-dot tank top? Some women should not be wearing tank tops in public. I don't care if it *is* hot outside."

My mother shook her head. "No, but the woman seated next to her is Deborah-Dawn. I'm not sure if that's her first name or the first and middle, but that's what the polka dot tank woman called her."

"It doesn't matter," I said. "What matters is what you heard."

"Well, if that's the case," Shirley went on, "I heard the tank woman say, 'Health and wellness need to come before fun and games. And we shouldn't feel bad making that happen.' There you go—an admission of guilt."

"Um, that's not exactly an admission of guilt, but it is a strong indicator that they could indeed be the culprits."

"Oh, honey, that's not all. Is it, Harriet?"

My mother straightened her back as if it was a military inspection. "We might not have gotten a confession, but we uncovered something far more important—their real weight-loss secret!"

Myrna helped herself to a complimentary cinnamon bun and shrugged.

"Not an issue for me. I only eat when I'm home and out!"

At that moment, the waitress arrived to take our orders and bring more cinnamon buns. As soon as she left, my mother continued with the weight-loss secret.

"It's those gummies. Those Restoration Youth Gummies that Samantha's stepson manufactures. They don't just restore your youth, they make the fat cells melt away until your body looks like it did thirty years ago."

I narrowed my eyes and fixed them on her. "Then why don't those weight-loss women look like they did thirty years ago?"

"They just started the regimen."

"Nonsense. Probably a bunch of hoopla."

"Hoopla or not, Samantha had quite a deal going with those women. She was the one supplying them with the miracle weight-loss solution. *That's* the piece of information we found out. And all we had to do was listen. Imagine that."

Yes. Speak less and listen more. And now they think of it?

"When our office spoke with Forrest, he indicated that his stepmother had no interest in his business."

"People lie, Phee," she said.

"But you, Shirley, and Aunt Ina didn't find any evidence of her involvement when you snooped in his office and killed his fish."

"It was an unfortunate accident."

"Okay, I'll ask Nate and Marshall if they'd pursue your latest lead."

"They've got too much going on already. There's no reason why we can't be the ones to pursue it."

"Dead fish!" I shouted. "That should be a reason enough."

"We won't go back to his house, but nothing prevents us from finding out who's going to carry on her under-the-table elixir business. All we need to do is attend their next meeting, but they make you join after the first visit. It's five dollars." Then she looked at Shirley and Myrna. "What do you think?"

"I can afford five dollars, Harriet." Shirley took a sip of her lemon water and looked at Myrna.

"I'll do it for the sake of the community. Their next meeting and weigh-in is Thursday. That's grilled cheese day at Betty's Rooste. Let's go there afterward. I want to get one of their giant muffins. Or maybe a scone."

And a double dose of Restoration Youth Gummies.

CHAPTER 26

Augusta was flabbergasted when I got back to the office and told her about the conversation at Cheddar's. She unwrapped her double order of cheese curds and smiled. "I'll wash these down with the can of root beer I have in the fridge, and you can give me more details. We can pick up the phone in the workroom and we'll hear if anyone walks in. No appointments until three."

I followed her into the room and sat at the small rectangle table. "The sleuthing saga continues. Those women simply cannot leave well enough alone."

"At least they're not breaking and entering or bringing your mother's dog to someone's place of business."

"Not yet."

"If what they claim is true, and Samantha was distributing those gummies, she might have upped the price, or worse yet, someone didn't lose weight and didn't look younger so they went off the deep end with that staple gun."

"Nate was right. You should be writing crime novels."

Augusta popped a cheese curd into her mouth and savored it. "I take it no gummies were found in her house, huh?"

"The deputies conducted a search along with our guys, and nothing."

"Time to think outside the box. And by box, I'm referring to one of those storage units that everyone around here has because they can't afford to part with their junk."

"Oh my gosh, Augusta. You might have nailed it."

"Yep. Who's writing crime novels now?"

When Nate and Marshall got back to the office from their gumshoeing, I informed them about my lunch conversation with my mother, Shirley, and Myrna. Then I mentioned Augusta's storage unit idea.

Nate rubbed his chin and grinned. "Great minds think alike, kiddo. But we cheated. We found a receipt in Samantha's house for a storage rental in Surprise just past El Mirage Road. Bowman and Ranston are going to check it out. We weren't thinking gummies, though. We were actually thinking a side business for Prosaic Puzzles. Guess all of us will have to wait and see."

"And if you're wondering, we're coming up with a big zero regarding perfume." Marshall sounded exasperated. "Since it obviously didn't come from Samantha, someone in that library *had* to be wearing it. Trouble is, it could be someone who only frequents that place once in a while."

"Believe me, my mother's nostrils are poised and ready. It's on the back burner for her since she's preoccupied with the puzzle sabotage, thanks to our manipulating, but one whiff and we'll all know about it."

Nate laughed. "I'm counting on it. Meanwhile, we'll keep on digging. I have a nagging feeling we're overlooking something, but I always get that feeling."

"It's what keeps us awake at night," Marshall added. "*That*, and calls from Phee's mother."

The two of us looked at each other and broke up laughing.

The next two days moved at a quieter pace but a productive one. The deputies secured a warrant to check out Samantha's storage unit but came up empty, unlike the unit itself, which was filled with lots of tchotchkes and boxes of jigsaw puzzles. Meanwhile, Nate and Marshall spoke with more neighbors on Samantha's street and ruled out anything from those folks.

"Do you think Samantha could have paid a friend or acquaintance to store those gummies for her?" I asked Marshall on Wednesday night.

"It's possible. Anything is at this point. We're still pursuing other leads, like her relationship with Carl and her possible fixation with Drake. In fact, I have a meeting with Drake in the morning at Einstein's Bagels on Bell Road, not the one on Grand. He didn't want to be seen in Sun City West."

"Understandable."

"Say, we haven't heard from your mother since yesterday. Any updates from the senior sleuths?"

"As a matter of fact, yes. She and Shirley plan on a direct approach tomorrow at the weight-watching meeting. They're going to come right out and ask if anyone is selling those gummies on the secondary market."

"It could work. Or it could blow up in their faces. Anyway, it's worth a shot."

"That's what my mother said. But when I asked what she'd do next, she told me that she and Shirley hadn't gotten that far in their thinking."

"That's the difference between amateur sleuths and actual investigators. That's why I always cringed when people told me about exploratory surgery. I prefer guide maps."

"Or GPS. We're in the twenty-first century, Columbus."

When I crept into bed, I tried to picture the scenario tomorrow when my mother and Shirley blurted out the million-dollar question. What I didn't picture was the response they got. It was a little before eleven the next day when the call came in on our office line.

"It's six hundred dollars for a ninety-day supply and you eat three gummies a day. And the six hundred dollars is the *wholesale* price. Those gummies retail for nine hundred dollars, so there's a hundred-dollar savings each month, but that's still outrageous."

"Uh, hi, Mom! Tell me, how did you leave it? And who's the new kingpin? That is, if Samantha *was* running a side business."

"Oh, she was running it. Shirley and I are positive."

"Did someone come right out and say so?"

"Not directly."

"We need *directly*."

"We came right out and asked the question bluntly. 'Is anyone here selling those restoration gummies off-market?'"

"And?"

"They said, 'You'll have to speak with Lettie Holton about that.' So then, Shirley asked if Lettie was holding the purse strings on it and then those women got all cagey and quiet. That meant someone was hiding something. In this case it might have been Lettie's relationship with Samantha. The fact that those two were co-chairs for the puzzle committee didn't necessarily indicate a friendship. Something more shadowy could have been going on."

"Hmm. I'll let the guys know."

"Hold off."

"Why?"

"Louise, Myrna and I will be in the Sun City West AquaSizers Class tomorrow morning at Beardsley pool. Lettie is in that class. We'll position ourselves near her and make like we're interested in a fast weight-loss supplement. We'll dangle the bait and wait for her to make a move."

"Dangle the bait? Goodness! Paul's certainly rubbed off on you."

"We can't just ask her directly. She'll want to know what we heard. And you know Myrna. She can't keep quiet. She's worse than Herb. I practically had to muzzle her during our last radio show."

"Uh-huh. I thought you were going to work on the puzzle tomorrow."

"LaVonda got all snitty and told Lucinda and Gloria that they needed to make room for others."

"What about her? Is she making room?"

"LaVonda only goes twice a week. Anyway, Shirley and Gloria are going tomorrow. Then we'll all meet up at Bagels 'n More."

"What about Cecilia and Lucinda?"

"Church ladies meeting, but they'll make it in time to chat with us, too."

"Don't go overboard with your performance. And it's a good thing Aunt Ina is still in Sedona."

"The minute the temperature goes to triple digits, my sister turns into a delicate flower that needs to be out of the heat. From what she told us, this new spa of theirs embraces life-energizing foods and exercises, not to mention massages, facials, and all sorts of body pampering."

I'd like to embrace all sorts of body pampering.
"Let me know how it goes at the pool, okay?"
"Too bad you're working or you could join us for bagels."
"Yes, I'm terribly disappointed."
"You're rolling your eyes, Phee. I can see them from here."

CHAPTER 27

I wasn't particularly optimistic about the book club ladies "yenta-ing" to find out if Lettie had a sideline with the late Samantha, but it wasn't as if any of us could pull it off. Then there was MCSO. One look at Bowman and Ranston, and even Mother Teresa would have froze up. Truth was, Nate and Marshall could be daunting. The very word *detective* conjured up all sorts of stereotypes.

Then there was Lyndy and me, total amateurs with a penchant for sleuthing and a passion for research. But we had full-time jobs, something the book club women no longer had to contend with.

Frankly, there was no way around it. If any progress was going to be made on the puzzle sabotage and the murder of its committee chair, it was going to involve a grassroots effort. With or without the weeds. Unfortunately, my mother's strategies and schemes left much to be desired. Today was the perfect example when she, Louise, and Myrna had no luck with Lettie at the AquaSizer class this morning. It didn't take a genius to figure out that eventually I'd have to get my own feet wet.

"Meryl Streep couldn't pull off a performance like that," my mother said when she phoned shortly before noon. I happened to be in the outer office, helping myself to a croissant from Panera Bread, when she called. Augusta put her on speaker phone and we both listened.

"Are you listening, Phee?"

"Yes. Go on."

"Here's what happened. Myrna was directly behind Lettie, and Louise and I were on opposite sides of her during the exercises. Thank goodness it was the AquaSizers and not the water mermaids. That class makes you sing along with the exercises."

Augusta all but spat out the croissant she had bitten into.

"Get to the point, Mom. Were you able to find out anything?"

"Yes. Time to escalate."

"What does that mean?"

"I need to backtrack. Myrna started by sighing and telling everyone around her how she followed a healthy food and exercise regimen and still couldn't lose weight. Then Louise added that her energy level was particularly low but her doctor attributed it to age. So I jumped in and announced that it would be wonderful if we could get our hands on something that would spunk up our energy and help us lose weight without a prescription."

"And?"

"She ignored us. Three or four minutes later, Myrna tried again. This time by telling everyone she'd be willing to pay for a safe alternative if it worked. When Lettie still didn't acknowledge her, I asked, 'Has anyone tried those restorative gummies that are advertised?' I figured that would get her attention."

In the meantime, Augusta finished the first croissant and bit into the second.

"Did she respond?" I asked.

"And how! She shushed me and told me I interfered with the routine because she couldn't hear the directions. That left me no alternative."

Oh no! Please do not tell me she splashed her. Or worse . . . dunked her.

"Did you do something that put you on probation like Streetman in the dog park?"

"Don't be ridiculous. I merely asked the official question and diverted it so that I didn't point to her."

"What did you say?"

"I said, 'It was no secret that your co-chair for the puzzle committee sold those wonderful gummies off-market. Would you know who's doing it now?' Then, that witch shouted to the instructor, 'This woman is annoying me and asking me about buying drugs.' At which point the class came to a complete stop and the instructor water-walked toward me and asked me to take another spot."

"That's it? 'Take another spot?' You're lucky that's all she did. She could have written you up or worse."

"I don't think so. Louise overheard her after the class. She told someone that Lettie was 'getting more obnoxious by the minute.' And here's the good part."

Finally, a good part.

Augusta moved closer to the phone even though it was on speaker.

"Betty-Jean Wiseman was in that class. She pals around with Celeste Blatt. And when Betty-Jean saw us when we got out of the pool, she told us that Lettie was just being cautious and that she and Samantha had a stash of those gummies that they sold. I asked how she knew and she winked at me. Winked! So now, it's escalation time!"

"Mom, I really don't like the word *escalate*. It connotes all sorts of scary scenarios."

"It only has to connote one. And we need to come up with it. Oh my gosh! We'll be late for the girls at Bagels 'n More. I can't wait to see what we come up with."

Before words could form in my mouth, the call ended and Augusta stood and patted me on the shoulder. Then she chortled and laughed at the same time. "I'll dig up our list of bail bondsmen."

"Don't bother. Just point to the nearest volcano and I'll jump in."

To make matters worse, Nate, Marshall and the deputies weren't having much luck with the investigation into Samantha's murder. That meant "casting a wider net." Nate's famous words. When they both returned to the office an hour or so later, they told Augusta and me that Bowman and Ranston would be looking into Lettie's possible involvement with gummy distribution, but, thanks to Sherman and his photos, our guys would be tracking down the people in that 2002 picture of the Sun Cities Puzzle Putters.

"That should keep those two busy," Augusta said and chuckled. "Especially when they get to figure out who's vertical and who's not."

"You're bad." I snickered. "Really bad. But right now, I'm on edge wondering what ill-conceived and preposterous plan my mother and her friends will come with." I looked at the time on my phone. "I give it an hour and a half. That's when I expect her to call with the details."

"I give it an hour. I'll just transfer the call into your office."

As usual, Augusta was right, and even though I had braced myself for something outlandish, I still wasn't prepared for the latest plan to emerge from the book club ladies.

"The simplicity of this plan," my mother said once I took her call, "coupled with the nuance of its layering, makes it the perfect means to unlock the truth."

"Huh? Is that taken from one of those TV recipe shows? Which one? *The Barefoot Contessa*? *The Pioneer Woman*?"

"Don't be silly. Do you want to hear it or what?"

"I suppose I'll have to, because you'll probably rope me into it."

"Good. Step One—We call it 'The Haunting'"

"The *what?*"

"You heard me. We begin by gaslighting Lettie into thinking Samantha's spirit has returned to hold her accountable."

"For what? A bad business deal or her murder?"

"We'll aim for both and see what sticks."

"I'm actually terrified to hear the details."

"That's why we need a few participants."

New word for flunkies.

"I'm listening."

"If there was bad business between Lettie and Samantha, we've got to make Lettie believe that Samantha's spirit won't let go. Lettie will be so shaken up, she'll be bound to confess."

"Maybe, if it's a raw financial deal, but I doubt she'll confess to a murder. Especially since there's no hard evidence pointing her way."

"That's exactly *why* we have to be the ones to do it. It's not as if those deputies are going to budge an inch from their protocol. And face it, your husband and your boss aren't about to play Charles Boyer any time soon."

Or associate that name with the movie.

"I'm curious. How *exactly* do you plan to haunt Lettie?" *This I have got to hear.*

"Sheer genius. Serendipitous, really. Remember me telling you that Gloria videoed people returning books to the library when she brought back the John Grisham novel?"

"I suppose. Why?"

"Because Samantha was there and her voice got recorded on Gloria's video. All we need to do is find out how to take snippets of it and use them to convince Lettie it's her ghost."

Boy, if that doesn't sound like a plot from some old movie, I don't know what does.

"I'm stunned. Absolutely stunned."

"Because it's so clever, right? I told you our plan was indescribable."

"Indescribable, but not infallible. And it better not involve creeping around her house after dark."

What the heck is going through my brain? Did I just put an idea in her head?

"That's only the beginning. First, we gaslight her into a ghost-driven guilt trip. Then we move on to—Oh, goodness. Streetman's pawing at the door. I have to take him out. We'll chat later. Once we nail down all the details."

She ended the call before I could muster a single syllable. Probably just as well. The ghost-gaslighting was enough to get my mind doing summersaults. I took a breath and then relayed everything to Augusta.

"I'm no techie-wizard," she said, "but I think I know how to separate parts of a recording. Old school. You get someone else to use their cell phone to video parts of *your* video as you play it."

"Mmm, that might work. But it sounds long and tedious, and most likely I'll be the one stuck doing it."

"Check Google. Or YouTube. They might have a better way."

They didn't.

According to Bing, however, all I had to do was "split an audio track from video clip 1 by selecting the video clip. Then right-click the video clip, and choose Audio > Split Audio." It said, "VideoStudio generates a new audio track, and once I split the audio track from the video clip, I can apply an audio filter to the audio track."

"That's what I just said." Augusta slurped a Polar drink and wiped her lips with a tissue.

"Fine. I'll see what I can do."

Then Augusta broke up laughing and some of her Polar drink dripped from her nose. "Got to hand it to you, Phee. This is a first. Impersonating the ghost of a dead woman. I can't wait to find out how that all works out for you."

Me too!

"They what?" Marshall asked when I told him about the book club ladies' plan to eke out a confession from Lettie regarding the sale of gummies. "I thought they were focused on the puzzle sabotage."

"You know my mother and her friends. Their minds flit around like moths circling a lamppost."

"But a fake haunting? It sounds like a bad Halloween movie. I'd tell you to steer clear but I know better. Someone has to be the proverbial adult in the room, and I guess you were nominated."

"I really don't know what to expect. Our call ended when the dog had to go out. I'm sure we'll catch up tomorrow. How does your day look?"

"Relentless. Everything's got tentacles."

And my mother's are far-reaching.

CHAPTER 28

For the remainder of the afternoon, all I could think of was that saying, "The devil's in the details," and my mother's plan, as far as I knew, didn't have any. But that changed at a little after nine that night while Marshall dozed on the couch and I channel-surfed. My mother had returned from her nightly walk with Streetman and secured "Fort Knox" with more locks and alarms than most apartment dwellers in high-crime areas. At least that's what she told me when she phoned.

"I thought you should know about our action plan for 'The Haunting,' so you'll sleep better."

"It depends. I might not sleep at all. Spit it out. What is it?"

"Logistically speaking, it's going to be really hard to have Lettie hear Samantha's voice while other people are around."

"You realized that just now?"

"Plans evolve and Lucinda came up with this one. She saw it on a Telemundo episode last year. Only it was a threatening boyfriend."

I stretched my neck and glanced at Marshall, who was in happy la-la land.

"First of all," my mother said, "we need to buy one of those burner phones. I think Walmart sells them."

"Uh-huh. Then what?"

"We use it so Lettie won't be able to identify the caller. We isolate the phrases and then spook her into a confession."

"Do you really think you can string those words together to do that?"

Because I really don't want to get stuck doing that. No matter what YouTube says. Or that Bing article.

My mother sighed. "No, but Mini-Moose can. Myrna told Paul and he said something to Mini-Moose. We should be ready to put the plan in action on Monday."

"And you think Lettie will drive to the posse office and confess her involvement with Samantha's gummy business?"

"Goodness, no. We expect her to drive directly to where she has those things stashed and catch her in the act of removing them. They're probably in her house. That's our cue to tail her and improvise."

"How about if you don't tail her and you don't improvise? If you insist on your Stephen King scenario, just gauge her reaction and let our guys know. Your interference could mess things up. Besides, shouldn't you be focusing on the puzzle sabotage? And what about those magazine people?"

"Oops. I forgot to tell you. Darcey said they got tied up with another story so they won't be here until the end of the week. By then, we'll have enough of the puzzle put together for a good photo shoot, and Darcey assured us that the library is taking every precaution to make sure no one tampers with it."

"Good. And don't you tamper with anything either. You know what I mean."

"Honestly, Phee. Stop being such a worrywart. These action plans always work on the Hallmark Channel."

"Of course they do. They have screenwriters who make sure they do."

"Tomorrow's Saturday. We'll run through the plan at Bagels 'n More. By the time Monday rolls around, it'll be a well-rehearsed operation."

Or an imminent disaster.

"Everything okay, hon?" Marshall's voice was soft and sleepy.

"Just ducky. The usual craziness from my mother. At least she gave me a pass on meeting the crew at Bagels 'n More tomorrow. Or she forgot about it in all her haste to move that haunting plan of hers along."

I looked over and Marshall had dozed off again. When he finally got up at eleven to go back to sleep in our bed, he muttered something about Nate finally meeting up with the lobster woman.

"Ask me about it in the morning," he mumbled. "And Tabitha, too."

• • •

I was up by seven and could hear him in the shower. A half hour later, we sat across from each other in the kitchen, hot coffees in one hand and warm cinnamon rolls in the other. I was on my third bite when I finally came up for air.

"Tell me about Josie Langostino and Tabitha. You mentioned them last night."

"Right. We're finally making headway. Nate had a long conversation with Josie and she told him that she, too, 'picked up the unmistakable scent of gardenia' when she 'waltzed around the puzzle table.'"

"Did she know whose unmistakable scent?"

"Afraid not, but she did know two of the women who were there, Lettie and Betty-Jean. We'll try to narrow it down. As for Tabitha, here's where it gets interesting. I met with her since Nate was tied up. She said she was in that photography club in Sun City and on a hunch, I asked her if she remembered anyone who was in the photography club as well as the Puzzle Putters. Guess whose name came up? Tisha Stoad."

"Anyone else?" I widened my eyes.

"Henry Longmire, the handyman at the mortuary, and Alfrieda Himmelfarb."

"Yes, Sherman mentioned Alfrieda but couldn't remember her last name."

"Maybe we're chasing shadows, but those two might have an idea of where Tisha could be found. I'll be working on locating them."

"And I'll be working on anything but."

"So you say." Then he winked.

"I'm not about to take part in any of my mother's schemes. I envisioned food shopping and some swim time."

"Let me know how that works out for you." Then he stood, kissed my cheek, put his dish in the sink and raced off to get to the office.

"Enjoy a free Saturday," he shouted as he headed to the garage. "Let's do takeout tonight."

My voice must have resonated "I love you" all the way down the block.

I knew my mother and a few of the ladies planned on puzzle work in the afternoon but I didn't plan on "yet another puzzle disaster." Her words. On a voicemail I played back when I got out of the pool around three.

"You won't believe this, Phee! 'Every precaution,' my foot! There's been yet another puzzle disaster. When Shirley, Myrna, Louise and I got to the puzzle, everyone was buzzing around it like flies. Apparently it was fine in the morning but then that crew left for lunch, and when we showed up—Is this voice message going to run out? I'll call again and make a new one."

I moaned so loud I was afraid someone would hear me.

"Like I was saying, Carl, the Bellowses, and a new lady got there before us and started on a different panel when they realized they had been foiled again. Again, Phee! Are you listening? They started putting the pieces together when they realized those pieces were from another puzzle entirely. The whole panel from the original puzzle was gone and, in its place—get this—was Mickey Mouse! This is outrageous. Call me."

I waited until I got home to change before I returned the call. By then, my mother had notified everyone in Maricopa County and possibly a few people in Yavapai County, too.

"It's about time you called." Her voice had the usual frantic edge when she's worried that Streetman ate something he shouldn't have or Essie didn't eat what she should have.

"Um, I think I got the gist of it from your voice messages. Did anyone notice anything?"

"No. Darcey was at lunch and the library volunteers were up front checking books in and out. Oh, there was one volunteer in the media section but that area is behind tall shelves so she didn't notice anything."

"What about the nonfiction area off to the rear?"

"I think I've only seen three people in there in the past decade. This is awful. We are never going to get that puzzle looking like something before *Senior Living* shows up."

"Mom, they won't know the difference. Keep Mickey Mouse. They're not doing close-ups." *At least I hope they're not.*

"When Darcey found out, she called Lettie to tell her. We're calling in lots of regulars to put a rush on this. Myrna came up with an ingenious plan to have a campout in the library until the puzzle is completed."

"What good is that going to do? It got sabotaged in broad daylight."

"True, but imagine what they could have done under the cover of darkness."

"Under the cover of darkness? Good heavens. Aren't you going a little overboard?"

"Myrna doesn't think so. And neither do Shirley and Gloria."

"Oh, no. I can see where this is going—the pajama party from Hades with Streetman and Thor."

"Watchdogs are important in these situations."

"Yes. Watchdogs. Not dogs that watch!"

"Anyway, Darcey's deciding whether or not to notify the sheriff's office. It wasn't exactly vandalism, but it does involve stolen property—our puzzle pieces."

"How about if I let Nate and Marshall know? That way, word will get out to Bowman and Ranston, but not officially."

"Good thinking. I'll let Darcey know."

"Do me a favor. Hold off on Myrna's brainstorm."

"Oh, I wasn't going to say anything. It was Myrna's idea. In fact, she's talking to the librarian right now. By the way, do you and Marshall have sleeping bags?"

If I did, I'd crawl into it and stay there!

CHAPTER 29

Since it was Sunday, Marshall and I would have slept in late had it not been for an early-morning phone call from my aunt Ina, who was still basking in the cooler Sedona weather.

"We had our auras read at dawn," she said, "and then Louis and I watched a glorious sunrise over the red rocks."

And here I was, happy to watch the insides of my eyelids.

"Uh, yeah. Good morning, Aunt Ina."

"I hate to disturb you on a Sunday, but I couldn't reach your mother. She's probably out walking that little ankle biter of hers. I wanted to tell her that our spa is selling those rejuvenation gummies but they cost a fortune. You'd almost have to remortgage your house to look thirty again, but I heard through the grapevine that there's a black market on them and it takes place right under your mother's nose in Sun City West. That's why I tried to call her. The scuttlebutt pointed to Samantha, but now there's a new player."

"Uh, yeah. She's been less than subtle tracking down her rumor leads. In the pool, no less!"

"Who was with her? Don't tell me Myrna or worse yet, one of the men."

"No men. But Myrna and Louise were there."

"Oy. Did she have a suspect in mind?"

"She's convinced it's Lettie. Almost got herself thrown out of there in the process."

"Tell her not to waste her time. It's not Lettie."

"How do you know?"

"The subject came up when I finished my mud bath with herbal rinse. I ran into a woman from Sun City West who echoed my sentiments—the price tag for those gummies is astronomical here. She told me that it was common knowledge Samantha sold them and may have had a male counterpart but couldn't provide a name. So you see, that gets Lettie off the hook."

"Her stepson denied any business involvement with her."

"What did you think he was going to do? Admit everything and put his business in jeopardy? No, they were more astute. First, they sell them at steep discounts to get people hooked. Then the price gouging begins. And as long as they stay under the retail price, not only do they get nontaxable income, but they acquire a whole new clientele."

"Hmm, so you think Forrest was complicit in all of this? That is, if it's true."

"Oh, it's true. And I believe he wasn't just complicit, he orchestrated everything. Which gave him a darn good motive to knock off his stepmother when she got too greedy."

"That's a lot of conjecture. What does Uncle Louis think?"

"To mind my own business. But he also gave me the nicest compliment. He said not to waste any of our money on youthful restoration. Said I was perfect the way I was. Between you and me, the man is most likely guarding our bank account, but who doesn't like to get a compliment like that?"

"Very true."

"Now that you know the sidekick in the gummy black market may be a man, feel free to drop this tidy clue in your husband's mailbox. Oh—I can't be late for my facial. Hydro-infusion and dermaplaning. I'll talk to you soon."

"Thanks, Aunt Ina."

"Any time. Say, let's do a girls' retreat sometime. They even have a special pet spa with a dog and cat resort."

"Shh! One word of it and my mother will book Streetman and Essie!"

"Everything okay?" Marshall asked when I got off the phone.

"Yep. Just my aunt. She couldn't reach my mother so I was the joyful recipient of her latest snooping."

"I thought she and your uncle were in Sedona."

"There were in Sedona and they still are." Then I unfolded my aunt's unsubstantiated information regarding Samantha working with a male partner in gummy distribution.

Marshall shrugged. "I'll see if we can prod more out of Forrest. Odd, but your aunt may have a point—get people hooked on a product and up the price. It's an old ploy but usually part of the original marketing plan. This sounds rather—"

"Far-fetched?"

"I was going to say unethical, but yeah, it may very well turn out to be far-fetched."

Too wide awake to go back to sleep, we opted for breakfast out at First Watch and got the shock of our lives when we spied Forrest holding the door open for Keenan Alcorn from the puzzle group.

"What do you make of that?" I whispered to Marshall. "He's a recent transplant from Washington."

"Could be perfectly benign, but it certainly prompts me to put a Forrest visit on the top of my docket tomorrow. This time at his place of business."

"My aunt would be proud of you."

"As long as she doesn't drag us to one of her naturalistic New Age spas."

"Ditto that."

• • •

And while Marshall added an impromptu visit to Forrest the next day, Shirley phoned the office that morning to let us know that "the *Senior Living* people will be here on Wednesday!" She went on to tell us that my mother asked her to call since she had to get her nails done.

"Didn't Mom get her nails done last week?" I asked Shirley.

"Yes, but she was worried they might be scuffed and would look awful if one of the photos showed them holding a puzzle piece."

Then Shirley went on to tell me that the salon squeezed her in for an appointment tomorrow to change her rose red nail color to spicy red.

I was dumbfounded. "Uh, that sounds nice. Please tell me my mother isn't about to alter her hair color. Her new champagne blonde with low light reds just made its debut."

"Heavens, no. She finally found a color she liked. For now, anyway."

I laughed and told her to have a great day. Twenty minutes later, Shirley called back and Augusta gave me one of those quizzical looks.

"Phee, you won't believe this. If you talk to your mother before I do, tell her they found the missing puzzle pieces that were replaced by the Mickey Mouse ones. One would think they would have been in the empty Mickey Mouse puzzle box, but whoever did it was really clever. The puzzle pieces were in one of those giant book-set boxes in the nonfiction section. It was for the post–Civil War years, and what I was told was that the man who wanted to read the books on the post–Civil War era was really distraught."

This gives the word *circus* a whole new definition.

"It has to be a prankster who's not very funny or someone who's intent on foiling the completion of that puzzle. But why?"

"Maybe they want to upset a particular person. If so, it's working. Lettie is running around here like a chicken without a head and Celeste has been downright irritable."

"As long as my mother is happy with her hair and nails, we're in the clear."

Then Shirley ended the conversation with, "Wednesday is only two days away."

At that point, I searched my desk drawer for a Tums.

Nate was in and out at lunchtime. He scarfed down a leftover sub he brought from home and told Augusta and me that he was on his way to chat with Betty-Jean, Lettie, and LaVonda at the library. Josephine ratted them out as possible perfume wearers and Nate hoped to verify the accusation.

"After that," he said, "I plan to pay a visit to the mortuary."

Augusta moved her glasses below the bridge of her nose. "So soon, Mr.

Williams? I just ignore those flyers from the Neptune Society and the local funeral homes. They'll get my business soon enough. Vultures! The whole lot of them."

Nate stretched his neck. "Not me. I need an address for Henry Longmire. I want to follow up with him. He was in that Sun City puzzle club and may be able to shed some light on where Tisha Stoad wound up."

"Just don't sign any pre-contracts on where you'll wind up," she replied.

He chuckled and rubbed his neck as he headed out the door.

"That was subtle." I grinned at Augusta.

"I always look out for everyone's best interests."

"And we appreciate it!"

CHAPTER 30

"Quite the operation at Restoration Youth Gummies," Marshall announced the second he walked into the office. It was shortly after Nate left and I had just stepped away from my desk to get something to drink. "Apparently the quest for youth is big business," he went on. "They've got one building for their naturally sourced ingredients and chemical lab, and another for packaging and distribution."

"Any headway on his relationship with Keenan Alcorn?" I asked.

"Yes, Mr. Gregory," Augusta added. "Tell us because your next appointment should be here any second. The two siblings in search of their birth parents."

"Keenan is a graphic designer and Forrest contacted him regarding new packaging. He got the man's name from his late stepmother, who met him in the library before her unfortunate demise."

"And you believe him? As the secretary here, I've learned to question everything."

"I know. And yeah, I believe *that* part but it seems too coincidental. I'll have Rolo do some digging on Keenan. See what we can pull up. Heck, everyone in that puzzle klatch is a suspect as of right now."

"It might get more interesting two days from now." Augusta pushed her glasses further up and turned her attention to her computer screen.

"Huh?"

I laughed. "*Senior Living* will be there on Wednesday for their photo shoot and interviews with the puzzle solvers. It's the lead story according to my mother and will be featured on the front cover. If you plan on getting a haircut, nails done, facial or any sort of beauty treatment, you're out of luck. Those businesses are jammed."

"Hmm, that would be a good time to be a fly on the wall." Then Marshall looked at me and I could see the smile creases in the corners of his eyes.

Rats! I know what's coming.

"In those situations, people tend to let their guard down. Not a doubt in my mind or Nate's that Samantha's killer is no stranger to the library."

"Shh!! My mother and the book club ladies are already nervous wrecks. Plus, they have the added concern that a heavily perfumed raving maniac may be on the loose."

Marshall shook his head and laughed at the same time. "They always have that concern. Like the time Cecilia was certain someone was trying to break down her front door. It turned out to be that gnome decoration on her door that the wind kept banging around."

"I suppose you and Nate will want me to drop by that event on Wednesday."

"Your presence won't raise as many eyebrows as ours. Or worse yet, Bowman and Ranston's."

"Are you serious? Don't tell me they planned to go to the library for the *Senior Living* photo shoot."

"You gals didn't hear it from me, but Ranston actually got his dress uniform pressed."

"Oh, brother." Augusta looked at me and I rolled my eyes.

"Fine, I'll go. I mean, how bad could it get?"

And then, the room went silent. Two days later, I knew why.

• • •

At a little past four a.m. on Wednesday, I found myself wide awake. My brain conjured up all sorts of miserable library scenarios, each one more horrific than the one before. Sadly, they didn't come close.

When I got to the library at seven thirty, a half hour before it was to open for the magazine people, I was astonished to see vans from all of the local TV stations, plus our own KCSW radio station manager and his news crew. And that was the least of it. Parking was a veritable nightmare. Every single spot appeared to have been taken.

At least it was early in the day so the long walk from the Men's Club to the library wasn't as bad as it would be a few hours from then, when the temperature was expected to hit 105 degrees.

So much for the parking. The line of residents and visitors waiting to get into the library was worse than the ones I remembered from Disney World. I snapped a quick photo and texted it to Nate, Marshall and Augusta with the following remark: *Why do I feel like I'm about to enter the Roman games?*

As I got closer to the entrance, I spied my mother. It was the new hair color that caught my attention and I immediately zeroed in to make sure she didn't tote the dog along with her. I heaved the proverbial sigh of relief and walked over to where she and Shirley stood.

"It's already ungodly hot," my mother said. "That's why I had to leave my little man at home."

"Good choice. I can't believe there are so many people waiting to get inside." Just then, the manager from KSCW made a beeline for my mother. Husky with wavy brown hair, the man looked to be in his early sixties.

"Harriet," he called out. "I've been keeping an eye out for you and Myrna. I already chatted with Paul. He got here right from his crack-of-dawn fishing and is in the library."

"How'd he avoid the line?" my mother asked.

"Same way you will. The feature editor at *Senior Living* agreed to have his staff interviewed by someone at our station and—"

"Don't tell me! We're going to interview their staff for a special mystery and fishing program?"

The man nodded. "You summed it up in a nutshell. You, Myrna, and Paul."

"Do you hear that, Shirley?" My mother elbowed Shirley and then turned to the people in line behind her. "We're going to interview the folks from *Senior Living*!"

I smiled at the station manager and politely asked, "When?"

"First thing tomorrow morning." Then he looked at my mom. "Be at the station at seven. Let Myrna know, will you? In case I don't see her prior."

Or hear her.

"You'll need to confer with them before they start taking pictures and talking to everyone in sight. The librarian said she'd let you in. Come on, I'll walk all of you right to the door."

"Lordy, this is unbelievable. I bet Herb will be kicking himself in the pants for not getting here early." Shirley was inches behind my mother and I struggled to keep up. Three or four yards from the door, we heard Myrna's unmistakable voice.

"Harriet! Shirley! Phee! Robert! Wait for me! Wait for me!"

I whispered to Shirley, "Must be the manager's name is Robert. Guess he's not great at introductions."

"It's a lost skill, sweetie."

Darcey, who let us inside, looked relieved. Paul had her cornered by a table that displayed at least two dozen of his eight-by-ten photos of the fish he'd recently caught.

"I have the staff from *Senior Living* in our conference room," she said. "There are plenty of bagels and donuts to go around. Also, lots of coffee. They wanted to chat with the hosts of your radio program before we have them meet with the puzzle regulars. Then, the general attendees can greet them in the large reading room. From what I understand, they'll have lots of questions about the puzzle process while their photographer takes pictures of the puzzle in progress and the seniors in our community who keep this tradition going."

"Um, have you seen that line out front?" I asked Darcey.

She grimaced. "And how. We'll usher everyone to the reading area and tell the regulars to go into the conference room once the radio station staff finishes."

I nudged my mother. "That means you can't take all day, Mom. And don't show them Streetman's photos. Or worse yet, Essie's. I'll wait out here in the entryway with Shirley while you, Myrna and Paul chitchat with the folks you'll be interviewing tomorrow."

"Let's go into the conference room, folks," Robert announced. "I have another meeting in twenty minutes."

Darcey gathered up Paul's photos like a blackjack dealer in Vegas. "Don't want you to forget these," she said.

Paul took them and scurried after us. "Remind me to show you and Myrna these," he called out to my mother. Thankfully, Shirley and I had moved further away.

Once my mother, Myrna and Paul were inside the conference room, Shirley and I sat near the giant puzzle.

"Is it my imagination," she asked, "or are those ants crawling all over the puzzle pieces?"

"Oh my gosh! They are! Tiny ones, but definitely ants. I don't see any food or anything that would attract them. Then again, syrupy stuff may not be easily noticeable. Like that glue."

"Darcey!" Shirley shouted. "Darcey! Lordy, take a look at this!"

Darcey rushed over and leaned against the giant table. "Oh, no. That's why we don't encourage food in the library. It's most likely cookie crumbs that those ants already devoured. Hold on! I've got a can of Raid in my office and one of those computer vacs."

Shirley and I looked at each other, speechless at first, until she asked, "Do you think those cookie crumbs or whatever it was were left there on purpose?"

"Aargh. I hope not. If so, someone's bound and determined to stop this puzzle no matter what."

A minute later, Darcey emerged from her office, bug spray in hand. She aimed the nozzle and didn't quit until all movement from the ants ceased. Then, like an experienced computer tech, she aimed the special vacuum, and within seconds blew the dead insects off the table and onto the floor where they wouldn't be noticed.

"It's going to take a lot more than some mischievous ants to get the Sun City West Library to stop the completion of our giant puzzle," she asserted. "Not after all of this!"

The second she said that, I knew, without a doubt, it was an open invitation for disaster to strike.

CHAPTER 31

"I'll run the vacuum, just to play it safe," Darcey said. "We have an old Dyson in the closet."

As she walked off, Shirley bent down and picked up a small piece of paper. "Might as well start with this." She started to ball it up when, "Lordy, Phee! It's an open sugar packet. Sugar! Crumbs, my patootie. Someone did this on purpose. Who opens a sugar packet in a place where drinks aren't allowed?"

"Someone who wants to invite ants to the party. And foil this event."

"Not on my watch. Shh! Here they come—your mother, Myrna, Paul and the staff from *Senior Living*. Will you look at their faces? They look bewildered. And that photographer is holding on to his camera as if it was Pandora's box."

Darcey immediately ran the vacuum cleaner and then called out, "Thank you, everyone. As you can see, this is our giant puzzle in progress. We expect to have it completed before August. I've asked our regulars to seat themselves around the table and chat with you. Then, we'll open things up to the public. Feel free to move about for a closer look."

The photographer took a few shots and then said, "I'll need to return for a photograph of the completed project. Meanwhile, this will be ample for the layout and design, along with snapshots of the participants." At which point, my mother added, "And a lovely photo of the KSCW radio show hosts would naturally be in order."

When no one was looking, I gave her the eye and ran my thumb across my neck. As the magazine staff circulated around the puzzle, Darcey ushered the regulars to the table. I heard her announce to the public that they, too, could enter, but must proceed directly to the larger reading area in the back.

LaVonda was the first to make her way to the table, followed by Carl and the Bellowses. Then, Lettie and Keenan joined them. Seconds later, Celeste and Betty-Jean raced to get seated as if it was a game of musical chairs.

"What happened to the Mickey Mouse section we substituted?" Norva asked. "I'm staring at a rather large empty space."

LaVonda motioned her forward and kept her voice low. "Lettie and I thought it would look ridiculous. If they ask, we'll tell them we work in sections. Lettie put the Mickey Mouse pieces back in their original box."

Shirley took a seat next to my mother and was joined by Gloria, Cecilia, and Herb. Opposite them were Myrna and Paul, who appeared to be shaking their heads at each other. The other regulars were scattered about the table, eyeballing the empty space and muttering to one another.

"Everyone," Darcey said, "please welcome the feature editor and writers who will be chatting with you today. I'll let them introduce themselves. Also, their photographer, Ray."

I tried not to laugh when I watched a few of the women sneak quick looks at their pocket mirrors and cell phone cameras.

A fortyish woman with white streaks in her dark hair looked up from her iPad and said, "We've gotten the history on the puzzle process as well as this puzzle in particular. What we're looking for now are those unique anecdotes regarding the process for putting this gigantic piece together."

"Don't you want to hear about our backgrounds first?" Carl asked.

The woman's eyes popped wide open as she shook her head. "No. This is not a memoir piece or biography." At that point, Herb nudged my mother. "Or an obituary."

"Not even Samantha's?" LaVonda asked.

"Who?" the woman asked.

"Samantha. Our committee co-chair who was murdered in the puzzle room. Didn't they tell you? It was all over the news."

The woman's face turned ashen and she looked at the other two writers, who shook their heads.

"News to us, Becky. And the New York office never said a word."

At that point, Darcey interjected and tried her best to do damage control. After a solid ten minutes of her explaining about the investigation, Becky turned to her writers and declared, "This story just got a whole lot more interesting."

I rubbed my temples and closed my eyes for two or three seconds while I awaited the catastrophe that would surely follow.

Then Drake cleared his throat as if he was about to deliver the Declaration of Independence, but instead, delivered his own proclamation— "I believe we should speak about the process. Let me begin." And with that, a mind-numbing two minutes followed as Drake explained how the pieces are initially arranged, how puzzle workers "troll" for pieces that wound up in other sections, and how color and shape determined the individual preferences for completion.

When he was done, Becky looked at the other writers and said, "When we meet with the general attendees in a few minutes, we'll move about the room speaking with individuals. Pull out as much information as you can about that murder as it pertains to the puzzle. Imagine—the seniors in this community have a real puzzle to contend with as well as the forty-two thousand pieces that're sitting right in front of us!"

I gulped and clenched my hands. At least the next few questions coming from the other two writers dealt with the actual puzzle and not the one that spelled *murder.* Finally, Becky thanked everyone and asked Darcey to escort her crew to the large reading area. I was relieved Paul didn't provide a discourse on fishing or worse yet, sharing one of his techniques for gutting a trout. But in retrospect, that would have been better. Much better.

As the photographer leaned over for a close-up of one of the sections, he asked, "Why are some of these pieces chewed up, as if some animal had gotten to them?"

I glared at my mother, who feigned total innocence before the biggest fib left her lips. "That puzzle is old. Wood dries out. Moisture gets in. It tends to chip and crack."

In what scientific world can wood be dry and moist at the same time?

"Why then are some pieces without color?"

Because that's what happens when you use nail polish remover to get rid of glue.

"Age and lots of handling," she said. Then, she mimicked Augusta and fluffed her champagne-colored hair. Her move didn't go without notice and the photographer snapped a photo of her with a puzzle piece in her hand.

"Let's move to the reading room, shall we?" Darcey said. "The attendees are anxious to chat with *Senior Living.*"

As anxious as I was to leave, I feared some new horror would unfold in the next phase of this *Senior Living* "meet and greet." Not willing to take a chance, I followed the crowd into the large reading area. My mother and her entourage were already a few feet ahead of me, because, heaven forbid, she should miss something. Behind me, I could hear Keenan and Celeste talking, but the noise level made it impossible to discern what they were saying.

"Our crowd is much larger than we anticipated," Darcey said as she held the door open for the magazine crew to enter the large reading area. "We'll have to engage this first group for about a half hour and then have them exit so another group can enter. I believe we'll be able to accommodate everyone in two groups."

Terrific. I'll never get out of here.

Unlike the roundtable chitchat, this was more of a cocktail party without the drinks or hors d'oeuvres. I milled around, catching tidbits of conversation that got me nowhere. Then, Herb tapped my shoulder and leaned over. "I know what you're up to, cutie. You're gathering intel for your husband and your boss. Good thinking. Don't waste your time on the mindless chatter. Get names. Who's in the buzz? See if you can find out why. I haven't read all those Robert B. Parker books for nothing."

"I can't walk around with a pad and pencil."

"Make like you're sending yourself a text message and write the names. Kill two birds with one stone. Gee, I should be working for your office."

"Wow. That's a good idea. About the names. Not working for our office. Enjoy your retirement."

"Herb!" Bill shouted. "I've been looking all over for you. Wayne called from the woodshop. The guys are meeting for some brewskis."

"Gotta go, cutie. Good Luck."

As Herb sauntered out, I took his advice and kept my ears open for names. It was unbelievable—the guy was right. Lettie's name came up at least a half dozen times, but that was to be expected. She was, after all, one of the puzzle committee chairs and a fixture in the library. But Keenan's name came up as well and that *did* surprise me. He was new to the area and not that well known. LaVonda and Betty-Jean got a few hits, but other than that, nothing.

I figured maybe I'd glean more with the second shift, so I held back and waited.

"No sense sticking around," my mother said, catching me off guard as I stared into my phone. "Lettie's been a royal pain in the rump, and don't get me started on Celeste. She all but told one of the writers that she thought the puzzle was cursed, but luckily, Carl scooted her away on some pretense."

I didn't want to tell my mother that I planned to stick around for fear she'd read more into it and go off the rails with a new rumor or two. So, I walked out with her, got into my car, drove to Starbucks for an iced coffee and hightailed it back. By then, the parking lot had cleared up a bit and I was able to nab a decent spot and work my way back into the library.

Other than Lettie and LaVonda, who stood like sentries near the puzzle, the crowd had changed to one I didn't recognize. Still, I took Herb's advice and circulated around the reading room, ears at the ready for names and anything out of the ordinary.

The magazine writers made their rounds as well, iPads poised in their hands, while Ray, their photographer, snapped a few shots of the seniors. Again, the same two names came up—Lettie's and Keenan's. No mention of any others, but it wasn't as if I caught every conversation.

As I was about to head back to the office, two men walked past me and I couldn't help but hear, "It was family business gone bad. Too bad they can't catch the stooge who took her out."

"Took her out?" As in murder? Or on a date?

Thanks to Lyndy, I used the same trick we did in the ballpark a while back. I took out my phone and pretended to take a selfie while photographing the men. There was not a single doubt in my mind one of those book club ladies or pinochle men would know who they were. Cecilia referred to it as "that small-town feel," but Augusta put it much more bluntly—"You can't pass gas there without somebody knowing!"

CHAPTER 32

"How was your undercover surveillance?" Augusta asked the second I walked inside the air-conditioned office. I made a beeline for the fridge, nabbed a Coke and rolled my eyes. "Like being in one of those surrealistic paintings. You know what everything is supposed to be, but no matter how hard you try to make sense of it, you can't."

"That bad?"

"Bad enough. Although I should have anticipated it."

"The chaos?"

"Nope. The loose lips. One of the women just couldn't wait to announce Samantha's murder, and that spun the magazine crew into an entirely different direction for a few tense minutes."

Augusta pushed her chair back and stretched. "Then what?"

"Thankfully Drake Bellows decided to give a discourse on puzzle strategies. Remind me to call him if I ever get insomnia." I took a long gulp of my Coke and started for my office.

"Hold on, Phee. Our office picked up another case. Thought you'd like to know."

"Not another murder?"

"No, vandalism. Although it may turn out to be industrial sabotage. And you'll never guess where."

Before I could utter a syllable, Augusta went on. "In Sun City. At Sunny Skies Mortuary on Del Webb Boulevard. Their insurance company contacted us. Mr. Williams and Mr. Gregory are there now."

"Sunny Skies? That's the mortuary Sherman mentioned. You know, the guy from Sun City who was in their puzzle club. He had all those pictures. In fact, Nate went to the mortuary the day before yesterday to track down Henry Longmire from the club. He was hoping Henry knew the whereabouts of Tisha Stoad. He didn't mention anything about vandalism."

"Because it happened last night."

"What kind of vandalism?"

"Hang on, I'll get to it." Augusta fluffed her hair and then patted it down. "The mortuary is expanding its outdoor mausoleum. According to Mr. Williams, the construction is in the rear of a rather large building. Anyway, the project required excavation, and well, someone put a halt to that by tampering with the equipment. And we're talking major machinery. That's why the insurance company contacted us."

"What about video surveillance?"

"Not in the rear of the building. Funeral homes and mortuaries aren't exactly big retail stores, although the cost of some of those coffins can be more than a new snazzy SUV. At least the funeral parlor had video cameras at the front entrance. I'm sure it's one of the first things our guys are looking at. Oh—I almost forgot—did I mention Mr. Williams was able to track down Henry Longmire? Apparently his son works at the mortuary but Henry is in a care facility in Sun City. Advanced neuropathy. Remind me not to get old."

"Does Nate plan on seeing him soon?"

"He *was* planning on today until he got the call about the vandalism. Too bad it's the older Mr. Longmire and not the kid. Otherwise Mr. Williams could have killed two birds with one stone."

"He may not have to."

"What do you mean?"

"At eight a.m. tomorrow, Sun City West and surrounding areas will be graced by a special KSCW radio show hosted by my mother, Myrna and Paul. They have to be at the Men's Club station at seven."

"A new murder mystery and fishing hour?"

"More like an acid indigestion and migraine hour. They were approached by the station manager to interview the writers from *Senior Living*."

Augusta's grin rivaled the Cheshire cat's. "I'll pick up donuts and get here early. I don't want to miss this baby."

"I do. If I'm lucky, the thought of it won't keep me up all night."

"Do they have a running agenda for the program?"

"Are you kidding? All they run are their mouths. I'm just keeping my fingers crossed they don't mess up Samantha's murder investigation."

• • •

And while I tossed and turned all night for fear that one of those three would drop a bombshell on the air in a few hours, Marshall slept through the night and was up by five and eager to get going.

"We've got way too many loose ends, hon. I'll be meeting with Ranston first thing while Nate heads back to the mortuary to review video footage again. MCSO dusted for prints on the machinery, but my take is that whoever did this was savvy enough to wear gloves. And when I say whoever, I mean more than one person."

"What exactly did they do?"

"Cut fuel lines to the backhoe loaders and excavators. Used some sort of tire iron, or the like, to smash the glass on more than one of the medium-size bulldozers and slashed the tires on the concrete mixer that was off to the side."

"A disgruntled employee from the construction company?"

Marshall shrugged. "Could be, but doubtful. According to the owner of that company, the workers have a decent contract and there haven't been any issues. No one let go. Nothing of the sort. Still, we're checking it out."

I sighed. "I suppose that leaves the mortuary staff, huh?"

He nodded. "Yep. We're afraid it does. Hey, you don't have to be up this early. I can make a cup of coffee and head out. Go back to bed for an hour or so."

"If only. At exactly eight o'clock, my mother, Myrna and Paul will be interviewing the writers from *Senior Living*. Augusta is already camping out at the office, I'm sure."

"Oh, gosh. With all that's going on, I forgot you mentioned it yesterday. Maybe they'll be a bit more circumspect with their guests on the air." Then he looked at me and grimaced. "Pray this doesn't morph into something else that will land on our plates."

"Trust me. It will."

An hour and a half later, I walked into Williams Investigations to find Augusta at her desk, donut in hand. "Thought I'd get an early start. We need to turn on the radio at seven forty-five so we don't miss anything. Help yourself. Got an assortment of donuts."

"Thanks. I take it there are no scheduled morning clients."

"Not until this afternoon. Grab a coffee and buckle your seat belt."

Buckle my seat belt? More like put on a crash helmet.

Since there was no one in the outer office, Augusta asked our Alexa to turn to KSCW in Sun City West. "We should get another Alexa for the workroom," she said. "Much better than that antique radio. I'll mention it to Mr. Williams. At least we've got one out here."

A few minutes later, I heard my mother's familiar voice.

"Good morning, Sun City West and friends! We are your hosts, Harriet Plunkett, Myrna Mittleson and Paul Schmidt from our mystery and fishing shows. But today, we have a totally different program in store for you. We're interviewing the writing staff from *Senior Living*, who are here today to discuss their feature story on our library's giant puzzle. Not many communities can boast a puzzle of that magnitude."

"Or a murder to go along with it," Paul blurted out. Then someone must have shot him a look because he quickly added, "What? Don't tell me I wasn't supposed to mention that."

"You weren't, Paul." It was Myrna's voice and already my coffee curdled in my stomach.

"Moving along," my mother said, "allow me to introduce Becky, the feature editor, as well as writers Tina and Delphinia."

"Thank you, everyone. Our magazine is ecstatic about this project. As

Harriet mentioned, not many communities offer such intriguing activities."

"Other than the puzzle itself," Myrna asked, "what do you intend to showcase?"

Oh, no. A wide-open question.

"I would be remiss to not mention the murder. After all, the unfortunate victim was one of the committee chairs if I'm not mistaken."

"Yes, well, all of that considered, what else will you focus on?"

"We'd like to get a sense of the people who take part in that activity. Is it a respite for boredom? A mental challenge? An opportunity to socialize? Or maybe even a means to get into an air-conditioned building."

"Will you be able to do that?" This time it was my mother's voice.

"Hi! This is Tina, and yes. We had a wonderful chat with so many interesting folks last night. The notes section on my phone is overflowing.'"

"Was there anything that stood out?" Again, my mother.

"She means other than that murder." Ugh. It was Paul. *Can't he keep his mouth shut?*

"Interesting you should ask that, Mr. Schmidt. Last evening at our hotel, our photographer, Ray, brought up a rather startling idea. Do you, or anyone working on the puzzle, believe the murder was somehow related to that puzzle?"

And there it was. The proverbial elephant in the room that no one wanted to touch. Although Paul was doing a darn good job of feeding it peanuts.

"Hmm," my mother said. "That could explain the sabotage."

"What sabotage?" Becky asked.

The investigation, Mother! You're about to sabotage the investigation.

I reached for my cell phone and phoned the on-air line, hoping someone would pick up.

"Good thinking, Phee!" Augusta called out, just as a recording came on.

"Hello, you've reached KSCW's open-line but we are not taking calls at this time. Please enjoy our programming and listen for the next open-air mic time."

"Don't get in a tizzy, Phee. All they'll yammer about is the puzzle sabotage. That is, if Paul can keep his mouth shut about Samantha."

Fat chance.

I swallowed a mouthful of coffee and held still as my mother's voice permeated the airwaves.

"The puzzle process was fraught with obstacles from the very beginning. There was some discontent about the original choices and we wound up having to borrow a puzzle from Sun City's library on Bell Road.

As you know, the puzzle is twenty-three years old and features an actual photograph of one of their streets."

"Is that usual? An actual photo instead of a painting or graphic?" Becky asked.

"We found out the photo was a contest winner and that's how it was selected to be their puzzle."

"And now we're stuck with that monster," Paul blurted out. "If they wanted photos, I could have offered some terrific ones of the largemouth bass from Roosevelt Lake or the—"

"Enough with the fish." The annoyance in Myrna's voice couldn't be missed. "If we wanted a fish puzzle, I'm sure there's a Ravensburger out there somewhere with a fish theme."

"If you don't mind," Delphinia said, "I'd like to piggyback on what my editor asked. About Samantha's murder being related to the puzzle. Is that a possibility? Maybe anger issues over the puzzle choice? We could do a spinoff article on that alone."

No. No spinoff. The only thing I want to see off is this program.

Then my mother again. "There weren't any anger issues, were there, Myrna?"

"No. Just a bunch of upset people because natural and manmade disasters got in the way."

Delphinia's voice rose an octave. "What kind of disasters?"

"Oh, the usual. An earthquake that resulted in puzzle pieces being strewn all over, and a plumbing issue where the sprinklers got the pieces wet."

Suddenly, it was as if my mother remembered that they were supposed to be interviewing the writers and not the other way around.

"I have a question for you," she said. "Have you come up with the story title for the cover of the magazine?"

"Indeed we have—'Sun City West's Puzzle Pieces Spell Murder.' And speaking of which, rumor has it that the identification of the killer rests on the perfume or cologne he or she wore."

CHAPTER 33

"It could have been worse, Phee," Augusta said when the show ended. "Then again, we have no idea what they'll write in that article."

"How'd they find out about the perfume? Or the fact our office was working on that part of the investigation? Unless Lettie opened her big mouth. Or Betty-Jean. Or LaVonda. Maybe even Celeste. They were all questioned about it. I'll tell you one thing—it may have compromised the investigation."

"Or . . ." Augusta smiled. "It might have kicked it wide open."

Sure enough, Augusta was right. In the hour that followed KSCW's radio disaster, our office received three anonymous phone calls, one of which came from someone who claimed to be a volunteer at the library, regarding the perfume said to be on Samantha's clothing. And all of them said the same thing—a few weeks before Samantha's demise, a guest author distributed mini swag bottles of parfum to attendees, complete with her author logo.

I remembered my aunt Ina explaining that while the contents of a particular perfume were the same as the parfum, the concentration was different. It was much higher in perfume than the less costly parfum.

At a little before one, when we expected the men to breeze in for appointments, Augusta and I tried Bento boxes from the convenience mart. We continued our conversation about the radio show and the mini parfums.

"That's an easy 'grab and spray,'" she said. "Samantha's killer could have held one of those mini containers in the palm of one hand and the staple gun in the other."

"Oh my gosh. Those small cylinders always slip out of our hands. And roll! They roll over all. Lipstick. Eyeliner. Concealer. Oh my gosh!"

"What are you saying, Phee?"

"When those things roll, it's all but impossible to find them. They get wedged under furniture or wind up in closet crevices. I doubt the forensics crew looked for that kind of evidence once they determined it was a staple gun that dealt the death blow. Oh my gosh. I need to get to the Sun City West Library."

Without waiting for Augusta to respond, I raced back to my office, grabbed my bag and shot off for Sun City West. It was a hunch, but it was the best one I'd had in a long time.

A few puzzle workers were bent over the large table when I walked inside but I only recognized Lettie, Carl and Keenan. I imagined my mother and her crew would be back in the morning and that was just as well. I didn't need the drama with her there.

"I need to see Darcey," I told the staff worker at the counter. "It's important."

"Hold on. I'll get her."

The white-haired lady stepped away from the counter and rapped on Darcey's office door. Seconds later, she approached me and I explained my urgent need to get inside the puzzle storage room.

"Are you sure you'll find evidence in there? It's not as if the room hasn't been sifted through by the forensic crew and our own cleaners."

"I wouldn't have left work if I didn't think I'd find something. And if you're wondering why I didn't mention anything sooner, it's because I didn't know what I'd be looking for."

Darcey furrowed her brow. "Okay. I'll humor you. It can't hurt."

She unlocked the room and switched on the light.

"Do me a favor," I said. "Video this so that if I *do* find something, there will be ironclad credibility."

I handed her my phone and closed the door behind me. Then I walked to where I remembered the body had been found. The room looked the same as it did the last time I was in here. Floor-to-near-ceiling wooden shelving on the perimeter as well as stand-alone shelves for all-sized puzzle boxes, including the giant ones.

I retrieved a mini flashlight from my bag, compliments of my mother's HVAC company, and studied the bottoms of the shelves.

"See the edges on the bottom of those shelves?" I asked Darcey. "All sorts of things get wedged in there and it's impossible to vacuum there or even use a Swiffer because the opening is too small. And usually most people ignore what may be stuck there, unless it's really important. Like a ring or earring. Most of us wait until we move and then are astonished at what we find."

"Don't tell me you plan on getting down on your hands and knees."

I turned and saw the shocked look on her face. "No worries. I can get back up. And I'm wearing capris so my knees are covered." *They'll be filthy, but if I find what I'm looking for, it will be worth doing the laundry tonight.*

It was impossible to determine the position Samantha was in when her attacker caught her by surprise, so if the attacker dropped the mini parfum, or even the cap to it, I had no way of knowing where it would wind up. Therefore, I decided to systematically check all of the puzzle shelves, starting with the closest ones.

In retrospect, I should have known better. Items always wind up as far away as possible from where we think they should be. After giving my back more exercise than a workout tape, I came up short as far as the stand-alone shelving was concerned. Well, not exactly short. I did find a roll of

Scotch tape and a petrified half-eaten chocolate bar. Ew! Not to mention a few dust bunnies and some paper clips.

"I might as well start on the wall shelving," I announced as I dusted off my capris and glanced to my right. Two shelves took up all the wall space. Same deal on the other three sides of the room. At least I'd get my daily exercise in.

Like the stand-alone shelves, these didn't offer up a prize either. Unless I could get points for uncovering two quarters and more dust bunnies.

"I'm still videoing," Darcey said. "If you want to show this, you'll have to Airdrop it, it's going to be too long for regular email or texting."

"That's okay. It won't matter unless I find what I'm looking for."

"You never did say what it is you were looking for."

"A mini parfum spray canister or whatever you call them. You know, purse size. With a logo."

"You mean a name brand? Like Chanel?"

"Um, it could be Chanel, but it would have an author's logo. It was a swag gift."

"Oh my gosh—from Libby Klein. She handed those out during a book talk a few months ago. She writes funny cozy mysteries. I'm sure your mother's book club is familiar with them. But what does that have to do with Samantha's murder? You don't think Libby Klein did it, do you?"

"What? Of course not." Good grief. The librarian was as bad as the book club ladies.

I took a breath and scooched underneath the next shelf. This one was opposite from the door and it seemed a likely place for something to roll. Too bad it wasn't. That left three more shelves, and my options were running out.

I bent down and moved to the bottom of the next shelf. The food-handler gloves I had on were getting dirtier by the minute and I didn't have another pair with me. Yeesh. Our office bought them by the crate, but they weren't an item I used on a daily basis, unlike Nate and Marshall, who always seemed to uncover evidence.

The floor was dustier back against the wall and I envisioned my arms picking up every bit of grime. I flinched as I moved my left hand to the rear of the shelving. Nothing. Then I moved it forward to the cubby where misplaced items seemed to find a home. And that's when I felt the rounded edges of something with a circular opening. Wasting no time, I picked up the bright pink top to a parfum sprayer. "This is it!" I shouted. "It says 'Poppy McAllister Mysteries,' and if I'm not mistaken, it was used to commit a murder in here."

CHAPTER 34

To be sure I hadn't missed the actual contents of the parfum cylinder, I literally scoured the bottoms of the remaining shelving. Nothing. Still, I managed to unearth a valuable clue and no one was more surprised than me.

"I take it you found what you were looking for?" Darcey asked.

I held the cap up and smiled into the cell phone camera. "You can turn off the recording. I need to get this to the sheriff's office right away. You wouldn't happen to have a clean Ziploc bag or anything?"

"We've got a box of sandwich bags. Hang on."

Five minutes later, I was in my car and texting Nate, Marshall, Augusta, Bowman and Ranston on the same thread.

Augusta was the first to text back. *I'm printing out an application from the county for an investigator's license for you.*

I text her back a yellow emoji face with its tongue sticking out.

Instead of driving to the posse office, I went directly to the sheriff's office on Bell Road in Surprise. Luckily, Deputy Bowman had just pulled in and I rushed toward him in the parking lot.

"Wait! Did you get my text?" I shouted.

"Yes. I take it you didn't read mine. I sent a deputy to your office to secure the evidence, or clue, or whatever you found."

"Sorry I missed the text. I was driving."

"Walk with me to the office. My clothes are beginning to stick from this humidity. So much for dry heat. Monsoon season keeps coming earlier each summer."

As we walked into the building, I gave him the rundown about my parfum epiphany and the actual process for finding the cap to the spray bottle. "I even had the librarian video the search so that if it did come up in the courts, they'd know it wasn't fabricated."

"We're not at that point in time, Mrs. Kimball. Gregory. The lab will need to conduct an analysis and compare the scent with what was found on the clothing."

"When they do, and it does, we'll be one step ahead."

Bowman wiped the back of his neck with a bandana and crinkled his nose. By now we were inside the main entrance and walking toward his private office. "Explain what you mean about 'one step ahead.'"

"Oh, that. Here goes. The cap to the parfum spray, and it's parfum, not perfume, I'm sure, because parfum is cheaper." *Oh good grief. I'm off on a tangent like my mother.* "Um, anyway, the spray bottle was a swag giveaway from a cozy mystery author. You know, a promotional item. The lettering on it was from a Libby Klein mystery."

"And?"

"It was from a library event. The library keeps track of all the attendees with their names, emails, and rec center card numbers. So, whoever was in attendance was on that list. One of them had to be the killer. And here's the good news—I asked the librarian to email your office and Williams Investigations a copy of that list from the event. You can compare and contrast. Or whatever it is you do best."

When I finished speaking, it was as if my mouth had to recuperate from dental surgery.

"I do best with the evidence in hand."

"Oh my gosh. Here it is." I opened my bag and handed him the sandwich bag with the cap inside. "Don't worry. I used food handler gloves and the sandwich bag came right out of the box. I've been well-trained."

Bowman laughed. "More than I can say for your mother's dog."

"More than anyone can say."

"Thanks. But next time, please inform our office. What you did was fairly safe, but you never know in any of these situations. Do me a favor and let your office know we'll be processing this ASAP."

"Shall do."

"By the way, I missed your mother's radio show interview with *Senior Living*. Ranston caught it and texted me a series of those little hieroglyphics screaming their heads off. Couldn't figure out what he meant but I got the gist of it."

I bit my lower lip. "Trust me. It's just as well."

• • •

"I'll be darned," Augusta said when I walked into the office with club sandwiches from the deli. "If it isn't Jessica Fletcher bearing gifts."

"Enjoy! I'm starving." I unwrapped my sandwich, leaned against the counter and took a bite. "I know. I know. Not very professional, but we're the only ones here."

"For now. It's going to be a busy afternoon with clients."

"I intend to bury myself in spreadsheets."

"Bury, huh? That seems to be the word of the day. "

"What do you mean?"

"Mr. Williams called to let me know he'll be running late. A new snafu. The owner of the mortuary told him that he thought maybe the vandals believed something of value was hidden under the ground where the new project excavation is. He also mentioned that it was a few yards from where a prior building project took place two decades ago."

"Two decades? As in the time that puzzle photo was taken?"

"Yep."

"Sounds too Hardy Boys for me. What on earth gave the owner that idea? Disgruntled employees or customers are more likely to do a thing like that."

"Good question. You and Mr. Williams think alike. Back when the project was going on, a number of Phoenix jewelry stores were robbed and the goods were never found. The owner put two and two together and came up with six."

"Oh, brother."

"Mr. Williams said the same thing. But the excavation will continue as planned. All it means is if they uncover something out of the ordinary, the workers are to notify the owner, who in turn will call the sheriff's office."

Who in turn will call ours.

"I see."

"Meanwhile, Mr. Williams wanted to stick around longer while the excavation is going on. The insurance company sent their adjuster and the mortuary got the all-clear to restart the work. They've already secured another backhoe loader and excavator. Between you and me, it's men and their toys. They love to see heavy equipment move stuff around. Mr. Williams is no exception. If he wanted to see that, he could watch my aunt Tessa around the cows. She was voted strongest woman in Oakfield, Wisconsin, back in the seventies."

"Uh, very interesting. Well, back to work I go."

I grabbed a Coke and raced to my office before Augusta had a chance to regale me with her family history. With my computer refreshed and my workload on the screen, I leaned back for the steady computations and analysis. Very orderly, very sequential, and very familiar. I was so engaged that I didn't hear Nate or Marshall when they got back to the office for their appointments. But Augusta's voice was hard to miss. Especially when it was right outside my door.

"The email from the library that you were expecting just arrived." A second later, she swung the door open and handed me a sheet of paper. "Other than some of the book club ladies, I don't recognize any of the names on the list. Well, other than a few of the book club ladies and your mother."

"Thanks. Did you read the note on the bottom? Darcey said there were thirty-four attendees and that she was going to cross-reference the names with the daily lists they keep for people who work on the puzzle. Said we should have it in the next hour or so."

"I haven't met the woman, but I like her already. She's saved us a bundle of time. When we get everything all together, I'll put it on Mr. Williams's and Mr. Gregory's desks. Meanwhile, they're both tied up with clients. All minor cases according to my intake notes."

"That's a relief. Our plate is about to spill over."

I'm rarely prophetic but when I said "spill over," I should have said "bubble over." Or maybe even "Explode."

• • •

At a little after four, Darcey emailed us the cross-referenced list. I immediately highlighted the book club ladies and my mother, as well as Celeste, LaVonda, Samantha, Lettie, Norva, and Betty-Jean. As for men, there were two—Herb and Keenan. I knew Herb would be at Libby's book talk because "It's a cheaper way to meet women than going to a bar."

Then, there were three crossover names that weren't puzzle regulars but who had been to both events. All of them women.

"From the looks of things, there are really nine people to focus on." I counted the names again to be sure. "Samantha may have been at Libby's talk, but we certainly can't very well hold a séance." *Unless my aunt Ina has been to one of her bat-crazy spiritualist seminars.* "And our office has already exhausted Celeste, Lettie, Norva, Betty-Jean, and LaVonda. But Keenan is somewhat of an enigma. That's for sure."

"What about the three newcomers?" Augusta asked.

"I'll ask Darcey if they came as one-shot deals for the puzzle or if they were return workers. One of them could have had business with Samantha. Personal or otherwise."

"Good idea."

I meandered back to my office and worked for another half hour or so when Augusta burst through the door.

"You won't be making dinner tonight!" she announced. "None of us are."

"Huh? What are you talking about?'

"Ranston just called. He and Bowman are on their way over to the mortuary and—"

Just then, Marshall charged into my office. "Hi, hon. Nate and I are headed to the mortuary. You won't believe this. The construction company resumed its digging and uncovered skeletal remains along with some skin and sinew." Then, like an excerpt from Wikipedia, he continued to expound on the grim discovery.

"The teeth were intact so we may be able to match up dental records with any missing persons. We don't know much more at this point. Being buried in a dry climate slows down the decomposition and we've got one thing in our favor—the body was discovered where the prior excavation took place. Therefore, we've got a rough date for the disposal, for lack of a better word."

Augusta crinkled her eyes at the word *disposal*, and Marshall continued speaking. "The time of death and the time the body was placed in the ground could have been hours, days, weeks, months and maybe even years if someone had a deep-freeze and waited for the right time to, well, you know . . ."

"I suppose this will be on tonight's news, huh?" I looked at Marshall.

"All they can say at this juncture in time is that the remains of a body were discovered and the investigation is in its infancy."

"Just goes to show you," Augusta said. "People are dying to get into those places."

I don't know who groaned louder, Marshall or me.

"At least it wasn't found in Sun City West." Augusta turned and started for the door. "Imagine the hoopla and drama if it was. My money's on a murder hit. Sounds more exciting than a poor homeless person who succumbed to the heat and fell into an excavation pit."

"Is someone paying you to write crime drama?" Marshall laughed.

"Nah. I just like to keep the excitement flowing."

"I like to keep it as far away from me as possible, but something tells me that's not about to happen." He winked.

"Not after this latest text from Bowman, Mr. Gregory. What does the upside-down emoji mean? The text says: *Stinkin' news crews are already lined up. Tell your detectives to get a move on.*"

I looked at my husband, then at Augusta. "You were right about one thing," I told her as she left my office. "I'm not cooking dinner tonight."

CHAPTER 35

Marshall stepped behind my desk and squeezed my shoulder. "Unless you want to watch forensic techs move about and Bowman get testy with the coroner, I suggest you grab takeout and enjoy a night swim with Lyndy. There's nothing much you can do at this time. A body found buried on the premises of a mortuary or funeral home involves a complicated set of protocols."

"What do you mean?"

"The authorities need to determine that the victim wasn't a client or customer who, for some reason, was dumped in that spot and not officially buried or cremated."

"You don't really think that's the case, do you?"

Marshall shook his head. "No, I don't. But we need to rule that out. Then the normal procedure—age of the deceased, identification of his or her body, or, in this case, the skeletal remains. Then, notification to next of kin, determination as to cause of death, decision regarding any evidence of foul play, that sort of thing."

"I imagine the office staff at Sunny Skies Mortuary will have their hands full sifting through the records."

"The approximate age of the victim needs to be determined first, then it will narrow down the time frame for business records. Keep in mind, depending upon the decay, it could take days or weeks for a determination to be made." Then he looked at me and chuckled.

"What? What's so funny?"

"Sorry, hon. I couldn't help but picture your mother and her friends coming up with all sorts of explanations."

"Shh! Don't let that thought cross your lips."

Meanwhile, I pictured some poor neophyte office worker going through employee and client records, but Marshall envisioned something else entirely. "The prospect of it being ruled an accidental death is—and I hate to say it—unlikely. I mean, who would be wandering around a construction site unless they had business there. And face it, if it was an area person who had gone missing, the deputies would have combed the area. Especially if it was an elderly or disabled person, not to mention a runaway."

"You're wagering on foul play?"

He nodded. "Putting all my chips on it."

"Guess it will be a long night for you. Make sure you grab something to eat. But don't worry. If you're hungry when you get home, we've got plenty of summer salads in the fridge."

"Enjoy them. I'll be fine." He leaned over, kissed my forehead and closed the door to my office when he left.

I knew that as soon as the five o'clock news aired on all of the networks, my mother would be reaching for the phone like a contestant for the buzzer on *Jeopardy!* With that in mind, I decided to take control of the situation and call her first.

"Phee!" Her voice was unusually shrill. "Is everything all right?"

"Fine. Everything's fine, but I wanted to let you know that a body was discovered on the grounds at the mortuary where Henry Longmire used to work. Henry was the handyman from the Sun City puzzle club in the photo Sherman showed you."

"The Puzzle Putters."

"Uh, yeah. Sun City Puzzle Putters."

"How awful. Did you want me to call Sherman to see if he might recognize who it is?"

"No! When I said *body*, I meant skeletal remains. Remains that had been there a while. A *long* while."

"Like how long?"

"I don't know, Mom. It was skeletal remains. I don't know how fast bodies decompose. That's what the forensic scientists are paid to figure out."

"At least it wasn't recent. Not like Samantha. We're still on edge that a killer is running loose."

Yeah. With a staple gun, no less.

"Tell me, Phee, how come no one noticed a skeleton laying around on the ground by the funeral parlor?"

"Okay, I need to backtrack. A skeleton was *not* laying around. It was remains. And they were unearthed during an excavation for a building expansion project. It wasn't as if someone stumbled over a corpse."

"Oh my gosh! You think this was related to Samantha's murder, don't you? That's why you called me."

"What? No! They were decades apart. Decades! And no one knows if the recent discovery was a victim of foul play."

"Of course it was a victim of foul play. People don't wind up in excavation sites out of the clear blue skies. I'm telling you, if those remains belong to someone in that Sun City Puzzle Putters, then this may very well turn out to be a serial killer."

"A serial killer? After two decades? I think you can cross that off your list. The reason I called you about the unfortunate discovery is because you're always bugging me about not letting you know these things. Well, now you know."

"Is that the only reason?"

"It's about to air on the news, and since the mortuary is in the neighborhood where that puzzle photo was taken, I wanted to be sure you had the facts straight before you phoned the book club ladies. And Herb."

"I don't always phone Herb. He has a tendency to gossip."

I swore, my eyes spun in their sockets. "Uh-huh."

"I take it Williams Investigations will be adding it to their homicide list."

"It hasn't been deemed a homicide." *Yet.* "And we don't have a homicide list. But yes, Nate and Marshall will be working the case along with Samantha's murder and that cold case from the sheriff's office. Remember? Arthur Stoad from Sun City."

"Of course I remember. His wife was in the Puzzle Putters. Even in that old photo, I could tell the woman needed a session of dermaplaning. Thank goodness the women in our family were born with light-colored hair. But still, who wants all that facial hair?"

Oh no. I've got to end this call before she moves on to body sculpting or worse.

"Uh, yeah. Light facial hair. Well, I've got things to do. Enjoy your evening."

"I'll be working on that puzzle tomorrow. Call me if you find out more. Especially if it involves Sun City West."

"Trust me. It won't."

When I finally ended the call, it was as if I had just testified as a star witness in a high-profile trial. I turned my attention back to the spreadsheet on my monitor and concentrated on something that made sense, unlike my mother's logic.

At a few minutes before five, I took Marshall's advice about swimming with Lyndy and texted her. The temps were in the hundreds and the humidity had started an unwelcome upward trend. The only solution as far as I was concerned was to immerse myself in water and stay there until Labor Day.

Seven-ish okay? she texted back.

I gave it a thumbs-up.

"Let's get out of here, Phee," Augusta shouted. "Before another body crops up."

I shut off the lights in my office and followed her to the front door. "What do you think the odds are that those remains will have something to do with that puzzle club in Sun City?"

"Null to zilch. Why?"

"I don't know. My mother put that stupid idea in my head and I can't get it out."

Augusta burst out laughing.

"What? What's so funny?"

"Wait until tomorrow when those book club ladies have had enough time to speculate. Meanwhile, it all rests with the coroner and the forensic lab. And let's hope they don't drop the ball on the first case. Too bad our guys will be stretched so thin. With that cross-reference list, they need to come on like Columbo and nag those people until one of them cracks."

"Holy cow, Augusta! Maybe I should get *you* an application for an investigator's license."

"Nah, I hear it's highly overrated."

CHAPTER 36

My sojourn in Nirvana with Lyndy ended when I walked into the laundry room to toss my swimsuit and towel into the wash. The red light on our landline blinked and I knew it was my mother.

"Your voicemail box is full, Phee. Who gets so many calls?"

Half of them are yours, Mother!

I listened to the full message and decided it could wait until morning. Unfortunately, my mother couldn't wait and she phoned again twenty minutes later. I picked up the receiver and her voice nearly blasted my ear off. "Lucinda is going to call you. She wanted me to relay a message but I can't pronounce those Spanish words. Anyway, she's going to call you in a few minutes. Stay off the phone."

"I'm only on the phone because you keep calling me."

"Well, now Lucinda will. I'll talk to you tomorrow. Unless you hear something."

And with that, she hung up. Seconds later, I said hello to Lucinda.

"Phee, this is really important. When I watched that news broadcast about the skeletal remains at that mortuary near the street from the puzzle picture, I remembered this movie I saw years ago, *La Llave Debajo el Cuerpo*.

"La what?"

"*La Llave Debajo el Cuerpo. The Key Under the Corpse.* It was a psychological thriller about skeletal remains that were found underneath a city street in Guadalajara when they razed some old buildings to put up an apartment complex. Anyway, underneath the skull they found a key. Of course, they had to do some digging around, but they unearthed a house key. It was a major clue to a murder. But then, the murderer, who fooled everyone into believing he was a police officer from a neighboring city, found out and one by one he poisoned the investigators who were on the case. Oh, dear. I'm ruining the plot for you, aren't I?"

No, but you're coming close to ruining my evening.

"No, not really. I rarely watch movies with subtitles."

"I understand. But that's not why I called. Don't you see? *La llave!* The key! You have to tell your boss and your husband to make sure they dig around that corpse and look for a key. The victim could have had a house key on him. Or her. Do you know if it was a man or woman? The news didn't say."

"That's because they don't know until a complete forensic examination can be made."

"All the more reason to poke around in the dirt and look for a key. Wallets and paper could disintegrate but keys don't. And neither does jewelry. Tell them to dig around in the dirt. That's what they did in the movie."

"I will. That's very helpful. You do realize that Nate and Marshall aren't the ones who'll be doing the digging. Unless it's the verbal kind. But I'm sure the forensic team will do a thorough job."

"If by 'thorough' you mean 'taking forever,' then it will be months. Goodness. I don't think they've gotten very far with Samantha's murder. And that should be a county priority! This is a senior community. We can't run that fast anymore. And forget about being armed. Half the population are blind as bats."

"I'm certain they're making headway. They just can't release information to the general public in an ongoing investigation. Anyway, I'll let everyone know to look for a key."

"Good. If I think of any more thrillers that involve decayed corpses, I'll let you know."

"Wonderful. I look forward to hearing from you. Thanks again, Lucinda."

When Marshall finally made it home, I was in a light sleep and apparently able to mumble the word *key* a few times. Thankfully he didn't press it until the following morning.

"Glad I didn't wake you when I got in last night, hon," he said. "Although you kept mumbling something about a key. You must have been dreaming." He switched on the lamp and walked to the bathroom.

"Not exactly. Lucinda called to tell me about some Spanish movie she saw where a key was buried underneath the skeletal remains of someone. She wanted me to pass along that vital piece of knowledge so when you and Nate confer with the deputies and forensic crew, you can have them dig around to see if there's a key underneath your corpse."

"Good grief! Those ladies are something else. Trust me. The forensic crew is scouring everything. Plus, these days they have equipment like metal detectors to see if they can find jewelry, key chains, belt buckles, you name it."

"I don't suppose you have too much info to share at this point."

"Not really. Unless you're interested in hearing about Ranston's root canal."

I laughed. "I'm not."

"It's a tedious forensic process, that's for sure. But that part is in the hands of the sheriff's office. And until they're able to share those tidbits of information that help to narrow down suspects, we've got to rely on what little evidence we have."

"Like what?"

"Employee time sheets from the company that did the initial building project as well as time sheets from the mortuary itself. Some of those folks are still around."

"Like Henry Longmire?"

"Uh-huh. I plan to chat with him today. It was on Nate's schedule but that got all turned around. Anyway, I know Henry suffers from advanced neuropathy but I'm hoping his cognition is good. Meanwhile, Nate's meeting Tabitha Stephens for coffee in Scottsdale. Since she's in Chandler and we're up here, he asked if they could chat someplace in between."

"I think I know where this is headed. The original mortuary construction took place around the same time as Arthur Stoad's disappearance."

"Bingo!"

"And you and Nate think the body might be his?"

"We can't discount it. The timing is close. Still, assumptions always get us in trouble. Are you going into the office today? Things have been so frenetic I can barely keep up with my schedule, let alone yours."

"I planned on it. Official workday or not. It sounds like Augusta is going to be busy and I can handle some of those office tasks."

Marshall walked back to the edge of the bed and kissed my forehead. "You're a trooper, hon. I'm taking a quick shower and I'll be out the door. I'll grab coffee on the way."

"Grab some food to go with it."

"I haven't starved yet. But I love how you worry about me."

"More than you know."

• • •

By eight thirty, I was comfortably seated at my desk going through some invoices and taking over the office phone calls since Augusta was "on the chase" to track down Alfrieda Himmelfarb for Nate.

"Found a Mildred Himmelfarb in Carefree," she called out, followed by, "we had a lovely conversation."

"You called her?" I was louder than usual since we were the only ones in the office.

"I wanted to be sure it wasn't Alfrieda. For all we know, Alfrieda could be a middle name."

"And?"

"Mildred's middle name is Eloise. And her nearest relatives are in Pennsylvania. Back to the drawing board."

I fielded a few phone calls from potential clients and one former client who made an appointment to discuss another matter. It didn't sound urgent.

When the phone rang again, I was certain it was a business call, but when my mother's shrill voice penetrated my eardrum, I literally shuddered.

"I'm at the library, Phee. It's a nightmare at the puzzle table. Shirley and Lucinda are with me. Everyone's yammering about the skeletal remains in Sun City as if it was in our backyard and not theirs. Then Betty-Jean and Lettie got into some sort of a private spat and the next thing anyone knew, Lettie threw her coffee at Betty-Jean. She got coffee all over the table and we had to scurry around for paper towels to clean up the pieces."

"Do you think you'll get the puzzle done in time for the photographer?"

"Not at this rate. We have to start that wet section all over again. Lettie threw down paper towels like a barbarian delivering a wild boar to the table. She managed to spread the pieces everywhere, including the floor. We got the pieces back but they need a few minutes to dry, so we're taking a short break. Do you have any news on that body they found?"

"Since last night? No."

"Did the deputies and Williams Investigations find a key under the body? We're very fortunate Lucinda watches all those Spanish movies."

"I don't know *what* they found. *If* they found anything other than bones and a skull. It's not as if they have me on speed-dial."

"Let me know. I've got to get back to the table before something else gets spilled."

The call ended as soon as my mother ran out of breath. Then I caught mine and got back to work.

The rest of the morning flew by and it was noon before I knew it. Augusta ordered us a pepperoni pizza and we decided to eat it while watching the noonday news. All of the local channels reported on the skeletal remains at the mortuary with the same party line—"A complete forensic examination is underway. Until we have results, we are unable to disclose gender or approximate age of the remains. This is a developing story and we will keep our viewers informed."

"I could have told you that," Augusta said as she finished the crust of her third slice. "Maybe the weather report will be more interesting." She helped herself to a fourth slice and that's when the next story caught our attention.

"Forrest Frost Wiggins, the CEO of Restoration Youth Gummies, whose warehouse and manufacturing plant are located on Cotton Lane between Surprise and Buckeye, suffered minor injuries when a pallet of those gummies overturned and trapped him underneath until firefighters could free him. According to Forrest, one of the wheels came loose and in a freak accident, the pallet overturned as he walked through the warehouse."

"Freak accident my foot!" Augusta said. "I better be quiet. They're still talking."

"As we were telling our listeners," the announcer continued, "Forrest refused to be taken to the hospital for observation, insisting he was fine. Too bad that couldn't be said for the cartons of gummies that broke free from the packaging."

Then there was a pause before he added, "Hmm, do I see a major sale in the near future?"

CHAPTER 37

"I'm still not convinced that guy didn't have something to do with his stepmother's murder," Augusta said. "There are too many unanswered questions. Like where she got the gummies to sell at a super discount. Was he in on it? Or did she pay someone at his plant to pilfer them?"

"I know what you mean. Nate and Marshall are still digging into it. They've got a hunch Keenan Alcorn was involved but nothing that can be substantiated. Not yet, anyway."

"At least they have time to concentrate on it since it will take the county days or even months to figure out name, rank and serial number for that decayed corpse. Then, once they do, it'll be a race to see which murder gets solved first."

"It had better be Samantha's. I don't know how much longer I can deal with my mother and the book club ladies insistent 'there's a killer in our midst.'"

"I thought they were focused on who's behind the puzzle tampering."

"Ha! They can't stay focused on anything. They flit from one disaster to another. And if there isn't one, they find one!"

I stayed at the office until two and then headed home. Augusta assured me she had everything under control and would let me know if anything of interest wafted her way between two and five, when she planned to join a canasta game with "the gals."

"If I find Alfrieda Himmelfarb," she said, "I'll send you a flare."

As I drove home, I wondered if Henry or Tabitha were able to provide our guys with the information they needed, but nothing prepared me for the text I would get later in the day from Marshall.

I had treated myself to a quick swim, followed by indulging on a hundred-calorie Yasso coffee chocolate chip yogurt bar. Two bites in and my phone tinged: *We hit pay dirt! Tell Lucinda no key but a pacemaker with a serial number!*

I texted back: *Who?*

Then: *Do not disclose to anyone. Only you and Augusta know. The remains are Arthur Stoad's. Will call later. Got to run. Should be home by six-ish.*

Then, like clockwork, Augusta phoned. "Hold your horses, Phee. The rotting skeleton belongs to the late Arthur Stoad. Mr. Williams called me. Said Marshall was going to get in touch with you. Holy cow! A pacemaker. Never figured on that one. Want to hear the best part? Based on forensic evidence, the coroner classified it as a homicide. Did Marshall call you?"

"He was in a hurry and sent a text but no details."

"Well, now you know. It's all very hush-hush at this point but Mr. Williams said the timing couldn't be any better since he was already meeting with Tabitha."

"Did Nate mention what classified it as a homicide?"

"Blunt force trauma to the back of the skull. Now those lab techs will spend an eternity figuring out what kind of instrument. Back of a gun? Hammer? Heavy vase? My money's on a paperweight. They were very popular years ago."

"They go by the shape of the indent or whatever you call it. Then, the depth. Of course, with a skull and not flesh, it might be different."

"One thing's for sure. Turn up your AC, Phee. The cold case just got hotter. Does this make those photos of Tabitha's the prima facie evidence? They corroborate the physical evidence on the skull."

"Hmm, I'm not sure. But they may provide a really good timeline."

"Guess it's 'one down, one to go.'"

"Huh?"

"We know where Arthur wound up. Now it's Tisha we need to find."

"Oh. Right. Maybe Tabitha had some ideas. She did say she thought Tisha was hiding right under everyone's nose. Then again, why hasn't anyone noticed?"

"Once you reach a certain age, no one notices you because we all look alike. Ever take a good look at couples in their seventies and eighties? Need I say more?"

"If you're telling me I'm going to resemble Marshall in a few decades, I don't want to know."

"If I hear anything else, I'll call you. Have a good weekend."

"You too, Augusta. And same here, if I find out anything, I'll give a holler."

As much as I itched to share this information with Lyndy, I kept mum. Instead, I did a load of laundry and vacuumed the house. It never ceased to amaze me how much dust accumulated in a day or two. I attributed it to the fact that I actually saw the dust on the furniture tops and the tile floor. That's because, unlike my hometown, Mankato, Minnesota, the dust showed up really well in the sunshine. And that was three-hundred and sixty days out of the year.

By the time I finished up, Marshall arrived home and couldn't wait to tell me everything that had ensued, including his chat with Henry and Nate's conversation with Tabitha. I grabbed us some cold Powerade drinks and a bowl of nacho chips and salsa.

"It's not dinner," I said and laughed. "Just conversation food."

"That's a new name for it." Marshall scooped salsa onto a chip and devoured it.

"Okay, spill it. I want to know everything. Augusta already told me it was blunt force trauma to Arthur's head and that it's officially a homicide."

"The type of indentation is indicative of a sharp object. Something wielded and not trauma from a fall or hitting one's head against something. Bowman informed us that the sheriff's office called in forensic specialists from Phoenix who've been working nonstop for the past two days. And nights."

"When will this become public?"

"Sooner than the sheriff's office wants. They don't want to be barraged by reporters and the like but it's inevitable. My guess is it'll be public knowledge by Monday morning the latest. Hopefully we'll enjoy a quiet Sunday tomorrow. Maybe an early swim and breakfast out."

"Sounds wonderful. By the way, what were you able to find out from Henry? Anything notable?"

Marshall shook his head. "Funny, the guy was pretty chatty. Even showed me old family and workplace photos, but clammed up when I mentioned the discovery of skeletal remains. I didn't disclose a name, even though I was made aware of it."

"Did he say *anything?*"

"Only that the construction was a major project at the time and involved a number of contractors and workmen. I asked him if he remembered the area being secured so that unauthorized people and vehicles couldn't get in."

"And?"

"Said they had temporary chain-link fencing with chains and locks to prevent entry and that no one had mentioned a break-in or one of the chains being cut." I asked if he had any idea how a body could go undiscovered during the project since the excavation area would have been wide open. He said that the operators of those excavators and backhoes don't always have a good view of the pit and that when the dirt is filled back in, it's not as if someone is looking for something. At least that was his take. Wish he was a better help, but after two decades, I suppose that's to be expected."

"What was his reaction when you told him about the remains? You said he clammed up."

"The news may have surprised him. I thought he might have heard it prior but apparently not."

I looked at the nacho bowl and it was nearly empty. "Or maybe there are things he doesn't want to reveal. Anyway, we probably should eat something more substantial. I can whip up chicken salad or make cold cut sandwiches."

"Let's pull out the cold cuts and have a field day."

"Done!"

Minutes later we chomped on ham, genoa salami, sliced turkey, tomatoes, spinach and jalapeños on sourdough bread.

"Did Nate have any better luck with Tabitha?" I washed down my first bite with the Powerade.

"More blanks got filled in and that's always a bonus. When he asked her why she suspected Tisha of killing her husband, Tabitha said he often confided in her at work and told her that his relationship with Tisha was 'on rocky ground.'"

"How rocky?"

"Arthur told her he took antianxiety medicine because things were so toxic at home and that he planned on divorcing her. That was shortly before she reported him missing. I'd say that was pretty rocky."

"Hmm, and on top of it all, Tabitha winds up photographing those cryptic shots of the white van in front of the Stoad house only days before Tisha made the missing person report."

"Yeah. About those photographs . . . She told Nate she wanted to enter them in that giant puzzle contest but thought the subject matter was too disturbing. But he got his wish after all."

"What wish?"

"He kept saying that without an actual *body*, it would be difficult to prove murder. Well, now we've got the body. All we need is to track down the killer."

"Oh my gosh! The contest. Is it possible to find out who *did* submit the winning photo? Maybe they could help with the investigation."

"They *could*, if they had the name of that person. And his or her whereabouts. But they don't."

"It's like one step forward and half a dozen back," I whined.

"What do you say we give our brains a break and zone out in front of the TV?"

"You read my mind."

No sooner did we make ourselves comfortable when the landline rang and I shouted, "Let the machine get it." It was the best decision I had made all day because it was my mother and she left me the following message: "Your aunt and uncle are back from Sedona. They want to have brunch with us tomorrow at Bagels 'n More. Louis missed his kippered herring. I'm inviting the book club ladies and Herb. Don't be surprised if the pinochle men and Paul show up. Ten thirty. I'll call and remind you tomorrow morning."

I nudged Marshall. "Shall I tell her we're starting an extended fast tomorrow?"

"Nah. I'm in the mood for kippered herrings too!" He kept a straight face and for a minute I almost believed him.

"You know, she'll nag us to death if we don't go."
"That's okay, hon. Truth is, I could go for a cinnamon churro bagel."
"And the never-ending chitchat and gossip that will surround it."

CHAPTER 38

My aunt's yellow and pink sundress nearly blinded me when Marshall and I walked into Bagels 'n More Sunday morning. She and Louis were glued to the menus even though they could recite the choices in their sleep.

"Good morning." I slid into the seat across from my aunt with Marshall to my right. "Looks like we're early for once," I said as I helped myself to the carafe of coffee on the table. "How was Sedona?"

"Splendid! Absolutely splendid! Full body massages, exfoliating facials, mud baths, crystal therapy, light therapy, I could go on and on. Isn't that so, Louis?"

My uncle darted his eyes back and forth until he had no choice but to respond. "Yes, dear. You could go on and on."

"That's not what I meant and you know it. Don't be silly."

My uncle sighed. "It was pleasant but I could have found the same food in the plant aisle at Lowe's. Right now, I want to sink my teeth into kippered herring with bialys." Then he looked at Marshall. "You might as well enjoy this free minute because Harriet's going to be here any second with the ladies and they'll pester the daylights out of you to find out if any murderers have been apprehended."

"They can pester away, but the result will still be the same—we're working on it."

Then my aunt spoke. "That's your mother's response too when it comes to that puzzle. Good heavens. Someone is either dropping something on it, spilling something on it, or knocking over the pieces. When did she say the final magazine photo will be taken?"

"In a week, I think. The librarian extended the hours after the last fiasco so it'll be done in time. My mother's been adamant they make the cover."

"Speak of the devil, there's my sister now. Hmm, Cecilia's got a new hairdo and Lucinda doesn't look as frazzled as usual."

"That's because they're coming out of church. Oh, and there's Myrna and Louise as well."

"Good morning, everyone," Myrna called out. "Pass the mini bagels, please. I'm starving. And when Herb gets here, make sure he sits at the other end. He keeps reaching over my plate for the bread and condiments and it's really annoying."

"Yo-ho, folks! I made it!" I recognized Paul's voice at the same time I caught a whiff of freshly gutted fish. "I just got back from a productive morning on Lake Pleasant with Mini-Moose from the bowling alley. He'd join us but he had to be at work by noon."

160

Please tell me Paul left his catch at home and not in here somewhere.

My mother pulled out the chair next to mine and sat. "Sorry I'm late but I decided to refresh the ice cubes in Streetman and Essie's bowls. The cat's not particular but Streetman likes to see ice cubes in his water. He's been quite distressed about not being able to accompany me to my usual haunts, but I can't schlep him in this heat."

Thank you, Arizona!

"We made it!" Gloria announced. "Shirley's with Herb at the bakery case. They're checking out the desserts."

"Does anyone know if Bill or the other guys are coming?" Paul asked. "I found a new bait that seems to be promising. It's—"

"Don't say it out loud," my mother all but shrieked. "It'll ruin my appetite."

Paul narrowed his eyes. "Honestly, Harriet. In some Asian countries, they eat that stuff for breakfast, lunch and dinner." Then he looked at Gloria. "No offense."

"Honestly, Paul. Just because I'm second-generation Chinese doesn't mean I eat like my ancestors. I suppose you think we use chopsticks at home and not silverware."

"I don't know. I eat a lot of fish and tacos so I use my hands."

"Ew!" Cecilia recoiled. "I don't eat anything I don't recognize and that's that."

"Always a smart move." This time it was my uncle Louis who had to offer his two cents.

"We're here!" Shirley announced as she and Herb squeezed into two of the remaining seats.

"Wayne can't make it," Herb said. "And neither can Kenny, but Kevin and Bill are on their way."

"While we're waiting for them," my aunt said, "I have a wonderful surprise for all of you. Look!" She reached into her large satchel, which was last used on the set of *Gone with the Wind* for one of the carpetbagger scenes. "Restoration Youth Gummies. Only a few chews away to roll back the years."

"Aunt Ina," I gasped. "You must have spent a fortune."

She shook her head. "These are promotional packs from the spa. Thirty gummies in each. We'd have to take out a second mortgage to purchase them. Take a whiff. They're a combination of blackberries, strawberries and blueberries. Quite the enticing aroma."

Lucinda gave a sniff. "Thanks, Ina. They'll be even more enticing if they work."

Herb studied his packet and looked at Lucinda. "It says *restoration,* not *resurrection.*"

"I don't care what it says, I'm giving them a try." She put the packet in her bag and then grabbed a mini bagel.

"They must do *something*." Shirley turned the packet over to read the information. "Or else Forrest wouldn't have such a thriving business."

"A thriving business and a target on his back." Herb looked directly at her.

"What do you mean?"

"I caught that quip on the news. About a minor accident in the warehouse. The wheels on those rolling pallets don't just loosen on their own. In fact, they need to be unloosened with a screwdriver. Remember when we had to deal with them for that show at the Stardust Theater?"

"Don't remind me," Shirley said. "That place still gives me the willies at night."

Just then, we heard Bill's booming voice. "Did you leave anything for me? We would have gotten here sooner but Kevin wanted to gas up before it got too hot."

"That's what you're supposed to do. Gas up in the cooler part of the day." He plopped himself down next to Herb while Bill took the seat on the opposite side. The seasoned waitress wasted no time getting our orders and rushing them off to the kitchen.

"Here, take these." My aunt handed the two men the gummies. "You can't put a price on youth."

"What are these? A new kind of edible?" Kevin smiled to himself until my aunt broke the news. "No, a health vitamin. Or mineral. Or whatever. Not marijuana."

"From Restoration Youth Gummies," I said. "The company that belongs to the stepson of our library murder victim, Samantha Wiggins. And before you say anything, Forrest indicated on more than one occasion that she had no part in his business, even though my aunt would beg to differ with you."

"What do you know that you're not telling us, Ina?" my mother asked.

"I know how politicians and businessmen spin the truth around like sticky little cobwebs so acting definitions and legal definitions become all tangled up. By the time everyone unravels it, the players are no longer in the game."

"Dead?" Cecilia asked.

My aunt nodded. "I was trying to be subtle. And Forrest, I believe, was rather clever with his definition of 'working in the business.' Technically, he wasn't lying. According to the paperwork, or lack thereof, that we found in his office the night of the fish tank disaster, nothing indicated she was an employee, a manager, or a part owner. However, and here's where the semantics kick in, I'm certain Samantha had a side business. Or 'feeder'

162

business, like I told Phee a while back."

"What's a 'feeder' business?" Myrna reached over Kevin's plate and snagged two mini bagels.

With her elbows on the table, and her head propped up in the palms of her hands, my aunt drew a breath as if she was about to deliver a proclamation. "Samantha sold discounted gummies as a means to bring in new customers for the regular business. And she did it with Forrest's blessing. How else would she get the product? Like I said, it's a technicality. But maybe something went wrong."

"I'll say. How else did she wind up dead on the library floor?" Bill quipped. "And don't forget Forrest was the beneficiary on her insurance policies. At least that's what Harriet told all of us."

And so much for keeping matters to oneself, Mom.

"Before all of you go off on tangents, keep in mind the sheriff's office as well as ours are looking into all of this." Marshall poured himself another cup of coffee, but before it could reach his lips, my otherwise quiet uncle spoke up.

"Getting back to those gummies, they were all the talk at my last gig in Fountain Hills. But like musicians, those gummies played to a mixed audience."

"What do you mean?" My aunt cocked her head and stared at Louis.

"All of you know I'm a betting man, but I wouldn't place any money on those things one way or the other. The sax players and one of the clarinet guys thought they gave them an energy boost, but heck, a can of Mountain Dew could do that. And the guys didn't mention rewinding the clock of time."

"What about the women musicians?" Shirley asked.

"The flutists were adamant that they looked younger but to be honest, no one else thought so. And Giselle, the pianist, insisted her skin rivaled a thirty-year-old, but she didn't specify which species of animal."

"Louis!" my aunt shrieked. "That's a horrible comment. It's a good thing none of us are acquainted with her."

"Sorry, dear. My apologies. It was a bit crude and uncalled for."

Bill and Paul smirked while Herb whispered to them, "Remind me not to ask for her phone number."

"Never mind, all of you. I, for one, intend to try them, starting right now." Louise opened the small paper wrapper and removed a gummy from its packaging. "Oh my! The aroma of blackberries is amazing. So enticing." With that, she popped the gummy in her mouth and chewed. "This is heavenly. Like eating fresh berries."

Herb rubbed his chin and squinted. "If those laugh lines of yours disappear before dessert, I'll try one, too."

"You can make fun all you like," Louise said, "but that company has a zillion followers. They must be doing something right."

Yeah, advertising.

"So, what's everyone doing this afternoon?" my mother asked.

"If it involves another one of your treks, Harriet, I'm busy." Myrna smeared black garlic cream cheese on her salt bagel and took a large bite. "Besides, it's already a hundred and three degrees and it isn't even the heat of the day."

"Exactly," my mother said. "That's why it's the perfect afternoon to head over to the open water volleyball games at Palm Ridge."

"Water volleyball?" I nearly choked on my bagel. "You hate that stuff, Mom. What's the real motive behind it?"

"Why do I need a motive? I just thought it would be a very nice way for all of us to be active in this heat. And Ina and Louis can come as our guests."

My aunt looked at my mother as if she had suggested bungee jumping off a cliff. "I just spent a week relaxing and rejuvenating. All of that will come undone the minute some Neanderthal lobs a ball at my head."

Herb laughed. "Guess we can count Ina and Louis out."

"And me." Paul smeared garlic cream cheese on his bagel and then salted it. "I'm fileting some fish for a cookout tonight at the Elks Club."

"And I promised my daughter I'd help her rearrange her closet." Gloria turned to Shirley, who whispered, "That's the best you can come up with?"

In the end, it was just my mother and Myrna who went to volleyball, but that was enough to get trouble brewing.

CHAPTER 39

"Your mother never ceases to amaze me," Marshall said on the drive home. "Water volleyball. Of all things."

"Oh, trust me. She hasn't the faintest interest in water volleyball. She's up to something. I only wish I knew what. At least she didn't mention the dog. Thank goodness dogs are not allowed at the pools or Streetman would be all decked out in swimwear with those ridiculous goggles they get for canines."

"Don't underestimate her. And if the phone rings in an hour, let it go to voicemail. Meanwhile, what do you say we go for a swim? The air is stifling and I guarantee we won't catch a break tomorrow."

"Done deal. Mind if I call Lyndy to join us?"

"I took that as a given. Lyman, too."

By midafternoon, the four of us were in the shady end of Vistancia's pool, surrounded by splashing kids and frazzled parents. Usually we came at night to avoid the chaos, but given the early heatwave, we opted to put up with a little noise.

"Just think," Marshall said, "in another decade, more or less, we could live in Sun City Grand, where the only pool noise is the gossip."

"We have children's hours at West," Lyman said, "but they rotate it so one pool doesn't have to absorb it all at once."

"You guys sound as if you're dealing with an infestation." Lyndy ducked her head and shook off the water.

"We are!" Lyman laughed. "But I'll live with it."

We remained in the pool for over an hour before our bodies began to resemble *A Raisin in the Sun* as opposed to *Beach Blanket Bingo*. Then, just as we were trying to figure out if we wanted to go out for burgers or get a pizza, Marshall and Nate got a shared text from Bowman. And I use the term *text* lightly because Bowman never took shortcuts. Even with texting.

Break-in at the SCW Library. Place will be hopping with lookie-loos once posse responding vehicles get here. Could use your assistance. Do not share with Phee's mother, although I'm sure she's already in the parking lot over there.

"Why on earth would someone break into a library?" Lyman asked. "They can check out the books for free, and it's not as if they've got a safe or anything."

Marshall and I looked at each other but it was Lyndy who spoke up. "I think it's that puzzle. It's all anyone talks about according to my aunt. She thinks someone is being a poor sport and doesn't want the Sun City West library to get all the fame and glory from that feature in *Senior Living*."

"Then they need to get over it and grow up," Marshall said, "because now Phee and I will be lucky if we get to eat soda crackers instead of pizza or burgers."

"Do you want us to join you? I'm serious," Lyman said. "In case you need help or crowd control."

"Nah." Marshall shook his head. "Enjoy the rest of your night and eat a slice of pizza for us!"

We darted out of the pool, dried off, went home, changed and were in Sun City West in record time. Marshall texted Nate to tell him he had it covered and there was no need for Nate for ruin his Sunday night. Nate returned the text with three thumbs up.

"Oh, heck no!" I blurted out as Marshall pulled up to the library's computer entrance facing the pickleball courts. "That's Streetman! And Thor! In matching patriotic outfits! And the Fourth of July isn't even here yet!"

"It's always an occasion where your mother is concerned. Weddings, bar mitzvahs, anniversaries, birthdays . . . and now, break-ins. To be honest, hon, I kind of expected her to be here, dog and all. But I think she brought the entire sideshow. Look around. Thor's not the only dog."

"Oh, no! She must have gone to the dog park, heard the sirens because Bowman and Ranston can't go to Walmart without their siren blaring, and now the entire barrage of barking furballs is waiting outside."

"I'm swinging around to the bowling alley parking lot that faces RH Johnson. No sense getting into it with that crowd. At least not until I know what's going on. Do me a favor and text Bowman. Tell him we are at the front and not side entrance."

"Done!"

Minutes later, Ranston met us at the front door, where two posse members were stationed, and let us in. "Wouldn't you know it," he said. "I'm on the schedule to work until two this morning. It better not take that long. And Bowman's not thrilled either. We were on our way to In-n-Out Burger when we got the call."

Marshall gave a nod. "Smart move to position the MCSO vehicles by the other entrance."

"Yep. Wasn't born yesterday. Especially in this community. It's a sea of gray out there. And what's with all the dogs?"

I tried not to laugh. "What happened? Was anything destroyed?"

Ranston motioned for us to follow him as he spoke. "Nope. Only thing broken is my eardrum from their new alarm system. You'd think the noise would have scared off the perps but I guess not. They had enough time to— Well, see for yourself."

He extended his arm to the large puzzle table, where Bowman stood motionless with his arms crossed. Another deputy was taking photos, but it wasn't until we moved in closer when we realized what they were staring at.

"Yeesh," Marshall muttered under his breath. "Who does such a thing?"

"At least they were considerate with the tinfoil," I said. "Whoever it was wanted to send a message but didn't want to undo all that work."

"Send a message?" Bowman nearly exploded. "Try email. Or the postal service! What *is* wrong with these people? I'll tell you one thing—the forensic crew can deal with it. They'll dust for prints anyway and there's no need for me to take my uniform to the cleaners."

I walked around the table and studied the graphic message that was plastered over the tinfoil. It was spelled out in ketchup and spanned the entire length of the table.

"How many bottles of that stuff do you think it took?" Ranston asked. "Had to be the kind with the squirt tops. Most likely store brand. No one wants to shell out for a brand name."

"I suppose looking into the handwriting is out of the question, huh? It would be like signing an invoice on an iPad. Impossible to recognize your own handwriting."

"Got that right, hon." Marshall shrugged at me before turning to Ranston. "Did the security cameras pick up anything? And how'd they break in to begin with?"

"Idiots must have run out of ketchup because the cameras were squirted with mustard. Darn those squirt tops. Hmm, now that I think of it, the stores must be having sales on Fourth of July condiments. No sense checking out who bought mustard or ketchup in Sun City West. It could have been anyone for all we know. And they could have gone to Costco. Giant sizes over there."

Bowman stopped grumbling for a second and took a few steps toward us. "Want to know how they got in? Someone left the door by the back stairwell unlocked. We'll have to ask the staff tomorrow but no one's going to own up to it. And it could have been a patron and not a worker or volunteer." Then he rubbed the back of his neck and let out a long sigh. "Had to have been deliberate. Someone doesn't want that puzzle finished."

Then Ranston rubbed the tip of his nose and stifled a sneeze. "You know, Foothills of Verrado had a problem like that a few years ago, come to think of it. But it was their atrium by the club rooms. Turned out the ukulele club used it every year for ongoing concerts but the bell ringers wanted it too so they put glue on the seats when the ukulele players came. And left threatening messages too. We finally got a confession out of one of them but it wasn't easy."

"How so?" Marshall asked.

"Rather sneaky. We brought a few of them into our Buckeye office and told each one that the other one ratted them out."

I immediately jumped in. "We should do that here."

Ranston shook his head. "We had more evidence in Verrado."

Just then we heard a pounding on the front door and Bowman went to investigate. Seconds later I heard, "Sorry to bother you, but I really need to use the restroom. Can someone watch my little man?"

"Little man?" Oh no! It's my mother with the gladiator from hell.

I rushed over. "I'll take him."

"Phee! When did you get here? You should have called me. Never mind. I'm on my way to the restroom." She walked past the puzzle and then said, "Is that blood all over it? Is that why the deputy cars are all over the place? Those dog park people can pick up a scent better than their dogs. Good heavens, it's blood! I've got to tell everyone! And it's a message!"

She zoomed closer before I could block her.

Her voice rivaled Myrna's. "Let me see! It says, *'Stop the puzzle or it will be real blood next time.'* Hmm, fake blood. Guess I won't be telling them, huh?"

Thank our lucky stars.

"Well, Phee, that's good, isn't it? They used fake blood. Don't let Streetman near it. It could be poisonous."

"I doubt it, Mom. Smell it. Smells like ketchup. And it's evidence. For the time being."

Suddenly, my mother's urge to use the restroom disappeared. "I need to let the girls know what's going on before they come up with something of their own." She snatched the dog out of my arms and bolted for the door. Streetman turned his head and bared his teeth at Bowman before letting out a deep growl.

"He's working on his social skills," my mother said. "And he's doing much better." Then she bent over and kissed his forehead. "Remember what Momma taught you. No bite-ees."

Bowman immediately stepped back, and this time it was impossible for me to keep from laughing.

CHAPTER 40

And just as I thought my mother had left the library for good, she returned a minute later to announce, "Those deputies should call the librarian!"

Bowman, who was in earshot, shouted back, "*Those deputies* already did! And we notified the rec center's director. Is there anything else we forgot, Mrs. Plunkett?"

"I'll let you know."

This time it was Bowman who rolled his eyes and not me.

Marshall and Ranston stood over the puzzle table with mixed expressions. Finally Marshall said, "The good news is that it's an easy cleanup. Once forensics are done, the tinfoil mess can be rolled up and discarded. The puzzle should be intact."

Meanwhile, I walked to the front entrance to eyeball the security camera. "I don't understand how the perpetrator squirted mustard on those lenses. It's not like a hose." Then I glanced to my left. "Oh. I take it back. The aisles have step ladders. Easy-peasey."

"This should give the lab guys something to do," Ranston said.

"What happened?" Darcey's frantic voice came from the computer side of the library. "I can't believe that crowd. Please tell me there's not another body in here."

"No body," Bowman said as he walked past the puzzle table to where she stood. Then, he showed her the mess and rubbed his chin. "Do you have any idea who might have done this? The side door was left unlocked."

"Unlocked? That's not possible. I locked it myself on Saturday afternoon when I made my rounds before we closed."

Marshall approached them and nodded to Darcey. "It appears as if someone also made the rounds and unlocked it. Can you get us a list of who was in here?"

"Sure. We scan the rec cards, and manually add the guests. Hold on, I'll go into my office and pull it up for you."

"It's an easy cleanup," I added. "It won't stop the puzzle workers, will it?"

"I don't think a freight train could stop them. That photographer will be here by week's end for the final picture. And it can't come soon enough."

The evening wrapped up fairly quickly for us. Forensic workers remained to do their job and the deputies went about their regular business, telling the lab guys that they'd be back in a few hours.

"I'll text you and Nate with the details once we get them," Bowman told Marshall. "Thanks for coming."

The dog park crowd had scattered and I imagined it was because a ketchup-mess table wasn't as dramatic as finding another corpse. And while this latest incident remained a mystery, Marshall was right about one thing—we did eat soda crackers for dinner.

Darcey wasted no time emailing the library patrons with the news. And the rec center put it on their website under *Updates*. And while the deputies and Williams Investigations continued with the latest "incident" involving the giant puzzle, my mother phoned the office early the next morning with her own disaster.

• • •

"I'm at the veterinarian's office," she said. "I put that packet of restorative gummies on the kitchen table when I got home last night and I found Streetman eating them this morning. I counted and there were only twelve left. He was on a chair chomping away when I walked into the kitchen. I wondered why he was so quiet. I forgot how much he likes fruit jellies. He must have smelled it."

"Is he sick? Throwing up? Passed out? What?"

"He seemed perfectly fine, but who knows how that stuff could affect him. For all we know, they could be poisonous to dogs. At least Essie stays away from candies and such. The vet sent the remaining gummies to a veterinary poison control lab for testing. They put a rush on it but it still could take as long as twenty-four hours. Meanwhile, they don't want to give the dog anything because it might not interact well with the contents of those gummies. Until they know, they're just keeping him hydrated and monitoring him."

"Okay. Thanks for letting me know. If there's anything you need, call me."

When I told Augusta, she said the dog was probably fine since anything really toxic would result in visible symptoms. She said something similar happened to a favorite bovine that belonged to one of her uncles. Luckily the powder they found in its feed was from one of those sugar candy packets that the nephews ate when they were in the barn."

"How did he find out?"

"From the bright pink color when he went to feed Hazel. He didn't have vet labs near him but they did have Quest, Lab Corp and CRL. Cost him a pretty penny."

"My mother would drain her bank account for Streetman. You know how she adores her little prince. Do you know he's even in her will!"

"Let me guess. And you and Marshall would take ownership?"

"My mother better live to a hundred and twenty! And not a day sooner!"

About an hour later, my mother called again to tell me Streetman seemed to be doing fine at the vet's office. She also contacted all of the book club ladies and Herb to see if anyone had any sort of reaction to those gummies.

"Did they?" I asked.

"No. Louise said she still looked her age and Shirley said her wrinkles were still on her face. And Gloria's sciatic nerve was acting up as usual."

"Um, even if those things really unwound the clock of time, I doubt it would be instantaneous. Thanks for keeping me posted."

My mother's check-in calls were like clockwork, and by four fifty-three nothing had changed.

"Whatever he ingested had to be nontoxic," I said. "Will they keep him overnight?"

"He'll stay until nine when they close. They don't seem to be worried. They fed him a small portion of boiled chicken and he didn't have any issues. Oh, did I mention they ran urine and fecal tests?"

"No." But that should increase the bill.

"The vet expects lab results by ten a.m. tomorrow. Poor Essie keeps looking for him. I gave her a catnip mouse to distract her."

"Good."

Needless to say, my mother did not work on the puzzle that morning, but Marshall found himself there in order to question the regular puzzle workers and patrons. Meanwhile, Nate returned to the mortuary for his continued questioning and probing.

There was no news until Tuesday morning, and it had nothing to do with those ongoing investigations. Nate and Marshall were both out of the office at ten twenty when my mother called. Since it was our break time, Augusta and I had opened a box of the special edition Pepperidge Farm Milano London Fog cookies. We'd barely tasted a crumb when my mother exclaimed, "They were nontoxic! And that's not all. The contents of those gummies has to be the reason Samantha Wiggins was murdered. You can thank Streetman!"

"Come again. What are you saying?" The phone was on speaker and Augusta's eyes couldn't get any wider.

As if my mother's voice wasn't loud enough, she practically belted out her explanation. "The contents in those gummies were blueberry, apple, sunflower oil, gelatin, vitamin D, collagen, glucosamine and hyaluronic acid. All perfectly safe for dogs and humans."

"Okay. But that was never an issue. Samantha wasn't poisoned."

"Don't you get it, Phee? Those harmless contents won't do a thing to restore your youth. Might as well suck on a gumball. Samantha must have known it all the time and blackmailed her stepson. Or, confronted him for a cut of the profits. Same thing, more or less."

"Got to admit, it makes sense. I mean, we did theorize the possibility of blackmail, but that was before we knew about Forrest's bogus product."

"What I don't understand is how he was and is able to get away with it. Shouldn't he be arrested for false advertising?"

Augusta shook her head as the phone conversation continued and mouthed, "Tell her to look at the box."

I'd shown Augusta the freebie box earlier and she must have scrutinized it. I also offered her some gummies but she said youth was overrated.

"Hang on." The little box was still in my bag and I dug it out. "Read the list of ingredients, Mom. It says "Gelatin, blueberry extract, apple extract, sunflower oil and a proprietary blend of vitamins, minerals, and essential oils. Perfectly legal."

"Honestly. I can find those in the health food section of the supermarket. How on earth can they possibly be doing such a blockbuster business? And with those extravagant prices, no less. Even your aunt Ina was taken aback, and she spends Louis's money like a drunken sailor."

"Testimonials and clever marketing. Oh my gosh! Marketing!"

"Yes, you just said that."

"That's what Keenan Alcorn does. Well, graphic design, but it's practically the same."

"Puzzle Keenan who sits near Celeste? The transplant from Washington State? What about him?"

"He was doing some work for Forrest, according to Marshall. Packaging and marketing. And, get this, he and Herb were the only two men at Libby's book chat where she gave away those perfume sprays. Listen, Streetman may have us on to something after all. Please don't breathe a word of this. Especially to Herb."

"I know better than to blab to Herb. It's different with Shirley and Cecilia. They know what it means to be discreet."

"Shh! Not even to them. For now, anyway. I'll get back to you. And I'm glad to hear the good news about Streetman."

"We can all rest better tonight."

The call ended, but five minutes hadn't gone by when my mother phoned again. I was still nibbling cookies with Augusta.

"I've been thinking, Phee. I have to tell the girls. No one will get a really good sleep until we corral Keenan. He's got to be the staple-gun-wielding manic. Forrest must have put him up to it. Bribery, blackmail, who knows? Imagine—putting puzzle pieces together one minute and murdering someone the next. This calls for a plan. No, better yet, a trap."

And no! Not again. The plan . . . the trap . . . the headache . . .

"Let our office and MCSO take it from here. Not a word. You could compromise everything."

"Fine. I'll just tell Shirley."

CHAPTER 41

"That was loud and clear," Augusta said. "At least she didn't say Paul. He would have asked the radio station for a special fishing show just to put it on the air."

"Ugh. I know. Listen, Marshall mentioned something a while back about having Rolo look into Keenan. I forgot to ask about it. Did he or Nate say anything to you about that?"

Augusta shook her head. "Nope. It may be one of those 'back burner' things that need to move to the front of the stove."

"Nice analogy. I'll shoot off a text to Marshall. For once my mother may be on to something. And she doesn't have a good track record for waiting things out."

"My money is on 'the trap.' 'The plan' never gets off the ground."

"That's because all they do is talk about it."

I went back to the paperwork at my desk, expecting the rest of the day to drone on. And it might have, had it not been for Marshall's text.

Rolo's been swamped but he did get the lowdown on Keenan. Digital designer and marketer who crossed paths with Forrest at a trade conference in Seattle. Don't know how our guy finds these things out but he does. Relocated to Sun City West shortly after that conference. Want to guess Forrest made him an offer he couldn't refuse?

I texted back: *Are you going all "Godfather" on me?*

And then: *Keenan's bank account points that way. Am off to see if Forrest begins to sweat.*

I replied: *Be careful.*

I kept my fingers crossed that Marshall could eke a confession out of Forrest but I wasn't too optimistic. So far, the guy had managed to elude everyone. Even going as far as to say his stepmother wasn't involved with his business.

At a little past two, a fax came in from Bowman regarding the ketchup incident at the library. Had the whole thing not been so disconcerting, I would have laughed my head off when Augusta and I read, "Forget text. Am not a pigmy. No one's fingers are that small. Lab results in on ketchup threat. No prints at actual scene but sticky partials found on ladies' room door and faucets. Men's room clean. Make it somewhat clean. No prints though. Partials belong to Betty-Jean, Lettie, and LaVonda. I knew those biddies had to be retired state workers or school employees. Call me when you get in."

"Okay," I said. "So Keenan wasn't a participant in slowing down the puzzle, but that doesn't mean anything, does it?"

Augusta shrugged. "Hard to say. But the same names keep cropping up. When did you say that photographer was going to take the final photo?"

"End of the week according to my mother. Why?"

"I don't want to be the harbinger of bad tidings, but given the track record, I'm anticipating a grand finale that will put the final kibosh on that giant puzzle."

"Heaven forbid!"

A short while later, Nate came in and mumbled about Bowman pulling him in one direction and Ranston in the other. I had just finished making some invoice copies and was a few feet away from where he stood. He peered over Augusta's shoulder to check his schedule when she announced, "You and Mr. Gregory got this fax from Deputy Bowman." She handed him the paper and waited to see his expression.

"Happy day! More interviews. Do me a favor, call those women and have them meet me at the posse office first thing in the morning. Space it out. Tell them I need to clarify some information. And while you're at it, email Bowman and tell him to get a large keypad phone."

"Seriously? You want me to do that, Mr. Williams?"

Nate choked up laughing. "Nah, just let him know I'm off to ruffle the biddies' feathers."

"Will he understand?" She narrowed her eyes.

"On second thought, spell it out!"

When five fifteen rolled around, Marshall straggled in and Nate stepped out to the main office. I had already shut down my computer and was ready to call it a day.

"Anyone going into lock-up tonight?" Augusta asked.

"I'd volunteer," Nate said, "if it meant a good night's sleep without interruption. Between my aunt's parrot and the calls that come in, it's a wonder I'm able to get some shut-eye before the next day."

"Any luck with Forrest?" Nate didn't look too hopeful.

"He couldn't weasel his way out of the situation," Marshall said, "but he didn't confess to murder. He asked if we were going to report him to the Better Business Bureau regarding his product and I said no. First of all, it's not our charge, and second, since no complaints were registered, the report wouldn't be valid. In fact, it could be considered entrapment. Besides, the county has enough on its plate."

"You mean Bowman and Ranston?"

He nodded and pulled up a chair. "Forrest admitted that he had a deal with Samantha. She purchased those gummies, used them as directed, and nothing. She saw her stepson at a senior services expo in Peoria earlier in the year and threatened to expose him in front of a huge crowd if he didn't compensate her. He was certain she went there for that explicit purpose.

Needless to say, he offered her a deal—sell them wholesale and keep the bulk of the profits."

"What happened?"

"Lettie did."

"I don't understand."

"Lettie overheard them at that expo and thought she'd get in on the action as well. In order to minimize the damage, Forrest cut her in with the caveat that she and Samantha would work together so that they could maximize their profits while ensuring they kept it to themselves."

"And you believed him?"

Marshall nodded. "I did. He had nothing to lose. In fact, he told me that by having Samantha introduce the product at wholesale, word of mouth spread to the retail end of it."

Augusta crossed her arms and leaned back in her chair. "I don't get it. The product was gelatin. And some sugar stuff."

"Think placebo effect," Nate cut in. "Won't be the first time. I see all those anti-wrinkle cream commercials on TV, not to mention the 'performance enhancing' products for men. Face it, people will believe anything."

Marshall gave a thumbs-up. "He's right. That's exactly what Forrest told me, along with the reason why he needed Keenan to create amazing graphics and market it as if it could change the world."

"Boy, are people gullible." Augusta still sat with arms crossed. "But what about Samantha getting greedy and Forrest doing her in with Keenan's help? I rather liked that scenario. Neat, clean, and logical."

Nate rolled his shoulder blades and then stretched. "Neat, clean, logical and impossible to prove. We don't have the evidence." Then he looked at me. "We can't use evidence like those insurance policies without a search warrant. Same with evidence from Rolo. Although in her case, it didn't turn up much. He checked Samantha's bank accounts but there was nothing to indicate a windfall. Just moderate income that we deem came from her gummy sales."

"You're not going to stop pursuing this angle?" I looked at Marshall and then at Nate.

"No," they both answered at once.

I reflected for a few seconds and then spoke. "You know, Keenan could still be responsible for Samantha's death. He may have a motive that none of us have thought of. And he did get a sample of that perfume spray during the book chat. I wouldn't discount him altogether."

"We're not," Marshall said. "We just need to get creative."

"And hopefully without your mother's interference," Nate added with a giant grin on his face. Then he turned to Marshall. "Hey, buddy, I've got to have another chitchat with Lettie, LaVonda and Betty-Jean. It'll go faster tomorrow with both of us. Their sticky prints were found on the ladies' room door at the library, after it had been cleaned. Ketchup maybe? Could be we've got a trio of mischief makers."

Marshall nodded. "Sure. Besides, I was planning on a little talk with Lettie as well, seeing as she was in the gummy distribution business with Samantha."

CHAPTER 42

"I called to let you know that we're making great progress on the puzzle this morning," my mother said. "Without Lettie, LaVonda, and Betty-Jean here, it's been nice and peaceful. Even Celeste has been on her best behavior. Naturally Drake wiped down everything as if the puzzle had been in a Louisiana swamp, and Norva acted as if she was uncovering the secret to Tutankhamen's tomb instead of a giant community puzzle, but still, it was a far cry better than all of that tension."

Thankfully, that was a voice message my mother left for me on my cell phone. She'd called between the time I got out of my car on a donut run and got back in. The phone was on mute and I never bothered to look until I was back at my desk. There was no urgency in her voice so I made a mental note and went on with my business. I did wonder, however, if Nate and Marshall were having a banner morning as well with their interviews.

I think deep down all of us hoped Forrest was culpable for his stepmother's death since it would shore up one murder investigation and allow the men to concentrate on Arthur Stoad's demise. Bowman and Ranston felt the same way, especially since Samantha's insurance money was headed to Forrest's bank account. Motive with a capital M in my book, as well as means and opportunity if Forrest paid off Keenan to do the dirty work.

Unfortunately, we weren't the only ones to tag him as our suspect of choice. The book club ladies, spearheaded by my mother, were one step ahead of us. And my aunt Ina was a full half mile past that. I knew it was only a matter of time before one of them would "unleash the Kraken," but I never imagined it would spin so out of control.

By Wednesday morning, most of the puzzle had been completed, along with more interviews. In addition, our office was tasked with evidence-sifting at the mortuary thanks to a search warrant from MCSO.

"My gut tells me Henry knows more than he's willing to disclose," Marshall said when he joined Augusta and me for a quick coffee break. "I'm headed back to his care facility to up the ante."

"Bribe him?" I was astonished.

"Scare him. Hate to do it but this has gone on long enough. I'm going to tell him that an undisclosed witness said he was involved with Arthur's murder."

"That should work, Mr. Gregory. Those TV cops use outright lies all the time. Plus, the good-guy-bad-guy routine," Augusta said.

"Technically it's not lying. Tabitha pointed a finger at the mortuary staff. That works for me. Now all I need to do is to be more convincing than Robert De Niro. Nate's at the mortuary right now with Ranston. They're going through old boxes of photos to see if they can get something to stick."

"What kind of photos?" I pictured embalmed corpses in coffins and teary-eyed families.

"Snapshots of the original building project to match up the time frame."

"Sounds tedious."

Marshall laughed. "And then some."

He darted out the door and I returned to my office to work. A few minutes later, Augusta called out, "You've got a phone call."

She must have heard me groan because she added, "It's not your mother. It's your aunt. Said it had something to do with Matt and Harry, whoever *they* are."

"Oh, no! Every time my aunt mentions new names, it involves some bizarre plan she came up with, complete with a never-ending list of players who tend to be musician friends of my uncle." I imagined this was no different.

"Do you want me to tell her you stepped out?"

"No, I might as well take it. She'll only wind up calling again."

I picked up the line and greeted my aunt.

"Phee! I had the most brilliant plan for getting a confession out of Keenan. Your mother filled me in but everything is in limbo with her plans and traps, and who knows what else. So, I came up with this on my own."

"Um, I don't think—"

"Don't say another word until you hear it. I got the idea from *Little Mary Sunshine*. Our theater group at the Grand will be producing it in the fall. Anyway, we borrow the technique from Mata Hari."

"Matt and Harry?"

"Mata Hari. A woman. You know, the infamous spy who seduced men during World War I in order to obtain information."

"Oh. That Mata Hari." *Thank you, Augusta.*

"All we need to do is have someone wrap Keenan around their little finger until he blurts out the truth. A glass or two of wine never hurts."

"And who will do the wrapping? Cecilia? She scares men off the minute they say hello. She immediately buttons her cardigan to the neckline. And Myrna? One bellow from her and they'll run to the hills. Louise will frighten them off when she tells them she shares a bedroom with Leviticus. Oh, and don't forget Lucinda, Shirley and Gloria. They'll talk Keenan to death."

"We can always ask—"

"My mother? Don't say it! Don't even think it. There's a four-legged pest-deterrent living in her house if you haven't noticed. Besides, Celeste Blatt has been cozying up to Keenan from what I've heard, and believe me, I've heard plenty from the book club women."

"That's perfect! Better than I expected. We just need to get her on board and wait for his grand confession."

"That may be easier said than done."

"So you like my idea?"

"I didn't exactly say that."

"Fine! I'll call my sister and see if she would be willing to convince Celeste to play along."

"I think she's working on the puzzle right now. They only have another couple of days until the photographer arrives."

"Then I'd better snap to it. All of you can thank me later."

With that, she got off the line and I remained, receiver in hand, for a second or two, trying to process what just happened.

"Phee! Stop what you're doing. Great news! We caught a break in the Stoad case." Augusta's voice bounced off the walls. "Mr. Williams phoned from the mortuary. He found evidence that substantiates Tabitha's story. He'll secure it and get it to the sheriff's office in Surprise."

"What evidence?" I left my desk and rushed toward hers.

"Tabitha's photos showed a white van with a magnetic sign for Sudsy Dudsy Cleaners. Well, Mr. Williams uncovered that sign, and another one as well, in an old cardboard box with a number of dated photos that the mortuary had stored away. The sign was caked with dirt and grime, and his guess is that those are the ones from that van. It begs the question, if they weren't cleaning, what were they doing?"

"My gosh! It's all making sense. Arthur's body buried there . . . Tabitha's photos of a man wheeling a trash container to the van . . . We're getting closer to the truth. Does Marshall know?"

"Of course. It was the first call Mr. Williams made. We're next in line," she said and chuckled.

"Good! Now Marshall won't have to fabricate a 'silent witness' story. Gee, I would have thought he'd be done by now."

"Nate texted him a photo of those car door magnets. You know what they say about a picture being worth a thousand words. All he needs are three words—'I did it.'"

"I don't think it'll be that easy. Henry Longmire is up in age, and even the sharpest memories go dim, especially if you've committed a crime."

"Tabitha told Mr. Williams that Tisha murdered her husband. Tisha was the one with a motive. Miserable marriage, blah-blah-blah. Only thing I can figure is that she paid off someone to help move and get rid of the body. Bingo! Along comes handyman Henry, who happens to work for a mortuary where a major construction project is taking place. Talk about taking it to the grave. And they would have if the mortuary hadn't decided to expand a couple of decades later."

"Marshall will still need to get a confession out of him. Hmm, I think I know how we can help. Oh my gosh! Shoot me now. I'm beginning to sound like my mother, or worse yet, my aunt."

"What did you have in mind?"

"Henry's son works at the mortuary. Let's hope he'll want his father to live out the final days with a clear conscience." I glanced at the time and went to retrieve my bag. "I'll be taking my lunch break at the mortuary. Wish me luck."

"I'll do one better. I'll order you a deli sandwich. Not sure they have a great selection where you're headed."

I was headed west on Bell Road and about to turn left on Del Webb Boulevard in Sun City when my Bluetooth picked up Augusta's call.

"It's a horse race, Phee, and Mr. Williams is winning."

"What?"

"When he blew off some of the dust on those magnetic signs, he noticed a small label affixed to the metal frame on the back. It was the name of the company that made those magnets. Of course, that was over two decades ago, but the company address is on Alma School Road in Phoenix. And get this—there was a customer number on the label as well. It's a grand slam win for Williams Investigations." Then she paused. "That is, if the company is still in business."

"Didn't Nate try to contact them?"

"Uh-huh, but the phone number is no longer in service. He's having Rolo do some checking for him."

"Where is Nate now?"

"On his way to the sheriff's office in Surprise. If I hear anything, I'll let you know. Good luck with Longmire's son."

"Thanks. You know, if that company still exists, even under a different name, and they can pull the records by customer number, it will be a slam dunk."

"Since when did you start using basketball analogies?"

"Since I said 'I do' to Marshall."

"Oh, brother."

A few minutes later, I pulled into Sunny Skies Mortuary and parked under the scant shade of a paloverde tree. The main building was a few yards from my parking spot but I chose to skirt around to the maintenance building on my left, figuring that's where I could find Henry's son.

I noted the yellow crime scene tape that had covered the excavation area past the maintenance building was no longer there and the construction vehicles were once again operating. Looking down at the ground, I made sure there were no rocks or chunks of cement. Last thing I needed was to stumble and wind up on the hot pavement.

Before I reached the entrance to the building, I heard the rumbling of a weed whacker and looked to my right to see a man in his forties or early fifties trimming some brush from the side of the building.

"Excuse me," I shouted over the noise of the machine. "I'm looking for the son of Mr. Henry Longmire who used to work here."

The man cut the engine. "You don't have to look far. I'm Tim Longmire. How can I help you?"

"This may take a few minutes. Is it possible to go inside the building where it's cooler?"

"I can give you a few minutes, but I've got lots of work to do. We lost time during an investigation. The body of a man was uncovered here during an excavation as part of an expansion project."

"I know. That's why I'm here."

"Are you with the sheriff's office?"

"I work for Williams Investigations and they're consulting on the case. Phee Kimball Gregory." I held out my hand and he shook it. No need to tell him I was the bookkeeper/accountant. "I need to speak with you regarding your father's likely involvement with the victim's death."

The robust color on Tim's face seemed to fade gradually. "Come on, we can talk in my office."

He motioned me inside the building and nodded to two workers who rounded the other corner of the building carrying supplies. Once inside, he offered me a bottle of water and pointed to a small room with a desk, file cabinet, and round table that was piled with assorted hand tools.

"Tell me, what makes you think my father had anything to do with that case?"

I took a breath and explained about Tabitha Stephens's amateur photography club and the photos she took of the house where Tisha and Arthur resided. My description of the white van and the man who wheeled the trash container from the house to the van was straightforward. No accusation in my voice or tone, but Tim immediately jumped to his father's defense.

"Mr. Longmire," I said, "right now the sheriff's office is in possession of some key evidence regarding your father's involvement. My sense is that they do not believe he was the one who committed the murder but he may have been complicit in it."

"Complicit how?" Tim's eyes were wide and he clenched his hands.

"Moving the body from the Stoad house and disposing of it at the excavation site on this property."

Suddenly my phone vibrated and I glanced down to see a text from Augusta: *Get out of there. Now! Longmire's kid may be the killer.*

CHAPTER 43

"Everything all right?" Tim asked.

"Yeah. Just a reminder from my office."

"Okay. So, what's this evidence?"

"Time-stamped photos of someone who appears to be your father in the garage and the driveway of the Stoad house a few days prior to the wife reporting her husband missing."

He shrugged. "That doesn't mean anything."

"It does when the sequential photos show the man moving a large trash container to a white van. A van with a bogus sign for a cleaning service. That sign was recently uncovered on this property by our agency."

Tim rubbed his chin and stared directly at me. "What is it you wanted me to do?"

"Speak with your father. His description matched the photo of that man. Ask him if he was hired by Tisha Stoad to dispose of her husband's body. Explain that given his age and circumstance, he would most likely not serve time."

"My father can't remember what month it is, let alone events from two decades ago."

"Try to refresh his memory, because I guarantee the conversation he'll have with the deputies won't be as pleasant as the one we're having."

"In other words, true or false, get him to confess."

"Unless someone else, who looked remarkably like him, was the man in those photos."

I stopped speaking and held absolutely still. I read somewhere that silence was an excellent technique for extracting information from suspects. The very uncomfortable nature of remaining mum was supposed to get them to talk. But so far, the only one who was uncomfortable was me. Finally, Tim spoke.

"I'll take care of it today. But like I said, I'll be lucky if he knows what day of the week this is."

Reaching into my bag, I handed him a generic Williams Investigations card. "Let me know how it goes, will you?"

"Don't expect much, but sure."

I stood and started for the door when my eye caught sight of a photo on the wall near his desk. It was a whole crowd of folks, and given their attire, it wasn't recent. "Is that you in the back row with the plaid work shirt?"

"That's me, all right. The photo was taken in the early summer at a picnic. My father's on the lower left-hand side. I had more hair then but he was already losing his."

The mental math took only seconds. Henry was in his eighties now and I estimated the photo was taken thirty years ago. Back then, men wore boot-cut baggy jeans and Henry was no exception. Neither was Tim, who had to be in his late twenties or early thirties at the time.

"Tell your father that the authorities are interested in finding out who killed Arthur Stoad. That's what they really want. I'm certain if he provides them with that information, he could strike a deal to drop any charges for complicity."

Tim nodded. "Got it. Listen, I've got to cut you off. I need to get back to work."

I made a beeline for the door. "I appreciate it. Keep cool. It's getting hot out there."

Rocks or no rocks, I hustled to my car. The combination of Augusta's text and the unsettling feeling I had speaking with Tim didn't sit well with me. In less than a half hour I'd know what prompted Augusta to relay that information, but in the meantime, I wasn't about to take any chances by lingering any longer than I needed to.

"Your ham and Swiss on rye is in the fridge," Augusta said the second I opened the door to our office. "Marbled rye. With the good crust. Grab it and tell me what happened. The men are still out."

"Tell me first about that text. Yikes. I was inches away from the guy in his office, in a maintenance building with no one else around."

"You have that Screamer, don't you?"

"Thanks to Myrna, I carry a small arsenal in my bag. But still . . ."

Augusta looked at the computer screen and motioned to the fridge. "We've got time until the next appointment arrives. Mr. Williams should be back by then. Not sure about your husband."

"I'll get my lunch, but tell me about Tim Longmire. Talk about getting creeped out."

I pulled a chair next to Augusta's desk and unwrapped my sandwich. "Spit it out. What made you think he could be the murderer and not the father?"

"This." Augusta handed me a fax from Rolo. "It came in after you left. Mr. Williams had him do some deep-dive background checks on Henry as well as Samantha. And by deep dive, I mean HIPPA-protected medical information. Read it."

With a mouthful of ham and Swiss, I chewed as I read, "Spinal stenosis, foraminal stenosis, claudication." "I've heard of spinal stenosis since it's a hot topic of conversation at Bagels 'n More, but I'm not sure of the other two."

"Neither was I, so I googled them," Augusta said. "Foraminal means constriction in the smaller side tunnels of the spine and claudication is leg weakness as a result of the other crapola going on."

I nearly spat out my sandwich. "And which medical journal cited 'crapola'?"

"You know what I mean. Henry was in no condition to drag a body out of that house. Sure, he could do other handyman work at the mortuary but not lift really heavy weights. Especially dead weight. Hmm, I wonder why that weight is heavier . . ."

"Oh my gosh. That *does* leave his son, doesn't it? And now he knows that we're about to blow things wide open."

"Maybe. Maybe not. He could talk his father into covering for him. But he knows he's got to do something because the deputies will be paying a visit to Henry one way or the other."

"You don't think he'd do anything to his father, do you?"

Augusta shook her head. "Doubtful. He'll probably play up the fact that his father is not aging well and his memory is not to be trusted."

"Ha! The one who's not to be trusted is Tim. Knowing what we know, he helped a murderess dispose of a body."

"Hey, no one's perfect." Augusta burst out laughing. "Hold on, a fax is coming in. Boy, does that machine grind." She stood and retrieved the paper. Then rolled her eyes. "Rolo. Second time today. Wants our office to call him on a burner phone. Honestly."

I stood adjacent to Augusta and mouthed, "Speaker phone."

"It's Augusta, Rolo. What's going on?"

"Your office is piling more stuff on my plate than the Golden Corral. Good thing today's request was child's play. That company your boss was looking into on Alma School Road is now Media Designs and Graphics. They do all kinds of print advertising. Business cards, magnets, swag items, buttons, mugs, banners . . . want me to go on?"

"That won't be necessary. Are they still in Phoenix?"

"In Goodyear. Close enough. 15620 West Roosevelt Street."

"Thanks. I'll let Mr. Williams know right away."

"Tell him I'm still digging into the other side dishes on my plate."

"Will do." Augusta ended the call and wasted no time phoning Nate. Luckily, she caught him seconds before he turned on Bell Road toward our office. She winked and gave me the thumbs-up. "He's making a U-turn and going west to the 303. He should be in Goodyear in a half hour unless there's a traffic problem."

"Do you think they'll be able to go that far back and find the customer who purchased those signs?"

"Hard to say. Who knows what kind of software they were using at that time to keep track. Or worse yet, paper files."

"Guess we'll know soon enough."

I moseyed back to my desk and lost track of time as I focused on numbers and figures instead of bodies and murderers. When I heard Augusta chatting with Marshall, I glanced at the bottom of my computer screen and it was five ten. I finished the task I had been working on and exited the program. Unlike tracking a killer, those numbers weren't going anywhere.

As I flung my door open, I called out, "Hey, how did it go with Henry?"

Marshall grabbed a Coke from the fridge and pulled off the tab. "Like a root canal. Funny, but I'm beginning to think Henry isn't our guy. Oh, don't get me wrong, but even with some memory loss, he didn't display the usual reactions to that kind of an accusation."

"That's because he didn't do it. I'm sure his son, Tim, is our killer."

Augusta jumped in before I could continue. "Phee's right, Mr. Gregory. Want to know how I know? I'll tell you. Rolo swam in the murky deep and faxed us his fishing report. Henry Longmire had a long laundry list of health issues dating to way back when. Stenosis. Not the liver. The spine. Makes it impossible to lift weights. And there's more, calcification, too." She cocked her head and looked at me. "That's the right word, isn't it?" Then back to Marshall. "Phee chitchatted with him today on a reconnaissance mission. Don't worry. It was her lunch hour."

Marshall's eyes couldn't have gotten any wider. "You did what?"

"It was broad daylight. At a place of business. With Nate tracking down evidence and you prying a confession out of Henry, I had the sudden urge to move things along. I know I should have let you or Nate know but—"

"You're lucky he didn't try to silence you. I just don't want you taking these chances, hon. And neither does Nate."

"Don't worry, Mr. Gregory. She's got a Screamer and a cat laser toy."

"Wonderful."

I walked over and squeezed his elbow. "It wasn't like meeting someone in a dark, shady place."

And no mention of the maintenance building, Augusta.

"I know, but killers can react anywhere. So, where did you leave it with Tim?"

"He downplayed it. Of course, at the time, I told him it was his father who we thought was responsible for moving the body. Then I got Augusta's text after she heard from Rolo."

"I see. Hey, if Nate has any luck with that marketing company, we might be able to make things stick. Right now, we're in limbo."

"I'm not," Augusta said. "I'm on my way out with the canasta girls. It's barbeque rib night."

Marshall laughed. "Wouldn't want to hold you up. Come on, everyone, tomorrow's another day."

CHAPTER 44

The alarm went off a half hour earlier than usual but it seemed as if it was two hours before our usual wakeup time. Marshall was already out of the shower, dressed, and on his way to plunk a K-Cup into the Keurig.

"Got a few odds and ends to deal with in the office," he said, "before I pitch in to help Nate sift through files of old receipts."

"At least that company was willing to let you go through their records. Of course, Nate's pretty darn convincing."

"Going through decades-old paper files isn't fun. Even with customer numbers. According to the current owner of that printing company, receipts were filed by month, not customer number. But I must say this much, as tired as Nate was when he called last night, he was practically doing summersaults."

"And just watch—Bowman and Ranston will get all the credit."

"What else is new? Hey, if we find Henry or Tim's name associated with the purchase of those bogus cleaning service signs, we'll have enough evidence to have the deputies classify him as a person of interest."

"Not arrest them on suspicion of murder?"

"Not strong enough evidence. Yet."

"Oh."

"Don't look so crestfallen. With enough pressure, people have been known to crack."

Just then the phone rang and the caller ID was my mother's.

"You're right about that. I'm about to crack right now. It's my mother. Can't be good at this hour. She and her fur-babies like to sleep in. I'll put it on speaker phone."

My mother's voice was loud, winded, and fast. "It's a disaster, Phee. A total disaster. Gloria just called. Lydia had an early shift at the hospital so she took Thor to the dog park since it's still dark outside. When she passed the library, she saw firetrucks."

"Oh, no."

"That's not the worst of it. Lydia smelled something horrific and Thor went totally berserk. Rearing up and howling. She got him back in the car and drove toward the library to see. Everything was cordoned off. The posse told her it was a sewer main break. And the odor was putrid. Poor Lydia had to rummage around her car for a face mask."

"Uh-oh. I guess that means the library will be closed today so the puzzle won't be completed on time for the photo shoot tomorrow."

"Not if I can help it. I'll be darned if we miss our chance to be on the cover of *Senior Living* because of a little sewer water. From what Gloria

188

told me, the building itself is fine. It's only the parking lot that has standing water."

"Um, standing sewage water. I don't think they'll let you in, Mom."

"There's a side entrance and the computer room entrance. Worst-case scenario, we can access the tower."

"Access the tower? What are you? The Hunchback of Notre Dame? Forget it. Wait and find out what the rec center decides. Anyway, we've got to get going for work. Talk to you later."

"Just so you know, Gloria's calling Shirley. Then our phone tree will kick in. Of course, I'll have to call Herb and he can let the men know."

"It's a sewer main break, not a landing from Space X. Don't go over there. You'll only make things worse."

"Don't be silly. We're going to meet for coffee at Bagels 'n More. We do our best thinking there."

"Don't think either!"

Marshall chuckled as he headed to the kitchen. "Sounds like you'll have a fun day. Once I gulp this coffee, I'm out the door. We'll catch up later."

"Good luck with your paper pile!"

"And then some."

When I got to the office, the men were already in Goodyear and Augusta informed me that I had two messages. One from my mother asking me to call her back and the other from Tim Longmire. I immediately phoned Tim.

"Mr. Longmire? This is Phee Kimball Gregory, returning your call."

"Thanks. Listen, if I can get immunity for criminal prosecution, I'd be willing to let your office know how Arthur's corpse wound up on mortuary property."

I was so taken aback that I couldn't respond right away.

"Mrs. Kimball? Gregory? You still there?"

"Yes. I'm here. But I'm not the person you need to speak with."

At first, I was going to send him to Bowman and Ranston, but I thought better of it. I pictured those deputies mucking up everything I had accomplished, simply by their demeanor. "Can you drive to our office in Glendale? Say, in two or three hours? One of our detectives should be available to speak with you."

"Can't you do it?"

"I don't make the kind of decision you're inquiring about. Of course, you could always drive to the sheriff's office."

"Two or three hours, huh? Okay, figure three hours. I've got your address on that card you gave me."

"Good. We'll expect you then."

I hung up the phone before he had a chance to ask me any other questions. I had already overstepped my bounds.

Two seconds later, I had Marshall on the phone. "A confession beats a paper chase by a long shot. Tim Longmire will be here in three hours to tell all. You or Nate need to be here."

"Whoa! Slow down, hon. What happened?"

I told him about the call and he assured me he'd be here. "I know the written documentation will still be needed," I said, "especially if Tim changes his tune or if someone else was in cahoots with him. Maybe you guys will get lucky and find it."

"That's the plan. And by the way, thank you. But please, don't take chances like that again." Then he sighed. "Unless you can't help it."

"Love you, too."

When I got off the phone, I told Augusta what to expect in a few hours. But no one told me what I could expect in the hours and days to come. If they had, I would have booked a flight to Rio.

• • •

"Tim probably saw the proverbial handwriting on the wall," Marshall said when he returned to the office. "Nate should be along any minute. We found the receipt for the purchase of two large magnets and it was paid in cash by our guy. No way around it."

"That's fantastic. If he backs down, you've got one heck of a bargaining chip."

"It still puts us right back to where we were. Only now we have a credible source who can testify to Tisha's culpability. If only we can find a source to point us to where she's living."

"Didn't Tabitha say she thought Tisha was right under our noses?"

"Yep. But so far, no sightings."

"I wonder what made her believe Tisha was still in the area."

Marshall brushed some hair from his brow and took a Coke from the small fridge. "Something Tisha had told her years ago about not wanting to leave this community."

"That's kind of vague."

"Sure is."

Nate arrived a few minutes later and let us know he had contacted Bowman and Ranston regarding Tim. Said it took some convincing but the deputies agreed to let him and Marshall "deal with it."

I was back at my desk, going over some spreadsheets when I realized I hadn't returned my mother's call. I resigned myself to a one-minute chat and phoned her.

"I was about to call again, Phee. I'm still at Bagels 'n More with everyone. Library patrons got an email from Darcey. The library is closed today due to a break in a sewer pipe. They expect to have it fixed in a few hours and then have a company take care of the standing water. Or sewage gunk."

"Okay. So now you know what's going on."

"What's going on is that the photographer plans to be here between ten and eleven tomorrow to take a final picture of the puzzle. And *how* exactly is he going to do that with a gaping hole in one of the sections?"

"Maybe a close-up of another section?"

"That's what Darcey suggested but we were able to talk her into another plan. She just got it approved from the rec center administrator. Tonight at seven, they are going to open the library for the puzzle workers to complete the job. Security staff and Darcey will be there."

"Good."

"Myrna, Shirley, and Gloria will be joining me. Then, of course, there's the Bellowses, LaVonda, Lettie, Keenan, Betty-Jean, Carl, and Celeste. We'll be tripping over each other if they all show up."

"How long will the library stay open?"

"That's the best part—as long as we need to get it done."

"That's great. Now you don't have anything to worry about." Someone needs to cut my tongue off when I say things like that.

● ● ●

Tim kept his word and arrived at the office two and a half hours later. He, Nate, and Marshall met in Nate's office, and when the three of them emerged, Nate followed him to the sheriff's office in Surprise.

"Think he'll pull a fast one and hit the highway, Mr. Gregory?" Augusta asked as they left the office.

Marshall shook his head. "Don't think so. He knows what the stakes are if he does."

"You sure he's not holding back where Tisha is located?"

"He's not but he's pretty sure his dad might know. He was the one Tisha initially called about removing Arthur's body, but Henry passed the job on to his son. Anyway, I contacted the care facility and I'll have another chat with Henry in the morning. The manager on duty said Henry's cognition is better in the earlier part of the day."

"I'm keeping my fingers crossed you get this cold case solved, Mr. Gregory." Augusta held up her finger-crossed hand. "Then you can move onto Samantha's cold, rotting body."

"Thank you for that image. I'll be in my office for a bit."

"I have a bad feeling about tonight, Augusta," I said. "I can't put a finger on it, but something in my gut tells me something will be going on in the library, and it won't be puzzle solving."

"I'll keep Mr. Smith and Mr. Wesson at the ready."

CHAPTER 45

By four forty-five, when Nate returned to Williams Investigations, Tim had made his confession to the deputies and had acquired a criminal lawyer. He confessed to receiving a substantial sum of money for removing and disposing of Arthur's body.

"Did he tell you how the wife murdered him?" I asked.

The three of us, Marshall, Augusta, and me, hovered around Nate like fireflies.

"Blunt force trauma to the back of the head with a rolling pin. Tisha had apparently finished making strudel when she walked into the living room, where Arthur stood over a table by the window. At least that's what she conveyed to Tim."

"I don't understand why he didn't say anything to the authorities."

"Money can be a powerful silencer. I suppose he reasoned that it was a done deal so it wouldn't have made any difference if he profited by it. Funny, but Tabitha held off as well. She didn't want to risk losing her job."

"In this case, money didn't talk, it walked," Augusta said.

Nate gave her a sideways look and continued. "Tim wasn't afraid of getting caught. No one was at the construction site at the mortuary at that time. It was real easy to dispose of a body in a pit that was being filled in. He'd go about his business with none the wiser."

"What about the rolling pin?" Augusta fluffed her hair and studied Nate's face.

"It was never at the crime scene. Remember, Tim was the one who told me about it. If a forensics lab were to find it and test it, they would have come up empty. Tim said Tisha scrubbed it with Soft Scrub and sprayed it with Clorox spray while she had him retrieve a large dark blue plastic tablecloth from the pantry. Remnants of it were found with the body, by the way."

"Tabitha was close," I said. "She said her photos showed a tarp covering something in a trash can."

"Yep. Arthur Stoad."

"We've shown those photos of Tabitha's to all of the rec centers in Sun City and Sun City West. Twelve in all. Not to mention the two libraries. No one on those staffs recognized the woman who stood behind Tim as he wheeled the trash can to the van. All we know is that she's a very heavyset woman that some folks mistook for a man. And that was twenty-three years ago."

Augusta unwrapped a chocolate bar that was in her desk and took a bite. "Let's hope Henry has all his faculties with him tomorrow morning and that he knows Tisha's whereabouts."

"Better yet," Marshall said, "let's hope he's willing to talk."

Even with maximum air-conditioning in both of our vehicles, Marshall and I were dripping wet with sweat by the time we had gotten home.

"This may sound crazy, hon, but all I want for dinner is a bowl of Raisin Bran and anything cold to drink. Heck, I'll just lap up the milk from the cereal."

"Actually, that sounds pretty good. I don't even have the energy to prepare anything, let alone eat it."

We changed into lighter, more comfy clothes and Marshall poured us bowls of Raisin Bran. When we finished eating, I put the dishes in the dishwasher and retreated to the couch. "I don't care if I watch a test pattern all evening, I'm pooped."

"Test pattern? Boy, are you dating yourself!"

I flipped on the news and the local coverage showed footage of the sewer break in Sun City West.

"Must be a slow news night," I said. Then, an hour later, I got my own news, courtesy of my mother.

"I told you it was going to be a circus with all those people here tonight."

"Hello, Mom."

"Thought you'd want to know that Darcey split us up into two-person teams for thirty-minute shifts. That way, everyone will get a chance to finish the puzzle. If it's still not complete after the first round, the shifts continue. I'm with Myrna. Shirley and Gloria will be working together. And naturally the Bellowses—"

"Uh, I get the idea. What do the people do when they're not working on the puzzle?"

"It's a library, Phee. Hopefully they'll find a good book and wait it out. Excuse me a minute, Streetman is getting restless."

"You brought the dog??"

"What else could I do? He hates being alone in the dark."

"He has the cat."

"She doesn't like it either. I think she picked that up from him. But at least she calms down when I put *Animal Planet* on the TV. Anyhow, he's safe and sound in his doggie stroller."

Until he bites through the mesh like he's done a thousand times before.

"Good luck. Hope you get it done."

"Between you and me, no one intends to leave until we do. Lettie and Betty-Jean are working on it now. Myrna and I are after the Bellowses. Then Shirley and Gloria. I'll keep you posted."

"There's really no—" But before I could finish the word *need*, she had ended the call.

"Everything okay, hon?" Marshall asked.

"For now. The library is open to a few puzzle solvers and my mother is one of them. And, get this, she brought the dog."

"What else is new?"

"I know I'm being silly, but I have a queasy feeling that something will go wrong."

"That's because something always does. She's with friends, right? In the library. Relax for a change and zone out in front of the TV."

I took Marshall's advice and joined him on the couch, dozing intermittently until my mother called again.

"Can you believe it? Lettie and Betty-Jean only managed to find one piece and then Drake insisted we Clorox the table in between workers. Celeste had to get home and Keenan insisted on driving her. Then LaVonda said she was too tired to think so she left too. Next thing we knew, the Bellowses remembered they had an early exercise class in the morning so they ditched us as well. As they were leaving, Norva sneezed and that set Carl off. He's right up there on the cleanliness fanatic scale with Drake. He gathered his things and raced out as if the place was infected by a plague. This is a nightmare. Uh-oh. I'm up again. Shirley will join Myrna and me. Gloria had to get home to Thor. Lydia's working at the hospital tonight."

"Okay." I waited for a response but there was no one at the other end. Turning to Marshall, I muttered, "I don't think the astronauts on Apollo 11 gave as much feedback."

"I caught some of it. Sounds as if there are only a handful of folks left."

"Maybe they'll be able to finish that puzzle without all that hoo-ha. Meanwhile, Darcey is sequestered away in her office with the door closed according to my mother."

"Smart librarian."

Less than an hour later, the landline rang and it took me a few seconds to place the voice. "Sherman?"

"That's right. I went through some of my other old photos and newspaper clippings tonight. Not much else going on here. I wanted you to know I found out who took the winning photo from that contest. Thought it might be helpful. It was in a local announcement from the Sun City Recreation Centers before everything went to the newspapers."

"Who? Who was it?"

"A woman by the name of Samantha Wiggins. She must have lived in this community back then."

Oh my gosh! It had to be Samantha from the puzzle committee.

"Does it give any other information?"

"Nope. Just the name. I figured you might want to know, for what it's worth."

I could feel my pulse quicken as bits of my own puzzle began to come together. "Thank you. I really appreciate it."

"Any time. And sorry if I called too late. I lose track of time."

"No problem. Have a nice night, Sherman."

"Marshall! You won't believe this. Not in a million years."

"What?" He raced into the kitchen and all but collided with me.

"That was Sherman from Sun City. The person who took the photo for the puzzle contest was none other than Samantha Wiggins. This changes everything!"

CHAPTER 46

The two of us looked at each other, dumbfounded until Marshall finally spoke.

"That certainly gives credence to the supposition that she photographed something that someone didn't want seen. But what? Has your mother mentioned what that puzzle shows so far?"

"Just a street. At dusk. I can't believe I'm saying this, but I'm calling my mother back. If what you said was true, Samantha's killer could be at the library right now. Good grief. I can't even remember who left and who didn't. My mother yammered so much I ignored most of it."

"Hey, I'm wide awake. Let's pop over there just in case."

"Give me a sec so she'll know we're coming. That way, she can have Darcey unlock the side entrance."

My mother sounded distracted when she answered the phone but that wasn't unusual. "Myrna's with Shirley in the ladies' room. Darcey is getting some ice from their workroom refrigerator."

"Huh? What?"

"Lettie poked Shirley in the eye. She leaned over to see what Shirley was doing and jabbed her. Not on purpose. At least that's what she said. So now Lettie and Betty-Jean are at the puzzle and Shirley is getting ice for her eye. It's all red and runny."

"Listen, Marshall and I are on our way over. Don't say anything but Samantha was the one who took that photo. There may be something in that puzzle that no one was supposed to see."

"Gott in Himmel."

"Okay, see you in a bit."

"This could turn out to be a long night, hon," Marshall said as he backed his car out of the garage. "Glad we changed into jeans and T-shirts."

"Especially if Streetman is there. He's never gotten over that weird obsession about certain fabrics."

"If we ever get a pet, let's make it a fish!"

Only a few cars were parked by the pickleball courts by the library as we walked to the side entrance. The sewage odor permeated the dusty air and I held my hand over my nose.

"How's Shirley?" I asked when Darcey and my mother met us at the door.

"Not happy," my mother said. "Her eye is swollen and she's upset it will look terrible in that photo shoot tomorrow. *If* we can get the puzzle done."

Darcey patted her on the shoulder and smiled at us. "You folks are almost there. I have some things I'm taking care of in my office so I'll leave you to the work at hand."

With that, Darcey scurried off and my mother, with Streetman in her arms, led us to the puzzle area.

"He was getting antsy so I took the little prince out of his stroller."

Can you take him out of the country?

Lettie and Betty-Jean hovered over the incomplete section of the puzzle but neither of them seemed to be making any progress. My mother stood against a bookshelf as Streetman sniffed the air and made whiny sounds.

Suddenly he jumped out of her arms and charged at Lettie's capris.

"Good grief, no!" my mother shouted. "Must be a cloth he doesn't like." Then she yelled, "Streetman, stop! Streetman, stop this instant." As if that was going to do any good.

Marshall made a mad dash to retrieve him but the dog grabbed Lettie's leg like a pole and began to bump it at the same time as he started licking her knee cap. Swooping down, Marshall grabbed the dog and backed off. "I think your knee might be bleeding," he said.

Lettie looked down and immediately put a hand over her knee. "I'm fine. It's not blood, it's ketc—never mind. I'm fine."

I edged over to where Marshall stood with the dog and glanced at Lettie's capris. "Um, looks like a mustard stain, too, on the other leg. Guess you were at a picnic. Or maybe . . ." And just then, Streetman dove for the tote bag Lettie had hung behind her chair. In an instant, the contents spilled on the floor. Purse. Cell phone. Pens. Lipstick. Sunblock. Mints. And two small plastic squeeze bottles. One red. One yellow.

Then Betty-Jean shouted, "It was you! You're the one who sabotaged the puzzle with all that ketchup and mustard mess. And I'll bet you were responsible for the glue on the pieces and the water sprinklers and everything else we dealt with. Why would you do a thing like that? Who paid you off? The Summer Showcase Readers? I wouldn't put it past them."

"Don't be ridiculous," Lettie said. "I brought snacks to a party, that's all."

My mother and I exchanged glances.

At that moment, Marshall's phone vibrated and he handed the dog back to my mother.

"Got to take this. It's Augusta."

He walked out of the main room at the same time my mother announced that she and Streetman were going into the ladies' room to check on Shirley.

"Don't mind me," I said to Lettie and Betty-Jean. "You might as well keep working. And sorry about the dog. He's got a thing for ketchup."

Lettie didn't say a word. She retrieved her items, put them back in her tote and continued to ponder over the puzzle with Betty-Jean.

"Augusta and Geneva, one of her canasta ladies, are on their way over here," Marshall whispered to me when he walked back.

"What on earth for?"

Then he took me by the elbow, and in a louder voice, said, "I'm headed to the drinking fountain. Join me for a minute."

Lettie and Betty-Jean paid no attention as Marshall and I left the room.

"What's going on? Why did Augusta call?"

"Augusta described Tisha Stoad to her canasta ladies and Geneva said it might be one of the women who was in her TOPS—that's Take Off Pounds Sensibly—class when she lived in Gila Bend."

"Isn't that a stretch? I mean, Gila Bend?"

"Yeah, I thought so too, but then Augusta said that Geneva lived in Gila Bend for a number of years and a lady by the name of Letticia Holton, who went by Tisha, had moved in from the Phoenix area. She joined the same weight-loss group as Geneva and was fanatical about dropping pounds."

"And she thinks that Tisha is really Lettie?"

"When Augusta mentioned the freckle mustache, Geneva was positive it had to be her. Overweight or not, that mustache wasn't going anywhere. And, the freckles sort of resembled a handlebar mustache. Not likely to be mistaken for a woman who needed to have dermaplaning to remove facial hair."

"Yikes. If what Tabitha said was true, then Tisha has been under our noses all this time."

Marshall grinned. "Under our noses, huh? That's one way of putting it. Anyway, we'll find out soon enough."

"We're back!" Myrna yelled from down the hallway.

"Lordy, we're back but not the vision in my eye. It's still blurry." Shirley dabbed a tissue on it and blinked. "I put in some artificial tears so maybe that will help."

"It will if you quit rubbing it." Myrna took her arm and pulled her forward. "Let's hurry back and see if they made any progress."

When they were a few yards from us, we went to Darcey's office and knocked on the door. When she opened it, Marshall put a finger to his lips. "Keep it low. Two woman are on their way over here. One of them is pretty sure Lettie Holton is Tisha, or I should say *Letticia* Stoad, a woman who is a suspect in the murder of her husband."

Darcey's eyes couldn't have gotten any wider. "Do you think she could be armed?"

"I hope not but I won't be taking any chances."

We walked back to the puzzle room, this time with Darcey. Lettie and Betty-Jean hadn't gotten any further but that didn't surprise me. If Lettie *was* Letticia, she didn't want that puzzle solved.

A few minutes later, Marshall got a text that Augusta and Geneva were at the door. "Some visitors who are associated with my office are dropping by. Don't let that interrupt you," he announced to the people in the room.

He walked to the door with Darcey and me a few feet behind. Once inside, Marshall pointed to the puzzle table and Geneva stepped forward. Enough to see Lettie's face but not interfere.

Then Geneva turned to him and exclaimed, "That's her! I'd bet big money on it. Wow. She managed to keep the weight off all those years and her hair is lighter, but it's Tisha, all right."

I watched as Marshall sent off a text that I imagined was for Nate, Bowman, and Ranston before addressing Geneva. "Might as well pull the Band-Aid off and greet her. It's got to happen at some point. No sense waiting."

With a fast nod, Geneva charged to the puzzle table. "Tisha! Is that you? Oh my gosh! It is! You look wonderful. You lost all that weight and kept if off. Congratulations."

Lettie turned ashen and dropped the puzzle piece she had been holding. "I think you have me confused with someone else." She bent her head down and fixated on the puzzle.

Geneva stepped closer to her and raised her voice a bit. "Did you move here and take on a new name because you didn't want people to know how overweight you used to be? We all wondered where you went when you left Gila Bend."

"I'm not who you say I am."

"You don't have to pretend, Tisha. When my friend Augusta showed me some photos, I recognized you. Freckles don't lie. Then, when Augusta told me you were a suspect in your husband's death, I couldn't believe it. I was told he was found buried at a construction site at Sunny Skies Mortuary. Is it true? That you killed him? Is that why you moved to Gila Bend all those years ago? So no one would find out?"

"None of you can prove a thing, and I'll make sure you don't."

In the split second that followed, Lettie stretched out her arms across the puzzle. "Back away. All of you. Or every single piece of this puzzle will be scattered on the floor."

"Why?" I asked. "Then again, there's no need to tell me. I already know. Somehow that puzzle proves you murdered your husband. Isn't that true, Lettie? Or should I say Tisha?"

"All of you, back away now and I'll only abscond with the salient pieces."

"You figured out the puzzle all along, didn't you?" Betty-Jean looked directly at Lettie.

"Actually, Samantha did. That woman was always too smart for her own britches."

"Oh my gosh!" Betty-Jean shrieked. "You killed her! You were the one who murdered Samantha."

"Don't be so shocked and broken up, Betts. Everyone knew Samantha was a witch on wheels."

"That doesn't mean you had the right to do what you did."

"Give me a break." Lettie pointed to Geneva. "It will be that woman's word against mine. Nothing will stand up in court."

"Tim Longmire will," I said. "And he was very specific."

Lettie opened her mouth to respond but Betty-Jean shouted, "I can't believe what you did!"

As the two of them went back and forth, Darcey slipped out of the room. Next, I heard my mother whisper to Myrna, "I know you have a packet of ketchup in your bag. You put it there when we were at Burger King. I need it."

Then Myrna whispered back, "I have ketchup, medium taco sauce from Taco Bell, and Buffalo sauce from Chick-fil-A."

I can't believe this. An unstable murderess is pondering her next move and my mother wants ketchup. For Streetman, I'm sure. If only this night would end.

CHAPTER 47

"Your ruse is up, Lettie," Marshall said. "No sense making this worse than it already is."

Lettie shoved the far end of the table, jostling some of the pieces. Then she leaned over and took a handful of pieces that were positioned near the incomplete part of the puzzle. "Consider these my security for now. I'm leaving and all of you need to stay put. One move toward me and I'll—"

"What?" I asked. "Throw them?"

"No. Snap them apart until they're unrecognizable. Here—see for yourself." She took a piece and broke it apart. "The puzzle's old," she said and laughed. "And brittle."

Behind me, I could hear my mother yammering with Myrna about ketchup. Marshall was at the ready, but he couldn't very well pull out a gun considering Lettie gave no indication of being armed.

Then, without warning, my mother pushed in front of me and squirted a packet of ketchup onto Lettie's blouse. Then Myrna followed suit with another one. It took all of two seconds before Streetman pounced on top of Lettie. She tottered for a second, then lost her balance and fell to the floor. Streetman was like a bolt of lightning. He was on her chest licking the ketchup as she tried to shove him off.

"Lordy!" Shirley yelled. "Someone get that woman before the dog takes a bite of her face."

"Will he do that?" Betty-Jean asked.

"Dog's as unpredictable as the weather," Augusta announced. "But I've got to admit, he's a valiant little guy."

In the background I heard my mother say, "What a wonderful new nickname for my little man—Prince Valiant." I wanted to gag.

As I tried to ignore the nausea in my stomach, Marshall moved like a gazelle, lifted Lettie from the floor and grabbed her wrist. "I wouldn't go anywhere if I were you."

Then, like a really bad Western, Bowman and Ranston thundered into the room, followed by Darcey, who must have let them in.

"Drop your weapon," Bowman shouted at Lettie. "I'm placing you under arrest on suspicion of murder."

Lettie opened her hands and displayed puzzle pieces. Then, she dropped them. One by one.

Bowman turned to Ranston. "Cuff her."

The next five to ten minutes became a frenzied scene as Lettie was escorted out by the deputies. The cacophony of voices literally bounced off the walls.

"She killed Samantha because she lost weight?"

"The husband was murdered."

"Does anyone know why?"

"The little dog has ketchup all over his face."

"A double murder. Does that make her a serial killer?"

Marshall took me by the arm and leaned into my ear. "I need to go to the posse office. Stay here, but if the party ends soon, go home with your mother. I'll text."

I kissed his cheek. "Good job."

"Thank Augusta and Geneva."

"I heard that," Augusta called out. "I want extra donuts tomorrow."

Marshall spoke briefly with Geneva before he exited the library. I thanked both of them and told Augusta I'd make sure the donut selection would be outstanding.

"If it wasn't for you showing Geneva those photos," I said, "we never would have figured out who Lettie really was."

"Yep. Just goes to show, losing weight isn't all it's cracked up to be." Then she looked at Geneva. "They have a Thursday night special at Tailgaters. What do you say we go there before heading back?"

I chuckled as the two women hurried to the door. Like it or not, I was stuck here until Marshall finished up. And knowing Bowman and Ranston, it wasn't going to be anytime soon.

"We still don't know what that puzzle shows," my mother said to everyone in the room. "Let's be honest. None of us are going to sleep tonight unless we do." She bent down, picked up some of the pieces from the floor and took a seat in front of the open puzzle space. "What are you all waiting for? Get a chair and let's get going!"

"You'll have to work fast, ladies. It's getting really late. I'll be in my office for another hour and that's it."

"Thanks, Darcey," a few people muttered.

Shirley, Myrna, Betty-Jean and I joined my mother at the puzzle table. Streetman was returned to his stroller and given a Greenie to mollify him. Less than an hour later, we had all of the pieces in place except for the one Lettie had snapped into a few pieces.

"I think they have Gorilla glue on the counter," Shirley said. "Give me a minute. No fair peeking."

No one said a word when Shirley put the final piece in its place, but the gasps that emanated around the table were surprisingly loud. Mine included.

"That's the same house Tabitha photographed. Only at dusk, and the front room is illuminated from inside." I put my palm to my mouth for a second and then continued to speak. "If this had been taken in broad daylight, it would have been impossible to see why Lettie sabotaged it."

"Must be the woman had a penchant for heavy objects. Not messy like knives or loud like guns." My mother rubbed her chin. "I must say, she had good aim."

"Mom! She slammed her husband with a rolling pin! Ew!"

"Too bad we don't know what he did to deserve it."

"Lordy, Harriet, you'll just have to wait for the trial. Oh goodness! One of us should get Darcey out here to see the final puzzle."

"Do you think the puzzle will be safe here tonight?" We were all on our way out the door when I asked Darcey about it.

"And then some. I actually hired a private security officer to man the library until it reopens in the morning. He just texted me. He's waiting outside to be let in. Believe me, I wasn't about to take any chances."

When Marshall finally came to get me at my mom' s house, it was almost midnight. My mother and I were on the couch offering Jessica Fletcher tips on the murder case she had to solve. Streetman and Essie were in his dog bed snoring away and I couldn't wait until the same thing could be said about Marshall and me.

"Remind me to pick up the gourmet donuts tomorrow," Marshall said on the way home. "This really calls for a celebration. Who, in their right mind, would have ever imagined that Lettie Holton orchestrated Samantha's murder to cover up the one she committed on her spouse?"

"I know. And if Samantha had kept her mouth shut, she'd still be alive today. From what you told me, Lettie was pretty forthcoming about describing how Samantha had taken that photo and didn't realize she had captured a murder in progress. Or at least that's what Lettie thought at the time."

"Samantha must have been frustrated as heck when she tried to blackmail Tisha, only to find Tisha had moved from the area."

"Talk about a long time to wait for some moola. Twenty-three years."

"And all that time, Lettie never thought to have her freckles lightened."

We both tried not to laugh but it was impossible.

CHAPTER 48

"I can't believe I missed all the fun," Nate said when Marshall and I arrived at the office with a giant box of gourmet donuts. "Got your call last night. Then Bowman's. Talk about a cold case that heated up twenty-three years later."

Augusta wasted no time checking out the donuts. "I'm starting with the jelly-filled frosted strawberry donuts with sprinkles and chocolate bites."

"Go for it," Marshall said and laughed. "You deserve it."

Augusta took a bite and looked at me. "I still can't believe how your mother used ketchup packets to get that dog to go after Lettie."

"I'm glad he's a chiweenie and not a rottweiler."

Nate grabbed a maple bacon donut and a few napkins. "Does anyone know what time that photographer is supposed to be at the library? The puzzle is now evidence, but according to Bowman, a professional photo would be acceptable."

"Good," I said, "or those summer readers will pitch a fit if the puzzle stays up longer than it should."

"Speaking of pitching a fit, Bowman said Lettie gave the sheriff's deputies a mouthful when they transferred her to the Fourth Avenue Jail early this morning. There was enough evidence to make a full arrest."

"What about Tim?" I widened my eyes.

"He'll be an accessory, but not to murder. Only to covering it up as well as being the one who perpetrated the vandalism to the machinery. Once he got wind of the investigation, he wanted to be sure they didn't find who he dumped there."

"I can't believe Forrest wasn't the culprit. Along with Keenan. I mean, the insurance money pointed to him, and his relationship with Keenan was dubious at best. Then there was that accident at his plant. That seemed suspicious."

Nate shook his head. "It turned out that there was a crack in the metal piece that held the wheel to the pallet. Purely accidental. Believe it or not, Forrest hired his own failure analyst to make sure it wasn't foul play. I only learned about it recently and it went straight to the recesses of my mind. Sorry, folks, for not spelling it out. But let's face it—Lettie had a stronger motive, a murder to cover up."

"And all this time I thought she might have held her bad stock investment in Prosaic Puzzles against Samantha."

Marshall laughed. "We can't always get it right. But we can come close."

Just then, the phone rang and Augusta took the call. "Phee, it's your mother. The photographer is at the library and Streetman is going to be in the picture."

I rolled my eyes. "Of course he is. Prince Valiant will grace the pages of *Senior Living* and we'll never hear the end of it. Okay, hand me the phone."

"All of us are going to celebrate tonight at the Homey Hut. It's Friday pie night. Buy one get one free, whole pies and slices. You and Marshall have to come. And invite Nate, Augusta, and Geneva. Everyone is coming. The book club ladies. Your aunt and uncle. The pinochle men and Paul. Oh, and ask your friend Lyndy and her boyfriend too. This is an occasion for the books. Two murders solved and Streetman on the cover of a national magazine."

"Please don't tell me you're bringing him to the restaurant."

"You'll be happy to know he and Essie are staying home. It gets too crowded on Friday nights. I don't want anyone to bump into the stroller."

"Good thinking."

"See you at seven. We'll reserve a big table."

"What restaurant?" Marshall asked as soon as I got off the phone.

"How did you know?"

"It's your mother. Need I say more?"

I smiled. "The Homey Hut. And all of you are invited."

"Taking a rain check," Nate said and laughed.

Augusta reached for another donut. "Finishing last night's canasta game."

Marshall gave my shoulder a squeeze. "I have an extra set of earbuds in my car."

"I'll need them. Knowing my mother, they've got another earth-shattering event planned in Sun City West."

"You read my mind."

EPILOGUE

The fall edition of *Senior Living* featured a full-blown photo of the giant puzzle with all of its major contributors standing behind it, in addition to an obnoxious little chiweenie who sported a vest that read "Puzzle Over It," only the word *Puzzle* was crossed out and replaced with *Muzzle*.

The feature story centered on the murder behind the puzzle as well as the process for solving both. According to the librarian, the magazine was in such high demand that the company had to reissue it. Go figure.

Last I knew, a jury had been selected for Lettie Holton's trial, which was to begin in the late fall. We even learned that a surprise witness was going to come forth to testify for the prosecution—one of the custodians who got paid by Lettie to help her sabotage the puzzle. It was his voice and hers that my mother heard that night.

On a lighter note, a new puzzle committee was selected for the library and they unanimously agreed to do a Ravensburger or Disney puzzle with plenty of colors.

Forrest Frost's company faced numerous fines, but after all was said and done, he reestablished a new line of holistic youth-restoring products. I attributed it to the fact that the public had a short memory and was more gullible than anyone could imagine.

Aunt Ina and Uncle Louis spent the month of August at a spa in Utah. Something about the altitude restoring her mind and body. As for the rest of the book club ladies, it was business as usual, but I knew it would be short-lived. I only prayed the next fiasco would wait until the cooler weather made its way into the Valley.

ABOUT THE AUTHOR

Ann I. Goldfarb

New York native Ann I. Goldfarb spent most of her life in education, first as a classroom teacher and later as a middle school principal and professional staff developer. Writing as J. C. Eaton, along with her husband, James Clapp, she has authored the Sophie Kimball Mysteries, the Wine Trail Mysteries, the Charcuterie Shop Mysteries, and the Marcie Rayner Mysteries. In addition, Ann has nine published YA time travel mysteries under her own name. Visit the websites at: www.jceatonmysteries.com and www.timetravelmysteries.com

James E. Clapp

When James E. Clapp retired as the tasting room manager for a large upstate New York winery, he never imagined he'd be coauthoring cozy mysteries with his wife, Ann I. Goldfarb. His first novel, *Booked 4 Murder*, was released in June 2017, followed by ten other books in the series and three other series. Nonfiction in the form of informational brochures and workshop materials treating the winery industry were his forte, along with an extensive background and experience in construction that started with his service in the U.S. Navy and included vocational school classroom teaching. Visit the website at www.jceatonmysteries.com.

29134865R00133